THE ICY BREATH OF DEATH—

When the ice opened to swallow Grem, Alaric knew he was the only one who could save him. But as the others lowered him by rope into the narrow opening, he wondered if he was already too late.

"Grem!" he shouted, and the name echoed all around him.

A moment later, a splash answered him, and Grem's head broke the surface. He grabbed for Grem, caught the man's fur wrapping, and pulled with all his strength. He locked his legs about the other man and shouted to be lifted upward. Slowly, jerkily, he rose from the water. And then, of a sudden, the weight on his legs was too much, and the loop of the rope could not hold him—he was ripped down through it, and he was in the water, deep, deep. He and Grem sank together, and dizziness assailed him, as he felt rather than saw the yawning darkness below.

And a heartbeat later, the two of them were falling through air. . . .

IN THE
RED LORD'S
REACH

Phyllis Eisenstein

A SIGNET BOOK

NEW AMERICAN LIBRARY

A DIVISION OF PENGUIN BOOKS USA INC.

Copyright © 1989 by Phyllis Eisenstein

Portions of this novel appeared originally, in somewhat different form,
in various issues of *The Magazine of FANTASY AND SCIENCE FIC-
TION, Copyright © 1977, 1979, and 1988 by Phyllis Eisenstein.*

 SIGNET TRADEMARK REG. U.S. PAT. OFF. AND FOREIGN COUNTRIES
REGISTERED TRADEMARK—MARCA REGISTRADA
HECHO EN DRESDEN, TN, U.S.A.

SIGNET, SIGNET CLASSIC, MENTOR, ONYX, PLUME, MERID-
IAN and NAL BOOKS are published by NAL PENGUIN INC., 1633
Broadway, New York, New York 10019

First Printing, July, 1989

1 2 3 4 5 6 7 8 9

PRINTED IN THE UNITED STATES OF AMERICA

For George R.R. Martin

PART ONE

THE LAND OF SORROW

In spring, the mountains were wild and windswept, the passes treacherous with meltwater, the human forage sparse. Beyond the heights, said the peasants of the southern foothills, was land unknown: perhaps a vast, frigid desert, or even the half-legendary Northern Sea, where perpetual ice floated over the graves of hapless sailors. Alaric's curiosity urged him across the peaks, and his talent for traveling to any place he could see with his eyes or his mind saved him from becoming one more pebble in many a landslide. He was careful to take his time, to scrutinize his surroundings with a mapmaker's concern for detail. His knapsack was full of compact—if uninteresting—food, a thousand mountain streams provided his drink, and the scrubby trees of the uplands offered fuel for his fire. When he saw lowland birds wheeling overhead, he knew that the worst was behind him.

Through the final pass, he descended into a wide, fertile valley. Here, greenery was well sprouted, grasses cloaking the hillsides, flowers waving in the meadows. To the east, a series of cascades broke free of the mountains, glittering in the noon sunlight like ribbons of polished silver; below, they joined, settling into a river that flowed north and west until it broadened into a small lake. Beyond the lake lay more mountains, peak upon peak, a barrier to the north as effective as that to the south. During the winter, Alaric thought, the valley must be completely isolated from the rest of the world. He wondered if he were the first visitor of the year.

Peasant cottages, bordered by the varying tints of kitchen gardens, were scattered across the landscape. Near the river stood the fortification—Alaric made that

his destination. Now, with the possibility of human witnesses, he gave over the use of his power and worked his
way downward with the slow care of an ordinary man.
His eyes on the ground, on the two paces immediately
before his feet, he did not notice the watching goatherd
until he was suddenly surrounded by bleating goats.

"Good day," said Alaric, dodging a few butting heads.

The goatherd was a fair-haired boy of ten or eleven,
dressed warmly in gray woolen shirt and breeches, with
woolen wrappings round his legs and feet. He carried a
staff, which he held out before him defensively. He barred
Alaric's way.

"Are you guarding the valley?" asked Alaric.

"One of many guards," said the boy. "Stay where you
are." From his sash hung a goat's horn; he put it to his
lips and blew a long, thin note. From the west came a
faint reply.

"I assure you, I am a harmless minstrel," said Alaric,
bowing deeply.

"I am very good with this quarterstaff," the boy told
him. "Do not move."

"Not so much as a finger," said the minstrel. Briefly,
he debated vanishing, but that would mean returning the
way he had come, and he was in no mood for retreat. He
could hardly blame the folk of the valley for their vigi-
lance. If any people lived in the mountains, they must be
bandits, for no man could scratch an honest living in
those heights; therefore, any stranger entering the valley
must be suspect.

Alaric smiled at the boy, who did not smile back—he
took his guardianship very seriously, that one, and his
goats wandered where they would while he held to his
post. Soon, a man arrived, and then another, both armed
with long knives. They looked at Alaric and then up at
the mountainside behind him, shading their eyes against
the high sun.

"Who are you? Where do you come from?" they demanded. "Who follows you, and what weapons have
they?"

"No one follows me," Alaric replied, trying to smile
as ingratiatingly as possible. "I am a minstrel, traveling
the world, viewing its wonders. The mountains tantalized

me, and I crossed them in search of the Northern Sea or some other marvel. I find myself in your lovely valley— a welcome rest stop, a source of fresh bread and meat perhaps, and lively company. I will play for you to prove the truth of my words.'' Very slowly, he unslung his lute and brought it forward under his arm. He tested the strings lightly, found them well in tune, and when no one made any move to stop him, he sang of mountain climbing, spring, and a fair damsel waiting on a nigh-inaccessible peak. The men's arms hung limp at their sides while they listened, their knives pointing to the ground, but the boy did not alter his guardian stance; his goats wandered far up the steep incline, nibbling the fresh young shoots of grass, but he paid them no heed, all his attention on Alaric.

Alaric smiled sadly, in sympathy with the song, with its forlorn youth who could not summon enough courage to dare the heights and win his love. His listeners, how-ever, showed no emotion; unlike the ground, they had not thawed with the arrival of warm weather—winter lay in their souls and on their faces. Alaric was sure of his talent. He had wrung tears from common men, from kings and warriors, from peasants reaping grain under the blazing sun. Yet here was nothing, no reaction, no back of the hand dashing wetness from a cheek, not even a face half-turned away to hide a pitying sigh. Stony si-lence greeted his song, and he realized with dismay that though he had thought he understood the hearts of men, he was still young in wisdom as in years. Not yet eighteen summers old, he finished the song with a discord and stood uncertain before his listeners.

"I come in peace," he said. "Elsewhere, I have been welcomed.''

The men's mouths turned down, and their lips tight-ened, wrinkling like apricots left too long in the hot sun. Their eyes swung sidewise in their heads as they tried to look at each other while still observing him. They had wispy, fair hair, parted in the middle, and their cheeks were hollowed, fringed with pale beard.

"Many a lord has set me at his table of an evening," Alaric said, yearning mightily that they would leave off this silent scrutiny and make some gesture, whether for good or ill. "I was thinking to journey to yonder castle," he told them, indicating the distant fortification with a movement of his lute.

One of the men rubbed at his jaw with his free hand. Then he said, "Come along," and he gestured with the knife as with a naked, beckoning hand.

Alaric followed him, and the other man fell in line behind them. The boy remained, standing on the rough track and watching till the three were well away, and only then did he turn to his goats, flailing with his staff and bawling them into order. Glancing over his shoulder, Alaric saw him scrambling among the rocks like his animals. *Well, with practice enough, I, too, would be so agile*, he thought. He wondered if the goats grazed the very peaks in high summer.

Where valley met mountainside, Alaric could not tell. Gradually, the grass grew thicker and smoother, the rocks less numerous, the incline less extreme, until the three men strode along a level path well beaten by human and animal feet, a path that wound among sparse trees and between fields tilled dark by the plow and spangled with fresh growth of beans and barley. It looked a prosperous valley, low stone walls shielding the crops from wandering grazers, houses neatly tended, apple and pear and cherry trees crowding out most other kinds. The men guided Alaric to a house that stood in the shade of an ancient, sprawling apple, and they bade him enter. After his journey down the mountainside, and the briefer stroll through cultivated grounds, Alaric was grateful for the chance to rest his weary feet.

The two-room house was empty of humans, though there was a very young lamb swaddled in homespun, sleeping in a cradle by the hearth. Alaric assumed it was sickly and being fed by hand—in an isolated valley, all domestic animals were far more valuable than in the wide world.

"Will you have a bowl of porridge after your journey?" asked one of the men.

"I thank you for your kind hospitality, sir," said Alaric, and he accepted the bowl and spoon that were proffered. The porridge was cold and crusty, but not without flavor, for it contained more than a little honey. He had eaten worse fare in his life.

"You'll stay the night with us," said his host, "and in the morn go on to the Red Lord's castle." His friend nodded soberly, as if in agreement with sage advice. "We will go with you and present you to the Red Lord. He will be most generous."

"Very well," said Alaric. "If you wish, I shall sing for my supper here and then sleep well and long before presuming upon his generosity."

The men inclined their heads. "You may stay within," said his host, "and rest upon the straw if you will, while we work our fields. My wife will be home soon, and no doubt she will be able to find one or two small tasks you may turn your hands to."

"No doubt," Alaric said dryly, and then he shrugged. He often happened upon cotters who felt that no song could pay for food, who provided him with an ax for splitting rails or a churn for making butter. Only in the great houses were his skills respected as honest recompense for room and board. He resigned himself to these petty cotters and their petty values; upon occasion, he felt guilty enough to agree with them. Just now, he was too tired to trek the final leagues to the fortification; as soon as the men had left, he stretched out upon the straw for a nap. Later, he would pay, with a song or with the strength of his arms—what mattered one single day of labor, he thought, in return for the good will of his host, when tomorrow he would rest in luxury?

He drifted on the edge of sleep, and the voices of toiling men and calling crows and barking dogs intruded pleasantly into his dreams. At last, the soft sound of a woman's long skirt sweeping the floor nearby buoyed him into wakefulness. Without moving, he opened one eye the merest slit. In the late-afternoon sunlight that streamed through the room's two windows and open door, he saw a woman moving quietly. She was stoking the fire with split logs, a pot slung over her left arm, ready to set above the flames. Heat had reddened her face and brought forth beads of sweat to dampen her white cap and collar. She was a middle-aged woman, coarse-featured, big-boned, and fleshy. Damp tendrils of graying hair strag-

gled out from under her cap, and she swept them aside
from time to time with one plump forearm. After she
finished with the fire, she lifted the sleeping lamb from
the cradle and, cuddling it close to her ample bosom,
began to rock it and croon a wordless lullaby. The lamb
woke and struggled, but the woman held it tight and
paced the room, swaying from side to side, as if she
soothed a colicky child. She bent her head and nuzzled
the lamb's forelock, kissing its curly-haired muzzle and
whispering half-audible endearments between snatches of
melody.

Alaric stretched, yawning loudly, and he sat up in the
straw and scrubbed at his face with both hands. "Good
evening," he said to the woman.

"Good evening, minstrel," she replied, and then she
returned to her one-sided conversation with the lamb.

"Your husband said you might have some small work
for me. I would be most happy to perform whatever task
you might set."

She looked at him speculatively and then, placing the
lamb gently in its cradle and tucking the covers round it
tightly, she said, "Sing a lullaby for the little one."

He glanced around the room to make certain that there
was no human child she might be referring to. No, there
was only the cradle by the hearth and the little creature
that lay there, bleating feebly now and then but making
no attempt to escape its bed.

"If you wish, goodwife, a lullaby." He lay the lute
across his knees and strummed softly, feeling a bit foolish. But he sang a lullaby. It was easier than churning
butter.

She prepared supper swiftly and laid four places at the
table, four bowls, four cups, four pewter spoons. She
took a long loaf of bread from a cabinet behind the table
and set it in the center of the board. Then she drew an
earthen jug from a dark corner in the back of the room,
and she placed that on the table, too, and then she began
to weep, leaning over the jug, fondling it with her hands;
she wept as though her heart would break.

Alaric put the lute aside, not knowing what to do, not
knowing what had caused her sudden sorrow. He walked
toward her, stopping with the table between them, and

he reached out to touch her arm lightly. "May I be of some service, goodwife?" he asked in a low voice.

She looked up, but she did not see him; her eyes were focused on some inner vision, or on nothing at all. Her fingers gripped the jug convulsively, trying to knead the hard clay, or to gouge it. Tears streamed down her cheeks as she lifted the jug in both hands, wrenched herself away from the table, and stumbled toward the door. At the threshold, she lifted the jug high, as if consecrating it to some deity, and then she flung it from her, screaming curses. Striking the hard-packed path, the earthenware cracked into several pieces, and the pale fluid within splashed the ground.

The woman sagged against the doorjamb then, as if all the strength had drained from her body with that toss, and Alaric hurried to her side to support her, to help her back to the hearth and a stool. She leaned upon him heavily and would have fallen had he not been her crutch. She slumped forward on the stool, almost falling into the fire, and she wept, she wept, as if the world were coming to an end and she saw her loved ones tumbling into the pit. Alaric fanned her with one hand and held her upright with the other.

The men came in soon after—they must have heard her cries—and the one who had acted as host took her in his arms and shook her, calling her name over and over again: "Aramea, Aramea." The other man tended dinner, stirring the pot with a long spoon and tasting the contents frequently. At last the husband took his wife into the rear room of the cottage, and then he returned for the lamb, delivered it into her care, and closed the door between her and the men.

They ate in silence, a stew rich in vegetables, huge chunks of dark bread; they drank water. Afterward, the men asked Alaric to sing, but they seemed hardly to notice his music, lively though it was. He tried to cheer them with bawdy rhymes and gay melody, but they were cheerless, moody, seemed to find the flames in the hearth more interesting than the minstrel. In the back room, he could hear the lamb bleat occasionally.

At full dark, Alaric begged their leave for a stroll around the house, for his digestion's sake, and for the privacy that nature's processes required. The broken jug still lay in the path—full moonlight revealed a sparkle of liquid remaining in its curved bottom. He picked it up, sniffed the contents: wine, a fruity, aromatic wine. He set the earthenware fragment back on the ground. He wondered what it meant. He thought it might make a fine song.

The boy arrived shortly, and he penned his goats in a wooden enclosure behind the house before claiming his own late supper. He eyed the lute while he ate, and Alaric smiled and picked the instrument up and sang for him. Of all the household, only he paid heed to the minstrel's performance, and his foot wagged in time to the music.

Here is an acolyte, thought Alaric. *He is like myself at the same age.* "Can you sing, lad?" he asked.

"I can whistle," said the boy. He pursed his lips and blew a brief, lilting tune that Alaric did not recognize.

"Can you whistle this?" the minstrel inquired, and he plucked a melody on the lute. The boy imitated it without difficulty, and Alaric repeated the notes, adding chords and weaving counterpoint among them and finally singing softly, and thus these two amused themselves for quite some time while the two older men huddled together by the fire and said nothing. The boy frowned his concentration as the music waxed complex, and sometimes he closed his eyes as if visualizing his own part, shutting out the distractions of the quiet cottage; he moved his foot, tapped his fingers on his knee, even nodded his head to keep the rhythm as he whistled.

At last the master of the house—Alaric presumed him the goatherd's father—rose from his stool, and poking at the dying embers with a long stick, he said, "Dawn comes early tomorrow."

The boy hung his head a moment, his whistling stilled abruptly in mid-tune, and he sighed. But then he nodded slowly, not to anyone in particular, and he left his place near the minstrel to fling himself down upon the thick straw in the corner. His father's companion did likewise, and the father himself broke the stick he had used as a poker, cast it into the flames, and went into the other room, closing the door firmly behind him. No one bid Alaric good night, but the boy and the older man left him

ample room in the straw, so he settled himself and his
lute and soon passed into sleep.

He was awakened by the heavy sound of boots tramping across the floor. He opened his eyes to pale dawn
twilight and a room filled with babbling people. The cotters were all there, all talking at once, and the lamb was
bleating loudly above the melee. Listening silently was a
knot of armed men—five of them, in chain-mail shirts
and dark leather, hands resting on sheathed swords, heads
covered by brass-studded caps.

"We would have come," Alaric's host was stammer-
ing. "We would have come straight after dawn." His
wife wailed wordlessly, standing behind her man as behind a shield, clutching the lamb to her bosom. The other
man and the boy pressed close.

The leader of the armed men stared at Alaric, and when
he saw that the minstrel was awake, he stretched out one
arm and shouted, "You!"

The cotters fell silent as if their throats were cut, and
they all turned to look at Alaric.

He rose slowly, brushing straw from his clothing and
lute. "Good morn," he said.

"The Red Lord wants you," said the soldier. "We are
your escort."

Alaric smiled slightly. "I thank the Red Lord for his
invitation," he said. "I will wait upon him immediately."

"Give him some bread," said the soldier, and Alaric's
erstwhile host scurried to gather a crust and some scraps
of cheese, which he thrust into the minstrel's hands.
"And a draft of water as well, for the journey." The
cotter signaled the boy, who brought a bucket and dipper.

"Thank you," said Alaric, and he bowed to the family
and to his escort before dipping up a long, cold drink.
Then he shouldered his knapsack and lute and marched
out of the cottage munching his breakfast, surrounded by
armed and armored men. Behind him, he heard the
goatherd whistling a familiar tune.

The soldiers set an easy pace, as if they were in no
particular hurry. They had not taken his knife or searched
his baggage for other weapons, or drawn a blade on him,
so he felt safe enough. There was a sword in his knap-

sack, but he did not think of extracting it for defense; if real danger presented itself, he could always vanish. He understood the Red Lord's interest in newcomers, and belatedly he wondered if he should not have ignored his weariness and extended his journey to the castle instead of stopping the night at the peasant's home. He hoped the Red Lord did not consider his actions discourteous— there was a poor footing for a cordial relationship. He had noticed in his travels that royalty and nobility tended to be intolerant of faults in lesser mortals, whether such faults were real or fancied. He prepared himself to be as humble and charming as possible. He wondered if the Red Lord had a young daughter or wife; that usually helped in awkward situations. Alaric was fully aware of his own physical attractions.

He smiled at his escort and began to sing along the way, and to strum the lute, a marching tune he had heard once among the young warriors of a castle far to the south. The men fell into step about him, treading to his meter. They passed a few peasants, who turned to stare at the men marching to music, and Alaric smiled at them and nodded. But they never smiled back.

Has it been such a hard winter? Alaric wondered. *Or am I in bad company?*

The castle loomed ahead, pennants fluttering on its battlements, pikes visible on the shoulders of pacing guards at the top of the wall. The portcullis was up; Alaric and his escort marched past it, and it did not lower behind them.

Peacetime, he thought, seeing men-at-arms lolling at their ease in the courtyard, some half out of their armor, few practicing their skills against the wooden dummies that waited for mock attack. *Peacetime, but the peasants do not look kindly upon their protectors. High taxes, perhaps? A small valley and many soldiers to support . . .*

The keep was a massive tower, dark with age and pitted by weather. They entered. The Red Lord awaited them in the high-ceilinged central room, amid tapestries ancient and faded, amid fine furniture rubbed smooth with the touch of many bodies, upon a flagstone floor grooved by the tread of many feet. They followed that worn path to his chair.

The Red Lord was tall and gaunt and no longer young. His flowing hair and beard were blond—the blond that comes when red hair fades and silver mingles with the darker strands. His eyes were gray and cold like the winter sky, his skin as pale as ice. From throat to ankle he wore crimson cloth—tunic, cloak, and hose—and his shoes were of red leather. Upon his right hand, a massive ruby-tinted gemstone shone like the eye of a serpent.

The soldiers knelt before him, and Alaric instantly followed suit. The leader of the escort took his master's hand and kissed the ring. "This is the man, Lord," he said.

Alaric peered up cautiously as the Red Lord turned to him. A scar, paler even than the white skin, showed above the man's collar—lucky he was, Alaric thought, to be alive after such a wound.

"Your name," said the Red Lord, his voice deep and booming as a drum, carrying throughout the room. Alaric felt his skin prickle. There were other people in the room, men in addition to those who had entered with him, and their utter silence was a sign of respect beyond any he had ever seen. No seneschal needed call for quiet in that chamber, neither before nor after the master spoke.

"My lord, I am Alaric the minstrel."

"Your home," said the Red Lord.

"I have none, Highness. I travel the wide world, seeking food and shelter where I may, trading my songs for bread."

"Why have you come here?"

Alaric bowed his head. "I wander, Lord. I have no reason for going anywhere, merely fancy. The mountains were there, and I wished to know if I could cross them. I did hear tales of a great Northern Sea beyond them, and I thought it might be an interesting sight. I had no pressing obligations calling me elsewhere."

The Red Lord glanced at his soldiers. "We found no other strangers," said their leader.

"I had no companions, Highness," said Alaric.

The Red Lord extended his right hand toward Alaric's face. "You may kiss my ring."

Alaric touched his lips to the cool gemstone, smelled

a faint, sweet perfume on the hand that bore it. The white
skin was dry and taut against the bones, an old man's
head, but steady.

The Red Lord nodded. ''I will hear your songs at dinner.'' To his soldiers, he said, ''See to his comfort.'' He
waved a dismissal.

As a body, they rose, and Alaric also scrambled to his
feet. The master of the castle had already turned away to
speak to someone else. Relieved, Alaric followed his escort out to the courtyard, where spring sunshine dispelled
the chill that had settled on his heart in the chamber. The
Red Lord was a forbidding man, a fit match for the
mountains that ringed his realm, and Alaric could not
relish the thought of trying to entertain him.

The soldiers led him to their own barracks, a stone and
a wooden shelter built against the castle wall. Within,
straw pallets made two long rows on either side, each
pallet separated narrowly from its neighbor by a naked
strip of hard-packed earth. Above the straw hung weapons and armor and bits and pieces of clothing—every
man's possessions exposed for all his comrades to see.
Upon every bed was a pillow of sorts, either a wooden
box or a lumpy bundle, and Alaric guessed that these hid
whatever other fancies the soldiers might own. How they
kept their valuables secret, he knew not, unless they wore
them on their persons at all times. *Or else,* he thought,
they have none.

The minstrel was assigned a bare spot far from the
door, and his escort tramped up and down the rows, col-
lecting a handful of straw from each pallet until they had
enough for an extra one. They left Alaric to shape it
himself.

''You'll be called when you're needed,'' the leader told
him.

Alaric nodded and dropped his knapsack where a pillow should have been. Although his own escort marched
out of the barracks, he was not left alone; several men
sat about, polishing or honing their weapons, mending
clothes, or merely lying still upon their straw. Alaric was
certain that they all watched him out of the corners of
their eyes—he expected no less. When his bed was settled, he sat upon it, his back to the cold stone wall, and

let the lute lie across his lap. He plucked idly at the strings. He sang a pair of songs about summer, and presently the sun rose above the castle walls, and a narrow, mote-laden beam lanced through the doorway of the room. The soldiers seemed to listen, though they said nothing. When Alaric went outside to the courtyard, one of them followed him, to sit in the sunlight and sew a fresh seam in his jerkin.

'Dust had risen with the sun. The courtyard was dry, barren ground except where some horses splashed water from their trough. Alaric joined a group of men there drinking from a bucket. They eyed him incuriously and made no attempt to converse, though he greeted them affably enough. Unlike most folk he had encountered in his travels, they seemed to have no interest at all in the world beyond the mountains. For a time he watched their idleness, their occasional leisurely combat, their gambling with knucklebones, and then he returned to the barracks. Upon his pallet, the lute and knapsack still lay close together, but Alaric noted that the sack had shifted a trifle—they had searched it in his absence, as he had presumed they would. Now they knew that he carried a sword, but his unobtrusively probing fingers told him they had not taken it. Why should they? He was outnumbered a thousand to one.

He was not a warrior. He had never drawn blood with that sword. He doubted that he was skilled enough to do so. Sometimes he wondered if he ought not to rid himself of the sword—it would sell for a goodly price in any market—and thus avoid the chance of being put to the test. Yet when his fingers touched it, memory flooded through them to his heart . . . memory of two good friends and of his first love, left far, far behind. And he could not cast himself loose of this last reminder of the past.

He would not wear it into the Red Lord's presence. That would be bad manners for a stranger with peaceful intentions. Nor would it look well with his travel-stained clothing and worn boots, an imposing sword with fine, tooled scabbard. It was not a sword for a poor minstrel. Some would say he was a coward—and perhaps they had, behind his back—but he preferred to think of himself as cautious. He had never worn it.

He had washed at the trough, dusted his boots and cloak and tunic, run wet fingers through his hair. Now he waited. It was full afternoon before he was called to the keep, and he had begun to feel hungry.

The Red Lord's chair had been moved back and a table placed before it, and other chairs added all around. He was seated already, as were three more men, and an additional four were crossing the room to join him as Alaric approached. An armed companion guided Alaric to a high stool set some distance from the table.

"When do I eat?" Alaric asked of him in a low voice.

"Afterward," he replied.

Alaric sighed. If he stayed with the Red Lord long, he would have to change that. A growling stomach disturbed his pitch. A light snack before—a slice of beef, a chunk of cheese—and then a fuller repast later were, to his mind, the proper form of payment. Too many patrons treated their dogs better than their minstrels, and here was another: several large dogs circled the table and were tossed meaty scraps by the dining men, including the Red Lord himself. Alaric tried to ignore the aroma of warm, fresh-baked bread and juicy roast, and he sang of the wild wind that blew upon the mountains. He began softly, and when no one bade him shut his mouth, he increased his volume till the rich tones of his voice and his lute rose above the clatter of dishes and goblets. The Red Lord looked at him several times during the meal, but he said nothing, only chewed with slow precision and drank deep from a cup that was filled and refilled by hurrying stewards.

There were no young people in the room. Alaric himself was the youngest by thirty years or more: the diners were of an age with the Lord himself, and the servitors were much the same. Another nobleman might have a young cupbearer or a lively, bright-eyed wench to carry the bread, or he might have his children ranged about the board, listening and learning for the time when they would bear his burdens. *Well, the customs of another land*, Alaric thought, and he wondered if later he would be called to entertain a Red Lady and her children. Or,

judging from the Red Lord's apparent age, her grandchildren.

He was fed in the kitchen after the diners left their
table, fed with the scraps of a sumptuous meal, and it
was more than enough to stay the grumble of his belly.
The cooks watched him eat as they scrubbed their pots
and polished their cutlery, and they seemed to pass un-
spoken messages to one another—a lifted eyebrow, a
nodding head, a shrug of the shoulders. Alaric tried to
engage them in conversation twice or thrice, but they
would not speak to him; they pretended to be too busy
with their own concerns to hear his banter.

A soldier beckoned for him to return to the hall, and
he went back to his stool, now standing in a wide-open
space twenty paces from the Red Lord's chair—the table
and the other seats having been removed while he was
gone. He climbed atop it, his feet resting comfortably on
a brace at knee height above the floor, and he sang for
the Red Lord, who sprawled at ease in his seat. Deep
into the afternoon he sang, with none to interrupt him.
The silence in the room was like a blanket of snow; even
when men passed through, their steps were light though
the floor was hard stone, as if unnecessary sound would
call forth some harsh penalty.

Evening came, and as the light from high, slitted windows failed, torches were lit all round the room, and
flickering shadows brought a semblance of great activity
to the chamber. The master of the castle lifted one arm
in peremptory gesture, and a bent-backed servitor scut-
tled forward with wine. The Red Lord took a cup, then
pointed at Alaric; the servant bobbed across the inter-
vening space and offered a drink to the minstrel, who
took it gratefully and saluted his host with the upraised
cup before draining it dry.

"You may go," said the Red Lord.

Alaric slipped off the stool, bowed low, and headed for
the kitchen. A light supper was being prepared there, and
he snatched a share of it before it was carried out to the
hall. The cooks ignored him, but a pair of soldiers hung
about the door, clearly waiting for him, and after he had
satisfied his craving for supper, he let them escort him
back to their barracks.

In the north, the spring twilight seemed to last half the night. Before the sky had darkened completely, Alaric was lying upon his straw pallet, dozing, his lute clutched safely beneath his arm. Beyond the nearest window, he could see a small sliver of the pale western sky, and the evening star shining brightly in the wake of the setting sun. Few of the soldiers had retired yet; he could hear many men walking about in the courtyard. He fell asleep to those soft, scuffing sounds, his belly full and his heart at ease. His last drowsy thought was that they were a dour and silent lot, these northerners, but at least the Red Lord himself had an appreciation of good music.

He woke to the sound of a woman's scream. At first he thought himself dreaming, for the sky was dark, and all about him sleeping men breathed softly. Then the scream came again, a high-pitched, wild shriek, wordless, distant, yet clear. He sat up. Beyond the window, a single torch on the opposite side of the courtyard glittered like a yellow star. Alaric picked his way among the sleepers and stepped out the open door. One pace past the threshold, a guard stopped him.

"Go back to bed, minstrel," said the man. He held a pike against his body, leaning upon the straight shaft as upon a staff.

"A call of nature," said Alaric, and he gestured toward the shelter that all the men used in common. The guard let him go, and he relieved himself, and then he heard the scream again. It drifted to him from above, as if blown to his ears by the wind. Tilting his head, he traced the sound to the upper reaches of the keep, where a dim light showed through half-open shutters. Like a tangible thing, then, the scream tumbled from the gap.

He returned to the barracks still looking up, over his shoulder. "What is it?" he asked the guard at the door.

"Nothing," said the man.

Alaric shook his head. "That's not nothing."

"A girl, then. What business is it of yours?"

Alaric looked at the man's grim face and said, "None. None at all." And he went inside.

The next day was much like the first, except that Alaric managed to snatch some food before he was required to sing for the master of the castle. An escort followed him wherever he went—not always the same escort, nor always a formal guard, but still he was carefully watched. His stool awaited him in the hall, and the same silence greeted his songs; he wrung neither tear nor chuckle from any in his audience, though he tried mightily. He received wine from his host and the same curt dismissal afterward; there were no compliments for him and no criticism. He felt as though he were singing to the forest, to the mute trees and the uncaring stones. The food was excellent, but he knew that he could not endure much more of this valley. He had yet to see a single pair of smiling lips. Sorrow hemmed him in at every side; though no one spoke of it, it was nonetheless real, bleak on every face and heavy in every step. For all the green buds and new blooms in the meadows, winter had not left the Red Lord's domain.

That night again, the screams, and as he listened closely, lying on his warm straw bed, he thought he could hear weeping after them, though it was soft and far away. And all around him, strong men slept through someone else's misery. He wondered if perhaps she were a madwoman—perhaps the Red Lord's own wife or daughter—locked in the tower and screaming into the night for some reason known only to her sick brain. A thousand fantasies drifted through his thoughts; there was a song here, if only he could persuade someone to tell the tale.

In the morning he attempted to befriend the soldier whose bed was nearest his own. He was a man of middle years, though possibly a few seasons younger than most of his mates. He wore a beard and mustache, blond as his comrades, but above them his cheeks were unlined and his eyes only a trifle crinkled at their corners. Sitting on his straw, he mended a shirt, but Alaric thought his real reason for staying indoors was to guard the stranger. Alaric leaned against the wall and plucked aimlessly at his lute.

"Have you been a soldier for many years?" he asked the man.

"All my life," was the reply.

"I suppose bandits come down from the mountains in the summer."

"Not often."

"They must fear you greatly."

The man nodded. His skill with the needle was limited, and he sewed an awkward patch on an already patchwork woolen shirt. He stabbed himself a few times and swore loudly.

"Is there no woman to do that for you?" Alaric inquired.

"Not for me," muttered the man, and he persevered until the work was done.

"Has the Red Lord a lady of his own?" asked Alaric. "And sons, daughters, grandchildren? Tell me—I would know something of the man I sing for."

The soldier squinted at him. "Why?"

Alaric shrugged. "For my curiosity's sake, nothing more."

The soldier threw down the mended shirt. "He is a great commander." Having said this, he retired to the far end of the barracks, ending the conversation.

Shortly, Alaric went to the kitchen, knowing that soon he would be called to make music for his host. He ignored the soldier who trailed after him and instead sought out a grandmotherly woman he had seen among the cooks on the previous nights, a woman he had smiled at often in his attempts to win a friend or two, but who, like her countrymen, never smiled back. He found her at the hearth, drawing a spitted bird away from the flames, and she was not so proof against his charm that he could not wheedle a crisp brown wing from her . . . and its mate. "How will the creature balance on the platter with just one wing?" he said, and she gave him the meat on a wooden trencher.

He seated himself atop an unused table and watched the kitchen workers. At any other castle, in spite of the presence of a stranger, they would be chattering as they moved about their tasks. All the gossip of the tightly knit castle society would float through the kitchen; no one would be spared, from the highest to the lowest. Alaric had seen this often enough that he always repaired to the kitchen to have his curiosity satisfied. Yet here was quiet save for a few cooking instructions or a curse if someone sliced a finger instead of a carrot. He wondered if they feared foreigners so much that they kept silence rather than reveal their petty secrets to him . . . or if they merely never spoke. A strange, dead kitchen it was, and the blaze on the hearth was cold in spirit if not in essence.

He was called, as he knew he would be, and he found himself reluctant to go into the large, cold hall and face the large, cold man. He went, of course, in spite of that reluctance, for he owed the Red Lord songs in return for his hospitality, for the very meat he had just eaten. And there was nothing to keep him in that kitchen.

As the afternoon waned, his decision formed itself: no longer would Alaric the minstrel remain in this land of sorrow. He had had enough—enough to last him well into the summer, enough to bring back his own sorrows, which he had hoped to put aside with travel. He sang the better for his decision, to give the Red Lord full measure, to leave him well satisfied and perhaps a bit wistful for more, to leave behind him the tale of a charming young minstrel with a silver voice. Though he wondered if they saw him so. He wondered if, wrapped in their own private winter, they perceived any breath of spring.

At dusk, he saw the Red Lord shift in his chair, and Alaric left his stool to fall to his knees before his host could utter words of dismissal. "My lord," he murmured.

"What is it, minstrel?"

"Lord, I beg leave to continue my journey with the rising sun."

"Your journey?"

"Lord, I would see lands farther north while the season is fair, and then return southward for the winter. As I told you when I came, I seek the Northern Sea and as many other new sights as my life will allow. I never stay long anywhere."

The Red Lord fingered his beard. "The northern passes are scarcely clear. The way is rugged. More mountains bar your path. You would be wise to bide awhile with us."

Alaric bowed his head. "Lord, if my songs have pleased you, I am happy; yet the wild wind calls me and I would go."

"Your songs have pleased me, minstrel. I had hopes that you would sing them longer than these few days."

Alaric said nothing but only bowed lower.

The Red Lord rose from his chair. "I would gift you, minstrel, before you leave. Come with me now, if you are bound to go, and receive a fit reward for your services."

Alaric climbed slowly to his feet. "I need no reward beyond your kind hospitality, Lord," he said. "I have eaten and slept well. I ask no more of the world."

"You must come," the Red Lord said in a voice that brooked no denial.

Alaric slung the lute across his back. "If you insist, Lord, then let it be something small, for I prefer to travel light." He wondered: Gold? Jewels? What wealth could this isolated valley boast that would be easily portable?

The Red Lord turned, and with a gesture bade the minstrel follow. Behind them, the ever-present escort trailed. At one end of the room was the stone stairway that curved upward along the wall of the keep; the Red Lord climbed, and the guards lit torches and held them high as they followed him. At the top of the steps, one of the men opened an iron-bound wooden door for his master, and the party passed through that into the upper chambers of the keep, a ring of small, wedge-shaped rooms about the central tower.

In the first room, the Red Lord said, "Here we have silver." Chests of every size and shape were heaped upon the floor, wooden, bronze, brass, and iron, each with a massive lock upon its face. "Open these containers and you will find dishes and goblets, candelabras and mirrors and ornaments of many kinds. I count silver the least of my treasures."

A soldier strode ahead to open a second door in the chamber and reveal another room. Here were more chests, though not so many by half as in the first.

"More precious by far is gold," said the Red Lord, and he nodded at the coffers as he passed them, as if they were old friends.

Another door, another room, and a single brass-bound trunk in the center of the floor.

"Jewels," said the Red Lord. "We have few of these, yet their value is above that of all the silver and gold before them." He glanced at Alaric, who made no com-

ment, and then he paused by the farther door in this
chamber. "And beyond, the greatest treasure of them
all." He turned the key in the lock and pulled the massive panel open with his own hands. The soldiers crowded
behind Alaric, as if they, too, wished to see the greatest
treasure, and he found himself leaning forward with their
pressure, his heart beating expectantly.

A woman.

She was young and might have been comely before her
face was bruised. Her skin might have been fair and flaw-
less before it was torn. Her limbs might have been lithe
and straight before they were broken. Naked, filthy,
smeared and crusted with dried and drying blood, she
hung slack in manacles bolted to the stone wall.

Alaric shrank back involuntarily, but the soldiers were
there and kept him from going far. *This*, he thought, *this
is the woman who screamed.*

The Red Lord approached her till he stood at arm's
length, and then he stretched his hand out to stroke her
cheek. The gesture would have been a caress in other
circumstances; now it was a grotesque parody of affec-
tion. At his touch, she moaned and opened her eyes. No,
only one eye opened—Alaric felt his stomach rising to
his throat as he realized that the other eye was a newly
empty socket.

"No more, Lord," she whispered. Her feeble voice
was loud in the small room, at least to Alaric's ears. "I
beg you, let me die."

He took the jeweled dagger from his belt and, as Alaric
watched in horror, scraped the point across her bare
shoulder, drawing a deep and ragged gouge. Bright blood
welled out of the wound and ran down her arm and breast;
on her torso it was quickly lost among the marks of other
injuries.

"Please," she moaned, her lips scarcely moving.
"Please, my lord."

The Red Lord turned to Alaric, his mouth curved into
a cold smile. "Blood," he said. "The greatest treasure."

Alaric found his voice after a long moment. "What
has she done, my lord?"

"Nothing."

"Then . . . then why is she here?"

"She is mine," said the Red Lord. "There need be no other reason." He touched the woman's blood-encrusted hair, wound his fingers in the strands, and pulled her head sharply upright. A scabbed-over cut on her neck broke open at the jerk, and more crimson flowed across her flesh. When she moaned, he said, "Have you already forgotten how to scream?"

The woman fainted instead of answering.

He turned back to the minstrel. "Do you pity her, boy?"

Alaric could see the soldiers from the corner of his eye. They stood erect, swords and daggers sheathed; they stood between him and the only door. A single, half-shuttered window admitted night air to the room, which now seemed too stuffy for Alaric's taste. A scant arm's length away, the Red Lord toyed with his dagger.

"I would pity any wounded creature," said Alaric.

"You shall have ample time to practice your pity," said the Red Lord. He nodded at the soldiers. "Shackle him."

As they grasped Alaric's arms, snatched the knife from his belt and the lute from his back, he cried out, "My lord, I have done nothing to deserve this!"

"When you entered my valley, you became mine," said the Red Lord. "I do with you as I will."

Alaric let the soldiers chain him to the wall beside the woman, perceiving that they would offer him no violence if he offered none to them. Indeed, they were gentle, as if they fastened bracelets of gold to his wrists instead of iron. Alaric did not watch them lock the manacles; he knew no metal in the world could hold him without his consent. Instead, he looked to the master of the castle.

"My lord, this is a poor reward for one who has done his best to please you."

The Red Lord sheathed his dagger. "Your reward, minstrel, shall be that you will not be touched until this other one is dead." He slapped her face with the back of his hand, but she did not stir. Only her hoarse breathing showed her to be alive. "Tomorrow, perhaps, or the next day." He slapped her again, harder, and she moaned. "Do not sleep," he said to her. "We have an appointment later tonight." He gestured to his soldiers, and the entire party went out, shutting the door behind them and leaving Alaric and the woman in darkness.

Beyond the window, the moon had already risen high, flooding the courtyard with its pale light, and even sending a shaft through the half-open shutter. Alaric's eyes adapted to the dimness quickly, and then he moved in his special way, only a short distance, leaving empty manacles dangling upon the wall.

Lightly, he touched the woman. "I will take you away from here," he said. As gently as he could, he lifted her free of the floor and pulled her as far from the wall as her shackles allowed. She gasped, "No, please, no," and then he had freed her and journeyed, all in a heartbeat, to a niche on the mountainside. There he laid her on a grassy spot, on the spot where the goatherd had stopped him and he had waited so long for two men to answer the boy's horn. Her body trembled, and she clutched feebly at the air. He let her take his hands. Bending low over her face, he said, "He shall not touch you again." He could scarcely discern her ruined features, so softened were they by moonlight, yet they were graven in his memory; he knew that he would see them in his dreams for all the days of his life. *Where can I go?* She could not be taken to her own people, whoever they were—the Red Lord would surely look there first, come midnight and his pleasure spoiled. As a minstrel, Alaric had been welcomed into many houses, of high station and low—in his mind, the years unrolled, and the miles, as he selected among them. There had been kind hearts along the way, and good wishes for his travels; now he would have to bring some well-wisher the real tragedy and not merely the song.

He began to slip his arms beneath her, to lift her for the journey, but she stopped him with a gasp. "Please don't move me."

Gently, he pulled away. "Rest if you wish, before we travel on. We have a little time."

She turned her head slowly, to fix him with her good eye. "Who are you?" she whispered.

"I am Alaric, a minstrel. A stranger. I was able to free you. You are safe now."

"He will find us. He will take us back."

"He will never find us. I know a way to leave this valley that none can follow. Trust me. I will take you to a warm bed and kind friends who will nurse you back to health."

For a moment she was silent, then her voice came so soft that he had to bend ever closer to hear her words, and the stink of her festering wounds turned his stomach as he listened. "No one has ever escaped this valley."

"I can."

"Travelers who come out of the mountains. Bandits and merchants alike. Whole caravans." Her breath came fast and shallow, as if the sheer effort of speaking exhausted her. "He takes them to the tower room. None survive."

He touched her hair gently. "But you—you are one of his own people."

"In a long winter . . . he becomes restless. Then we must serve his pleasure."

"What sort of lord is this," cried Alaric, "who destroys those he is bound to protect?"

"He pays for us. With wine."

He remembered the cotter woman, and the jug of wine she smashed. Was the lamb a feeble replacement for some child lost to her lord? Alaric shivered, though the night air was warm enough. "Why have you not risen up and killed this man?"

She sighed, a long shuddering sigh. "It is good wine."

He looked back over his shoulder. In the moonlight, he could barely discern the castle, standing dark by the silver glimmer of the river. How long, he wondered, had it been going on? Why had no peasant assassinated this monster? Were his soldiers so fanatically loyal that they could stand by and watch their innocent countrymen—perhaps members of their own families—tortured to death?

"We must not stay here," he said. Once more he slipped his hands beneath her body.

Her arms fluttered weakly against his chest. "No, no," she begged. "Don't move me."

"Good woman, I must move you a little."

"No, no, I cannot . . . I cannot bear it." Her breath

came hoarsely now, and it gurgled in her throat. "Stranger, please . . . just one boon."

"I will do whatever I can for you."

Her right hand groped toward him, so he caught it in his own; that seemed to satisfy her, for she let it lie limp in his grasp. "I am broken . . . inside," she whispered. "There is too much pain. Too much. Stranger, I beg you . . . kill me."

Alaric could feel his heart shrink back in his chest. "Let me take you to friends," he said quickly, "to good and kindly help. You will be well again—"

"No. I will die. Let it be quick."

"No, no, I cannot."

"Please." Her head rocked slowly from side to side. "Please let it be quick."

He clutched her hand tightly, his whole body trembling. *No,* he told himself. *No. No.*

She moaned. "Would you let a mortally wounded creature suffer? Give me a knife and I will do the deed myself."

"I have no knife!" he cried.

"Then you must do it with your hands. Your strong hands."

Hot tears spilled down his cheeks. His fingers had no strength. How could they lock about her slender neck? How could they squeeze until she breathed no more? He, who had never killed in anger—how could he kill in compassion?

"Your strong hands," she murmured. "Oh please . . ."

And then he remembered the sword. Wrapped in his knapsack, it might still lie on his pallet in the barracks. And if not, there were swords aplenty hanging on the walls. The sky was full dark, the men probably swaddled in their individual blankets and snoring. In the barracks he would be a shadow among shadows. He stepped back among the boulders, that his abrupt disappearance might not frighten her. Then he was within the castle walls once more.

His pallet was gone, the space it had occupied empty, its straw probably redivided among the other beds. But in the corner lay all his property; he gathered it in his arms and vanished.

On the mountainside once more, he drew the sword from its scabbard. Moonlight glinted off the polished blade; since he had owned it, the sword had never drunk human blood. He looked down at the woman, saw moisture sparkle in her single eye.

"Strike," she said, and the word was loud as thunder to his ears.

Standing above her, the sword clutched like a great dagger in his two hands, he drove the point into her breast, felt the breastbone cleave beneath his weight, felt the heart yield and the spine snap . . . and then hard earth resisted him. His whole body shuddered for a moment, and he fought to clear his swimming head, his brimming throat; then he lifted the sword, and her whole body rose with it, till only her heels and hands touched the ground, and he had to shake the blade violently to free her from it. He would not touch her flesh with his own.

Blood gushed from the wound, black in the moonlight. Alaric stabbed again, and yet once more, and at last he was satisfied that he had sent her beyond pain. He turned away then, the bloody sword a leaden weight in his grip, weighing down his heart as well as his arm, and he wept for her and for all her kind that had gone before her, and he wept for himself as well, for the loss of something that he could scarcely name.

After a time, his eyes dried and he began to gather leafy branches to spread over her still form. It was only a gesture of honor for the dead, for leaves would not keep the scavengers away come morning and the warm sun, but he had neither time nor inclination to dig a grave. He had dug a grave once, for his beloved companion Dall, and he could not bring himself to dig another and, by that labor, to resurrect so many painful memories. He covered her, and that would have to be enough.

He rose from his knees, still gazing downward, though her body was now no more than a heap of greenery in the light of the moon. A voice brought him to alert: "Hist! Minstrel!"

He took a step backward, sword upraised, body poised for his own peculiar sort of flight, and then his brain recognized that voice. The goatherd. He saw the boy as a dark shape detaching itself from the darkness of a boulder.

"Where are your goats?" Alaric asked softly.

"Sent home. I saw you up here and decided to stay a little, and watch."

Alaric glanced all around, and he listened carefully to the night noises. He saw nothing but the peaceful, moon-touched landscape, heard nothing but the scratchings of insects. "Will the goats not stray without your guidance?"

"Once down the mountain, they go home happily enough," said the boy. He moved closer slowly, and Alaric could see that he carried his staff and his horn. There had been no bray of that horn, as far as Alaric knew . . . but he had been gone for a short while. He wondered if the boy had seen him vanish; probably not, from that distance and in the shadow-riddled night.

"So you watched," said Alaric. "Did you know her?"

The boy bent, drew a branch aside to expose her face. He studied her features for some time, and then he nodded. "I know her."

"She was chained in the Red Lord's tower. He was torturing her without reason."

Again the boy nodded.

"She told me that she was not the first innocent to be taken."

The boy stepped nearer to Alaric. "Are you leaving?"

"Yes. I have no wish to die by torture." In the space of a heartbeat, he recalled the boy sitting at his feet, listening and whistling counterpoint to the lute, and he made a decision. "Would you like to come with me?"

"Come with you?"

"You could be my apprentice, learn the minstrel's trade, and see the wonders of the wide world."

"No one leaves this valley," said the boy. "It is the Red Lord's law."

"I leave. Will you come along?"

The boy stood a long moment in thought, fingering the horn at his belt, and then he said, "Yes."

Alaric smiled stiffly—he feared it was more a grimace than a smile, for his face felt rigid, as if made of cold clay—and he stretched his free hand toward the boy. "Give me your pledge."

The boy clasped his hand firmly.

"What is your name?" asked Alaric.

"Valdin."

"Valdin, we shall be friends from this day forward."

"We shall be friends."

"Our journey begins now. Come, walk close beside me." Silently, he added, *And I shall show you a new form of travel.* He half turned away from the boy, to gaze up at the darkly looming mountain slope, and then a tremendous blow struck him across the back of the head and he fell, rolling, tumbling, down the grassy path until he struck and wedged among some rocks. The sword slid from his nerveless fingers, clattering away in the darkness, and his arms and legs seemed to float away with it. The moon rocked crazily over his head, and the earth heaved beneath him as he struggled for consciousness. Above him, the horn bayed again and again, its note mingling with the roaring in his ears.

Dizzy and sick, he lay still, denying the call to oblivion with all the strength of his mind, and at last the world steadied about him. Feigning a swoon yet, he looked out upon the landscape with slitted eyes. The boy stood above him, staff raised for another blow. Without moving his head, Alaric could see down the slope some distance; he chose a spot that he thought the boy would have some trouble scrambling to quickly, and he went there.

Behind him, the boy's startled cry was loud. Alaric oriented himself swiftly, then flitted still farther away. From a safe distance, he watched and listened to the boy beating the brush for his vanished quarry. Soon, two men were toiling up the slope to join the youngster—Alaric guessed that he knew those two men well enough. They had not been with the boy long when his cries indicated that they were beating him. Alaric hoped they beat him well.

After they had gone back to their cottage, he returned to the burial site and found his sword and lute and knapsack. He wiped the bloody blade on a clump of grass and sheathed it. The body was still there. He wondered if anyone but himself would ever mourn her.

Down at the river, the castle of the Red Lord sat grim and silent in the moonlight. Briefly, Alaric thought of vengeance, for himself and for her and for all those innocents that had come before—vengeance on behalf of folk too terrified or too resigned to seek it for themselves. Perhaps he was the one person who could wreak that vengeance and escape with his life. He grasped the pommel of the sword, and his hand shook and his head spun and he had to close his eyes against the memory of the black blood gushing out of her heart. *I have killed enough for now.*

He turned away. His head ached horribly, and he needed rest. The next mountain peak would be safe enough; he found a grove of stunted trees some distance below it and claimed their shelter for the night.

As he closed his eyes against the glare of the moon, he pushed away all thought that someday he might return.

PART TWO

THE MOUNTAIN FASTNESS

From his resting place deep in the mountains, Alaric could not see the valley of the Red Lord. Yet behind his eyes, its image lingered: thatched huts huddled like frightened sheep in the wide fields, the great stone fortress looming like a vulture over the river, the Red Lord himself clothed in the color of blood and striding through his peasants' lives like a god. And the high tower, most sharply etched image of all, where the Red Lord satisfied the darkest cravings of his heart. Alaric shivered, though the campfire crackled bright at his feet. Beside him, his unsheathed sword glinted in the flamelight. A mere wish could take him back to the castle, to a silent search and a silent execution.

Am I to begin righting the wrongs of the world, Dall? he asked of his beloved mentor's memory. He could have flitted to that lonely grave in an instant, stood above it to contemplate the pattern of the grasses on its mounded surface, but that pattern would yield no answer. Dall the minstrel had never killed another human being; in this, as in so many things, Alaric had surpassed his old friend.

He lay back against a tree. Supper had long since been served in the Red Lord's stronghold, and the scraps of the meal tossed to quarreling dogs. The courtyard would be quiet now, a few men-at-arms standing the weary watch till dawn. Alaric had not been inside the hall so late, but he was sure that only a handful of guards stirred there also, and probably one or two others at the door of the Lord's own chamber. This moment would be perfect for the killing, if only he knew where that chamber lay. But he did not. And so he waited, dozing by the fire, as he had waited for two days already—considering every possible approach, waiting for the perfect plan to come to him.

Waiting for the courage.

All his life he had run away from danger. If the sword had not been a keepsake, he would have sold it long since. But it was a treasure to him, a remnant of lost days of love and laughter with the Princess Solinde, her brother Jeris, and the mocking dwarf who was their father's jester. He could heft it with some grace, because those had also been days of sham combat with Jeris, their wooden weapons clashing beneath the summer sun, quilted armor soaking up their sweat. The blade which was the prince's parting gift had drawn blood only once, only that one terrible time; Alaric had never raised it in anger. Nor was it anger he felt now, only a cold loathing, as for a venomous spider. That loathing kept him in the mountains that hedged the Red Lord's valley, when he could be lazing on some warm hearth singing songs of love . . . but it was not a strong enough emotion to carry him back to the fortress.

Yet it was too strong simply to fade away. He was not a warrior, but he was one man who could do the deed.

He wondered if by now the Red Lord had chosen another victim to shackle in his tower. In that tiny prison room, in the middle of the night, one might kill the valley's dreadful master with only that helpless peasant for witness. Alaric's hand closed on the pommel of his sword. There would be guards standing beyond the door, he guessed, discreetly far from the Red Lord's pleasure; he would have to be quick, strike hard and sure before his quarry could utter a sound. Strike as he had done once already. His arms remembered the feel of the blade plunging through human flesh and bone, his inner eye the gout of blood which followed. His fingers shook, though he gripped the sword with whitened knuckles. *Tomorrow,* he thought. *Tomorrow.* He slid the blade into its scabbard; then he kicked dirt over the fire and curled up in his cloak. Sleep was long in claiming him.

He awoke to a foot prodding his shoulder. A man stood over him, a heavy staff in his hands, its charred and sharpened end pointing at Alaric.

Alaric smiled. "Good morn," he said.

The man grunted. He wore the ragged remains of a linen shirt and trews, with a goatskin pulled over his shoulders as a cloak. His feet were bare and horny, the nails dirty and overgrown like animal claws. He gestured peremptorily with the staff. "Get up."

Alaric obliged him slowly. He made no attempt to touch the sword, seeing the man's eyes flicker in that direction. "My name is Alaric," he said, "and I am a minstrel. See, over there, that bundle contains my lute. I'll play it for you, if you like."

The man scraped the sword toward himself with one foot, then picked it up with his left hand, cradling the staff in his right like a knight couching a lance for the charge. "A pretty piece of weaponry you have here, minstrel," he said, and he smiled, showing a mouth that was missing three teeth. "And you asked to use it, too, by burning wood most of the night on this mountain."

"It was a very small fire," said Alaric, "and I didn't think anyone lived in this wilderness to see it."

"Oh, we live here, if you want to call it a life. We live here." He made a sharp motion with the sword, and if the blade had not been sheathed, Alaric would have flinched, so close did it come to his belly. "Throw that knife down and step back from it."

Alaric did as he said, and the man scooped the knife up with two fingers of the hand that held the sword.

"Are you a bandit?" the minstrel asked.

His captor laughed. "Oh, yes, we are bandits. We plunder and live a soft life up here in the mountains." He jerked his head toward his right shoulder. "Come along, minstrel. You can entertain at our bandit feast."

"I'll need my lute for that."

"Well, then bring it. But mark you show me it's nothing more than a lute before we take another step."

Alaric unwrapped the instrument slowly, and when the man was satisfied with its identity, he wrapped it up again, to protect it from the morning damp. His knapsack contained little more than a change of clothing; his captor passed it with a glance, and Alaric slung both bundles over his shoulder. He started walking.

They took no path, for there was none, not even a goat trail. Underfoot were stones rimmed with tough grass, slippery with dew. The second time he fell, Alaric would have stopped to nurse his battered shins, but the sharp end of the staff urged him onward. "Up there," said the man, pointing to a boulder-strewn incline.

A depression, relatively free of obstructions, followed the base of the rise and curved around it in the distance. "Can't we go that way?" asked Alaric.

"Climb."

The minstrel could have reached the top of the slope in an eyeblink with his power, but so long as another human being watched, he dared not. Instead, panting, he clutched at the rocks with fingers scraped raw and climbed. His captor moved beside him, still carrying staff and sword and knife; he seemed not to need his hands for the ascent at all. They made slow, steady progress, and Alaric began to wonder what they would see at the summit.

He never found out. Well below the top, hidden from the view of anyone beneath by a broad ledge, was the entrance of a cave. Alaric and his captor squeezed through the narrow opening. Inside was darkness and a rank smell.

As his eyes became accustomed to the feeble illumination from behind him, Alaric was able to pick out nearby human figures. He also became aware of the walls and ceiling—the space around him was scarcely more than a pocket in the mountainside, and a few bodies filled it up. The smell, he realized, was that of their unwashed flesh.

"Here he is," said his captor.

"Does he have food?" asked a woman.

"No. He had food yesterday, but he ate it all."

The woman keened softly. "How can he travel without food?"

"He is a fool," said Alaric's captor.

"I planned to hunt," said Alaric.

"You *are* a fool," said another woman. "There's nothing to hunt in these mountains."

"There are wild goats," said Alaric.

"Goats!" said a man. "Shall we turn him loose and watch him hunt the goats of these mountains!"

"Let's eat him," said the first woman. At her words,

a hush fell over the crowd, not even the shuffle of feet marring it.

Alaric edged sideways till rock was at his back and he was no longer silhouetted against the entrance. "I can find you food," he said, "if you're hungry. But if you eat me, you won't have the benefit of my services, nor my music."

"My baby is hungry," said the woman. "I can't give milk without food."

"The stranger says he can find us food," said the other woman. "Where?"

"A secret place," replied Alaric.

"The valley," said the woman who had spoken of her baby. "He'll bring the Red Lord's men to hunt us down."

"Nearer than the valley," said Alaric.

"Show me," said his captor.

"I can't do that. You must trust me."

"We trust no one."

"Swear on your mother's grave that you will not harm me," said Alaric, "and I will swear on mine that I'll not bring you harm."

"As if such swearing would mean anything to the Red Lord!"

"I am not the Red Lord's man. I am not of the valley at all."

"You could have come to the valley since the last of us left. You could be his man . . . though I can't recall that he ever let an outlander live."

"He's done it now!" cried the woman. "To deceive us!"

"Let me leave," said Alaric, "and I'll return before the sun marks noon. I couldn't travel to the valley and back in that short a time."

"He has the Red Lord's men hidden in our mountains!" wailed the woman.

"Hush, Malgis," said the second woman. "We would know if they were in our mountains."

"I'll leave you my lute as ransom," said Alaric. "My sword, my cloak, all . . . but you must give me back my knife."

"He hunts with a knife," muttered one of the men.

"I have my methods. I promise you, you will not regret giving me my freedom."

His captor, having dropped the staff, the sword, and the knife in other hands, stepped close to Alaric and gripped the minstrel's shoulders with strong fingers. He turned Alaric's face to the light of the entrance and gazed at it long. "I brought you here because I thought you were the Red Lord's spy. You were too close to this meeting place. You didn't move on with yesterday morning, as any traveler would. But if it be true that you are nothing but a minstrel, that you aren't of the valley, then I have saved your life this day; for if you had gone on to the valley, you would surely be on the road to death right now. The Red Lord greets travelers most unpleasantly, minstrel, this I promise you."

"I know," said Alaric. "I have been to the valley, I have seen and heard terrible things, and I have narrowly missed the fate you are thinking of. I have no love for the Red Lord, believe me. And if you will conquer your fear of me, I can help you, I swear it."

"Why were you lying so long at your campfire, then, minstrel?"

"I was thinking of how I might kill him."

The gasp of the crowd sounded like a sudden gust of wind through the entrance to the cave.

"You *are* a fool," said one of the men.

"Possibly," said Alaric. "I wasn't quite sure that I would try it. Now I'll put off the decision while I find you food."

His captor let his shoulders loose. "Go," he said. He passed the knife to Alaric. "Bring the food back here before noon. We will not be here when you return, but we will see you. And if you should prove something other than a minstrel who owes no allegiance to the Red Lord, you will never see any of us again."

Alaric squeezed through the cave entrance. Outside, balancing on the ledge that hid the opening from below, he turned back. Darkness lay behind him, and he could see nothing inside now that his eyes were narrowed by sunlight. He said, "Who are you folk?"

His captor answered. "The Red Lord wanted each of us, and we cheated him. We are the exiles of the valley."

Alaric nodded and started down the mountainside. The descent was more treacherous than the climb had been, but shorter, because he did not intend to reach the bottom. He angled toward an outcropping of rock below and to one side of the cave entrance; behind it, he could not be seen from the opening. He vanished.

Many days' journey south was a dense forest where game was plentiful and scarcely knew the fear of man. Alaric hunted there when he could find no easier source of food, either in manor house or peasant hut. Among the trees was a clear brook where deer drank in the morning; he went to it, appearing some distance from the verge. No animals were within sight, so he settled down to wait, leafy bushes cloaking his body, wind blowing his scent away from the water. A short time passed before a doe peered out of the greenery on the far side of the stream. Alaric held himself immobile while she edged toward the flowing water, head turning from side to side as she sought signs of danger. At last she bent to drink. Alaric was beside her in an instant, and before she could startle he had plunged his knife into her throat, hooked an arm about her neck, and wrestled her to the ground. Their strengths were evenly matched, for the doe weighed near as much as he did, but hers ebbed fast with her life's blood. When she stopped struggling, he hefted the carcass across his shoulders and returned to the mountains.

He appeared a short walk from his campsite of the previous night, in a place he hoped none of the exiles would have reason to be watching. The spot seemed to be deserted. He dropped the deer and then wriggled his back and shoulders, which had been creaking under the heavy weight. After catching his breath, he bent to the task of skinning and dressing out the animal.

Some time later, just as the sun was reaching its zenith, he arrived at the bottom of the slope that led to the cave. He had walked there, using the same route that his captor had selected; though it was unmarked, he remembered every step of the way, as he always remembered such things. He had wrapped a forequarter of the deer in the skin, carrying it over his shoulder, and now he threw it down upon the rocks.

"Come get it, my friends!" he shouted. "I'm not go-

ing to climb with this load!'' He sat down on a boulder
to wait for them.

Noon passed, and no one came to him.

"Don't tell me I've done this for nothing!" he said at
last. He stood up, hands on hips, looking around in an-
noyance. "I haven't any army with me—surely you can
see that by now! I thought you folk were hungry!"

At that, a woman peeped out from behind a clump of
rocks halfway up the slope. Then she scrambled toward
him, and he could see the small head that bobbed just
beneath hers—her baby in a sling upon her bosom.

"Are you Malgis?" he asked.

She nodded and, laying hands on the venison forequarter, ripped a bloody chunk of meat away and
crammed it into her mouth.

Alaric felt faintly disgusted at the sight. "It would taste
better cooked," he said.

She cast him a wild glance but said nothing, just kept
chewing. She was a sun- and wind-burned woman of
middling years, so thin that her skin seemed to cling to
bone alone, with no fat or sinew to soften the lines. Her
hair was fair, though stringy with grease and dirt. Once,
Alaric thought, she had been pretty.

The other exiles trickled out of their hiding places to
converge on the meat, and they pushed and clawed at
each other in their eagerness to reach it.

"There is more," Alaric said. "Not far from campsite. I couldn't carry it all this far. If three or four of you
will come along with me, I'll take you to it."

"Where did you find this?" asked his captor.

Alaric shook his head. "That will have to be my secret, friend."

The man gripped Alaric's arm hard. "Where?"

"There is some game in these mountains," said Alaric, "but one must know where to seek it and how to
hunt it." He stared down at the man's hand, then up into
his face, and the man let go abruptly. "You have been
here a long time. What have you lived on?"

"Roots and berries," muttered Malgis, eating more
slowly now, and picking slivers of the raw meat from her
teeth with broken, dirty fingernails.

"We have caught a few of the wild goats," said Alaric's captor, "but that isn't easy."

"And we have stolen from the valley," said one of the other men. "That isn't easy either."

Alaric looked around at them, his first clear view of the whole ragtag group. There were eleven in all. Smeared with blood from the raw venison, their clothing in tatters, their feet roughened and scarred from climbing along the crags, they hardly looked as if they had ever lived in comfortable huts and drunk summer wine. "You have been here," he said, "how long?"

"Since I was young and pretty," said Malgis.

"Different times for each of us," said Alaric's captor. "Some of us have lost track of the number of seasons."

They had done eating by now, and three of the men and one woman had volunteered to accompany Alaric to retrieve the rest of the meat. On the way, they did not talk much, but they did give Alaric their names when he asked for them—the men were Daugas, Vitat, and Jogil, the woman Gedimina. And his captor, he learned, was called Berown. He had been in the mountains the longest of the group and had been their leader since an older man died of the cold the previous winter.

They divided the remaining meat among them, each man slinging a haunch over his shoulder and the woman carrying the deerskin—which they had brought back with them—full of the edible internal organs. Alaric took the head. When they returned to the others, the minstrel was relieved of his small burden by Berown, and the whole troop of exiles went off together, the empty-handed ones forming a tight knot about the meat bearers, like cows protecting their calves from marauding wolves. Only Daugas was left behind with Alaric, to keep him from following the others and discovering one of their secret places. In his hand, Daugas held a piece of deer liver that would serve as the minstrel's meal.

"You still don't trust me," Alaric remarked, "even now that I've filled your bellies." He shook his head. "Well, I hope you'll cook the venison next time—it tastes much better that way. I intend to cook mine."

"You have no fire," said Daugas.

"There's wood aplenty here. And I have flint and steel

in my pack. I suppose it's still up there." He indicated the slope and the cave with a wave of his hand.

Daugas nodded.

Sighing, Alaric began to climb. He was not as fresh as he had been in the morning, and Daugas had to help him. They found the pack and the lute in the cave, but—as Alaric had suspected—the sword was not there.

He built his fire in a sheltered spot, sliced the liver thin, and speared it on pointed sticks to sizzle over the flames. The rising aroma made him acutely aware that he had not eaten all day, and he pulled the first slice away from the heat when it was still rare. Daugas's eyes were so wide and so intent on the cooking meat that Alaric split the first slice with him.

"I thought you ate already," said the minstrel.

"It is better cooked," said Daugas.

Alaric looked at him thoughtfully. "You do have fire up here in the mountains, don't you?"

Daugas nodded. "Back at our camp, we keep a fire burning all the time. And Berown has flint and steel, in case it goes out." He licked his fingers. "I have never tasted anything so good."

"You've never had venison before?"

"No. There are some deer in the valley, but they belong to the Red Lord."

"Ah," said Alaric. "I can imagine what must happen to poachers."

Daugas looked down at the scrap of meat remaining in his hand. "Is this the Red Lord's deer?"

Alaric shrugged. "I didn't ask before I took it."

"Some of them are loose in the mountains, then." He shook his head slowly. "But they are swift creatures. How does a person hunt them?" He gazed expectantly at Alaric.

"One relies on surprise," said Alaric. "And considerable patience."

"The same way one hunts the goats," Daugas said glumly. "We are farmers, not hunters."

"Can you not farm in the mountains?"

Daugas sighed. "We raised a little barley last year— stunted stuff, though it fed us for a time. The soil is poor up here, not like the valley, and it is so very rocky.'' He kicked at some loose pebbles with his bare foot.

''I'm surprised you have stayed here so long,'' said Alaric.

''We can't go back.'' Daugas looked into the flames with weary eyes. ''I have wanted to, many times since I came here. I have wanted to go back to my father and mother. I've been to the valley, to steal grain. I've passed the house where I was born. But I didn't dare go in. I think they would hide me, but that would only mean their doom as well as mine. The Red Lord would find us out.''

''Why not go the other way, then?''

''Other way?''

''Away from the valley. Away from the Red Lord forever.''

''Away? But where?''

''South, to warmer climes. Or east or west. There is a wide world out there. You need not starve here.''

Daugas shook his head. ''The mountains are harsh traveling.''

Alaric had to laugh. ''You are hardy folk—hardier than I am, and I made the journey. And I have heard that merchants make it as well, whole caravans that pass through the valley on their way to the north. Surely if soft merchants from the south can manage the journey, so can you.''

''And bandits,'' said Daugas.

''If there are bandits,'' said Alaric, ''then the merchants manage to drive them off.''

''Perhaps only the best-armed caravans get through, minstrel.''

''I saw no bandits in *my* journey.''

''They *are* there. We are ringed by them, like a great wall around the valley, nine or ten days' journey outward. They are afraid of the Red Lord, so they rarely venture closer. Before his reign, though, they raided us often—I remember my grandfather speaking of those days. Everyone had to hide in the castle when the bandits came, and when they finally went away, they took everything they could carry and burned the rest. The people had to rebuild their homes, replant their fields, and raise new livestock from whatever animals they had taken into the castle with them.''

''In your grandfather's day.''

''Yes. When the Red Lord became our ruler, things changed. When the bandits attacked, he and his men drove them off; they killed many and brought others back for torture. Now the bandits stay away, but still the Red Lord takes his men up into the mountains after them sometimes.''

Alaric was puzzled. ''How is it that the Red Lord could drive the bandits away, and his predecessor could not?''

''His father kept only a small guard,'' said Daugas, ''and ill trained, so my grandfather said—no match for the bandits. But the Red Lord called in enough farmer's sons to make his army strong, and he trained them well. He is a great commander, minstrel. Ask Berown of that if you wish; he was one of the Red Lord's men, until he fell asleep on watch.''

''The Red Lord tells his people there are bandits in the mountains,'' said Alaric. ''Have you *seen* these bandits in recent years?''

Daugas shook his head. ''I was no soldier; I never hunted them.''

''And Berown—does he say he has seen such bandits?''

''He helped bring them back to the castle for torture.''

''But he has been here for many years, has he not?''

''Yes, many.''

''Then . . . perhaps there are no bandits anymore. Perhaps they have all been hunted down. Or have given up and run away from the Red Lord's wrath.''

Daugas frowned. ''Do we dare believe that?''

Alaric shrugged. ''You folk have told me that the mountains make an inhospitable dwelling place. Without the valley to raid for food—as you do yourselves—how could bandits survive?''

Daugas appeared to turn that over in his mind. ''I don't know,'' he said at last.

''Berown told me, though I think he meant it as a joke, that *you* were the bandits.''

''We?''

''You have taken their place, have you not? You steal

from the valley. You live in the mountains. And . . . the Red Lord hunts you?''

"He does.''

"Then how can you be afraid of yourselves?''

Daugas stood up. "I don't know what to think now, minstrel. You argue smoothly—too smoothly, perhaps. We still don't know who you are.''

"I am no more than I appear to be," said Alaric. Finished with the liver now, he wiped his fingers on a corner of his cloak and drew the lute out of its wrappings. "Shall I sing you a song, Daugas?''

"I don't care.''

"Sit down. Take your ease. Or are you impatient to do something?''

"No.''

"Not . . . impatient to kill me?''

Daugas frowned. "What do do you mean?''

"Oh, I thought you might have been left behind to get rid of the stranger.''

"No.''

"I'm glad I'm wrong, then. We're a near match, you and I. But you would not be able to kill me, Daugas. I hope you will remember that." He strummed a chord on the lute and then began a soft melody about a lost goat and the goatherd that hunted it in the high mountains. The child braved a snowstorm to search for the animal, only to find it slain by a wolf. The song ended with the goatherd facing the wolf with only an icy branch for a weapon, and the wolf's red eyes staring at him through the swirling snow.

"You sing very nicely," said Daugas, "but that is a strange ending to the story. It is no ending at all. What happens to the child?''

"What do you think happens," asked Alaric.

"The wolf kills him?''

"Perhaps. What would you think of your own chances in the same situation?''

"I don't know. It was a foolish thing for him to do, go out in the storm alone, ill armed.''

"Yes, it was.''

"What is the meaning of that song, minstrel?''

Alaric smiled. "It's just a song. Must it have a meaning?"

Daugas thought a moment. "We are the goatherd, and the Red Lord is the wolf."

"You have a lively imagination," said Alaric. "What is the goat, then?"

"The goat is a goat. Food. Life. We chance the Red Lord's retribution by stealing food from his valley. So far he has not caught us. Is that what the song says, minstrel?"

"If you wish it to say that." He strummed another chord. "Every song has many meanings."

Daugas half turned away, gazing at Alaric from the corner of his eye. "This day, my belly is full. It has not been so in a long time. Can you hunt again as you did today?"

"I think so."

"Then I hope you will stay with us."

"I don't intend to stay here forever, Daugas. And after I leave, you'll be hungry again."

Daugas shifted from one foot to the other, but he said nothing.

"And some winter," Alaric continued, "there will not be enough roots and berries, nor enough game of any kind, nor an opportunity to steal from the valley, and then you will be forced . . . to eat each other?" He looked up sharply. "Or have you done that already?"

Daugas glanced away from him.

Alaric plucked a series of high, sweet notes from his lute, a melancholy air that never failed to make him think of weeping women. "I wonder," he murmured, "how do you choose the victim? Do you draw lots? Or is it the weakest? The oldest? Perhaps one who—"

"Enough!" shouted Daugas. He faced Alaric, his hands closing into fists at his sides. "We live on the edge of death, and we do what we must to stay alive!"

"You *must* stay in these mountains and prey upon each other when there is no other prey?"

"We have no choice."

Alaric shrugged. "I don't agree. But you certainly have no courage."

"You are so sure of yourself, minstrel!"

"I intend to leave these mountains alive. I think you can do the same."

Daugas squatted and picked up a stick to stir the fire, which was burning low. "You have been very lucky, minstrel. I don't know if we could divide that luck among twelve people and have anything left of it."

Alaric made no reply to that, only strummed his lute and thought about his own journey to the valley of the Red Lord. He had used his power to travel faster and more comfortably than other men, and earlier in the season than most would dare. But he had seen no bottomless chasms, no unclimbable passes on his route. The land had been unstable with the thaw, and he had narrowly escaped several shifting masses of earth and rock, but with every additional day, summer came nearer, and the land dried and hardened. Already the runoff from melting snow had dwindled, as the lesser peaks showed bare to the sky. These folk, he thought, were surely mountaineers enough to manage a crossing.

"Do you plan to stay here with me all night?" asked Alaric.

Daugas nodded.

"And in the morning . . . what?"

"Berown said he would be back in the morning. He said they would all be back."

"To decide my fate, yes?"

"I'm sure they're talking about you."

"If I chose to stand up at this moment and walk away from you, Daugas, what would you do?"

"I'd try to stop you. But I don't want either of us to be hurt, minstrel, so please don't try to leave."

Alaric smiled. "I'm in no hurry, my friend. I was just . . . curious." And then he sang another song, and another, and so he amused himself for the rest of the afternoon, and Daugas listened.

Some time after sunset, Alaric laid his lute down, wrapped himself in his cloak, and pretended to fall asleep. He watched through slitted eyes as Daugas pushed the embers of the fire aside and curled up on the spot they had warmed. Daugas appeared to sleep almost immediately, but Alaric lay still until soft snores began to escape his guard's half-open mouth. Then, he edged away, pulling his lute along gently, his fingers flat on the strings, muffling them from even an accidental note. When he had melted into the shadows that surrounded the campsite, he vanished. He preferred to spend the night elsewhere, not because he feared Daugas, but because he did not know how early in the morning the others would return. He had no desire to be caught sleeping by people who might have made their decision to kill him. He knew a bower in the dense forest where men seldom hunted. He tore down some springy branches for his bed, and he rested well far from the hard and stony ground of the mountains.

He woke shortly after dawn and traveled back, lute slung over his shoulder, cloak rolled under his arm. He appeared some distance from the campsite and walked to it. Berown and the other exiles had already arrived, and they were all shouting at Daugas for letting Alaric get away. The first person to see the minstrel approach had to punch his neighbors to make them leave off their abuse and look behind them.

Alaric smiled. "Good morn to you all, friends. I hope you slept as well as I did."

Berown turned a tight-mouthed gaze on the minstrel. He wore the sword and the fine-tooled scabbard on a length of rawhide tied about his waist. "Where did you go?" he asked.

Alaric waved in the direction from which he had walked. "The wind was too brisk here last night, so I moved to a better spot. But Daugas was sleeping so soundly that I hadn't the heart to disturb him. He must have been very tired."

Berown glanced back at Daugas. "We could all be dead because of your tiredness."

"I hardly think so," said Alaric. "I'm really a harmless fellow."

"I watched him till he fell asleep." said Daugas. "I didn't think he could get very far in the middle of the night."

"You watched him till *you* fell asleep," said Berown. He stared at Daugas for a long moment, and then he slapped him in the face. "That's to remind you that he could have killed you."

Daugas rubbed at the red mark on his cheek with one hand. "I don't think he wants to kill any of us. I think he wants to help us."

"I told you to stay awake!"

Alaric said, "You can't expect soldiers' discipline from starving people."

Berown looked at Alaric once more. "You are a most unusual person, minstrel. You have shown that you can move about these mountains better than we can, that you can hunt where there is no game and pass through bandit country without being touched. You could have left last night, and I'm sure that none of us could have followed you, but you chose to stay. Why?"

"I do want to help you."

"Why?"

"Because I pity you."

Berown laughed, a short, hard laugh with no humor in it.

"Need there be another reason?" asked Alaric.

"And what can you do for us with your pity, minstrel? Hunt again? Stay and hunt for us forever? Would you do that, minstrel?"

"No," said Alaric. He looked around the group. "I suppose no one thought to bring Daugas and me a bit of breakfast?"

Berown motioned peremptorily, and one of the other men stepped forward to hand the minstrel a chunk of venison. Alaric thanked him, then set it atop a nearby rock as he knelt on the ground beside the ashes of the fire—they were still warm, but there was no live coal among them for a fresh blaze. Taking flint and steel and tinder from his knapsack, Alaric struck a new fire, feeding it scraps from the pile of wood he had gathered the day before until it burned brightly. Then he sliced the meat, as he had done the liver, and set it on pointed sticks to broil. He gestured for Daugas to squat beside him.

"You know," said Alaric, as if speaking to Daugas alone, "you have two choices. One is to leave the mountains and find a fresh life elsewhere, perhaps in some other valley or even on the southern plains. There are other lands than this one—lands whose lords are strong

enough to keep evil men away and yet are kind and just
and would be shocked to hear of a lord who used his
people as if they were his cattle. You could be farmers
again, and live without fear."

"And the other choice?" asked Daugas.

Alaric lifted a piece of meat from the flames and nib-
bled delicately at its crisping edges. "Has the Red Lord
an heir with the same love for peasant torture as he has
himself?" he inquired.

"He has no heir at all," said Daugas.

Alaric chewed a juicy morsel, then swallowed. "Your
second choice, then, is to return to your own valley."

"That is no choice at all," said Daugas.

"It would be, if the Red Lord were dead."

"Dead!" said Berown, his voice heavy with scorn.
"And how would you kill him, minstrel?"

"I have a plan. But I'll not tell you about it."

Berown shook his head. "Fool. You'll be the one to
die, not him."

Alaric smiled. "I hunt where there is no game, Berown. I travel without fear of bandits. When I say I can
do a thing, I mean it."

"Do you think it's never been tried? The last time, the
fool was a long time dying. And his head hung on a pike
above the battlements until the crows picked the skull
clean."

"I can kill him," said Alaric.

Daugas looked up at Berown. "What if he speaks the
truth?"

"He's mad."

"But *if*," said Daugas.

Berown stepped close to Alaric, stood above him, glaring down. "I'll tell you what would happen if you killed
him, minstrel, if by some impossible stroke of luck you
killed him. We might live well for a year or two or even
more, but someday the bandits would come down out of
the mountains, and there would be no Red Lord to stop
them."

"If they exist," said Alaric.

"You think they don't?"

"I think they are a tale told by the Red Lord to keep
his people from assassinating him."

"I have seen them."

"Years ago," said Alaric.

"I have no reason to believe they have gone away, and you'll not convince me of it. I remember the Red Lord burning his own fields to kill the bandits. And I remember their shouts as they vowed to return someday and destroy us all. Some of these others may be too young to have such memories, but *I* am not."

"You fear the bandits more than you fear him," said Alaric.

"Yes."

Alaric looked around at the crowd. "You others—you feel the same?"

There was much muttering from the group and, eventually, nodding. "We couldn't live up here if the bandits weren't afraid of him," said Gedimina.

"But you wouldn't be living up here at all if he were dead."

"And if he were dead," said Berown, "no one would be living down there."

"Don't kill him, minstrel," said Gedimina. "I'd rather be alive in the mountains than dead in the valley."

Alaric shook his head and looked at Berown. "It's you that has convinced them of this."

"No, minstrel. We heard it at our mothers' knees. The Red Lord keeps our valley safe, and long life to him."

"Long life," echoed the other exiles.

Alaric scanned their faces, shimmering in the air beyond the fire. "And if I should decide to kill him anyway?"

Gedimina sank to her knees beside him and clutched his arm. "No, please, no."

He looked at her contorted face. "You believe I can kill him?"

"Yes, I believe!"

He peered into the flames. "I was going to do it. For you, for all of you. And for the others, the ones who still live in the valley. But . . . they wouldn't thank me, would they?"

"No," said Berown. He frowned. "You really think you can, don't you?"

Alaric had to laugh, half in wonder, half in relief. "I

can, but it no longer seems the proper thing to do." He glanced at Daugas. "That leaves the first choice, doesn't it?"

"If you'll show me the way," said Daugas, "I'll go out of the mountains with you."

"Well, that's one less mouth for the mountains to feed," said Alaric. He looked up. "What about the rest of you? I'll lead you out."

"Past the bandits," muttered Berown.

Daugas said, "Malgis?" He lifted his hand, and after a long moment she came out of the crowd, the baby in one arm, and linked her fingers with his.

"Who else?" said Alaric.

They just stared at him with wide eyes.

Berown said, "We'll never see any of you alive again."

"That's true," said Alaric, "but not because the bandits will kill us."

"You'll be carrion within a few days."

"No, but perhaps *you* will be. That deer won't last much longer. And then what will you do?"

"We'll find something," said Berown.

Alaric thought of hunting for them once again before he left, but he saw the futility in that; they would not be able to eat what he brought them before it spoiled. *And after all,* he thought, *I owe them nothing.* He gathered up his pack and lute. "Get your belongings together," he told Daugas and Malgis. "We'll leave as soon as you're ready." He turned to Berown. "My sword, sir." With some reluctance, the leader of the exiles handed the weapon over, and Alaric slipped it into his pack.

"We are ready," said Daugas. "We have no belongings."

Alaric eyed their tattered clothing and the rags that wrapped the baby Malgis held. "Very well," he said. "As long as the weather is fine, let us go."

They walked easily in the spring sunlight, and they spoke little. Alaric kept a careful eye on the ground beneath his feet, and he hummed snatches of melody to the ragged rhythm of his step. Occasionally, he bade his companions stay where they were while he scouted the terrain ahead; at those times he walked beyond their sight and then used his own mode of travel to flit forward and determine the easiest passage. This was the route he had taken to the Red Lord's domain, and although he knew it could be traversed on foot, there were some difficult stretches. They camped that night at the very edge of the territory that Malgis and Daugas knew. The baby, which had not cried all day, whimpered now with the oncoming chill of night, and the small fire that Alaric built was not enough to comfort it. He gave Malgis his lute wrap for it then, and slept with the instrument close against his bosom.

In the morning, he stole a pair of chickens from a distant farmyard, not wanting to waste traveling time lying in wait for a wild creature. After the meal, they resumed their journey.

In his scouting forward, Alaric saw no trace of other human beings, but the farther they walked from familiar territory, the more nervous Malgis became. Her eyes moved constantly, and she walked a little behind the others, always glancing back, as if expecting someone to follow. At first Alaric just smiled and reassured her that there were no other people nearby, but as the sun sank in the west, her nervousness began to communicate itself to him, and he ranged farther in his scouting, both forward and back, seeking some source of danger. That night they camped under overhanging rocks, and she begged Alaric not to make a fire. Unable to calm her fears, he acquiesced.

The following day dawned gray. The rain had begun while the sky was still dark, and their rock shelter was scarcely enough to protect them from the wet. Daugas and Malgis huddled together, the baby between them, and Alaric sat shielding his lute for a time before he decided that he was too hungry to let the rain deter him. He went out, leaving his cloak to wrap the lute, and returned, drenched, with a rabbit. They had no small trouble cooking it while the rain spattered their fire. Malgis stamped the flames out as soon as the meat was done enough to suit Alaric.

"No one would be out in this weather to see the fire," he said.

"You were out," said Malgis.

"If the bandits were as desperate as I was," he replied, "they would do well to find some other way of life."

"How is it," said Malgis, "that you always find game when you go out, and yet *we* have found so little?"

Alaric smiled. "I'll tell you a secret, my friend: when I was a child, we had a bad summer, and the crops on my parents' farm died; and then we had a bad winter, and the game in the woods disappeared. My parents were almost starving, and though they gave me more food than they took themselves, I was a sack of bones barely covered with skin. And so we decided to make a pilgrimage to the Holy Well at Canby. We walked, though it was far, and all along the road we begged crusts of bread and rinds of cheese from travelers. At last we came to the well, and my father threw in the only coin we had in the world, and he prayed that we might not starve. I prayed, too, as I recall, though I really didn't know what I was about—I prayed hard. And after a while, other pilgrims wanted to pray at the well, for it was a very popular shrine in those days, and so we went into the woods to gather fuel for that night's fire. We had not been among the trees for more than a few moments when a rabbit bounded out from behind a stone and stopped in front of us, sitting up on its hind legs and looking at us as if it expected us to perform some wonderful deed. My father took the knife from his belt very slowly, raised it very slowly, and still the rabbit stayed where it was. Then my father flung the knife and impaled the creature, and very soon we had a delicious meal. Ever after that day, my father was able to find game when we were hungry, and so am I."

"Where is this Canby?" asked Daugas.

"Far from here," said Alaric. "You would have to walk half a year or more to reach it."

"And does the well always grant the prayers of pilgrims?"

Alaric shrugged. "I cannot speak for anyone else." He glanced toward his lute, but decided against unwrapping it while the rain still fell. Having just made up the tale of the pilgrimage, he rather liked it, and he stored it away in his capacious memory, to be set to music on some other day.

"Perhaps that's the same good fortune that keeps you safe from bandits," murmured Malgis.

Alaric made no reply but only gnawed the bones of the rabbit and watched the sky for a glimpse of sun. That came at last, well past noon, and with it the end of the rain. Alaric stood up and stepped into the sunshine. "Shall we go on?"

Pools of water lay everywhere, hiding sharp or slippery stones in their muddy depths, and the streams were indistinguishable from their banks. Soon all three travelers were spattered with mud to their waists, and Alaric's boots, stout though they were, had begun to leak. He called a halt before dark, for they were approaching a steep descent, and he preferred to make it when the light was fresh and the ground dry.

Once more Malgis balked at building a fire, but Alaric argued that they were wet as well as cold and would all have fevers by morning without a blaze. They built it, finally, among large boulders, and they leaned so close to it that Alaric doubted any light got by their screen of flesh.

The next day, Malgis gazed down the plunging slope and did not wish to go farther.

"It isn't as difficult as it looks," said Alaric.

She sat down on the ground. "I can't," she said.

"I'll take the child," said Daugas. "It will be easier for you then."

She clutched the baby to her bosom. "No."

"Malgis!"

She looked up at him with wild eyes. "Listen to me. They're waiting for us out there." She pointed sharply at Alaric. *"He's leading us to them."*

Daugas shook his head. "The minstrel is our friend."

"He's been lighting fires to show them our path. Why should they come after us when we'll be walking right into their camp?"

Daugas knelt and closed his arms about her. "No."

"He tried to make the others come, too, but they weren't foolish enough to believe him." She pulled away from him. "But *you,* you were!"

Daugas glanced at Alaric, despair on his face. "I

thought she would be all right," he said, "with a full belly."

Alaric looked down at the woman. "I mean you no harm, Malgis."

"Liar!"

"Have I not fed you? Have I not given you the wrapping of my most precious possession for your baby?"

Tears welled from her eyes. "Take me home, Daugas," she pleaded. "Oh, please, take me home."

"I'll take you to a new home," he said, catching one of her hands between his own. "Across the mountains."

She shook her head violently. "Please!"

"You don't want to go back there," said Alaric, squatting beside her. "There's nothing for you there but cold and hunger."

"She means the valley," said Daugas. "She always means the valley." He stroked her dirty, tangled hair with one hand. "Oh, Malgis, trust us and come along."

As if in reply, she jerked Alaric's dagger from its sheath at his belt.

In the instant that her hand reversed its arc to strike him, he vanished.

He found himself in the forest, in the bower where he had spent the night when Daugas watched him, and he cursed the reflex that had sent him there. Another man would have caught her wrist and forced her to drop the blade; another man might have suffered a scratch on the shoulder or chest wrestling the knife from her grip. But Alaric had vanished into thin air, proving himself something other than a normal human being.

Proving himself a witch.

It was a name he had never wanted. There was too much fear attached to it, too much hatred, too much danger of an unexpected arrow or an unseen dagger. For a known witch, death was always near.

Almost, he did not go back. He was vulnerable to Malgis and Daugas now and would never again dare turn his attention away from them, even for a moment. Yet he felt responsible for their lives, having brought them so far, and now that he had exposed himself, he thought he might as well cut their journey short and take them out of the mountains in his own way. After he had found some secure place for the knife.

For safety's sake, he reappeared a short distance from the spot he had left. He had been gone a few heartbeats. Daugas still knelt at the top of the steep slope.

Malgis was gone.

Alaric glanced about quickly, to see if she had run away, but even as he did so, he knew what had happened. He remembered precisely where he had been squatting, with his back to the brink. The force of her knife thrust had plunged Malgis over the edge.

Daugas rose slowly, like a man in a dream, and started his descent. He did not notice Alaric following softly after. He clung to the rocks as he climbed down among them, and his hands left each surface as if pulling away from honey. When he reached her, he eased his arms around her and gently lifted her head to rest on his thigh.

She had fetched up against a boulder halfway down the slope, and there was blood on her face and arms and knees. The baby lay nearby, silent. Alaric looked at it and then wished he had not.

Daugas was whispering her name.

Alaric saw his knife wedged among the rocks farther down the incline. He made no move to retrieve it.

Her eyes opened. "Daugas?"

"I am here."

"Where is the baby?"

He looked around slowly, saw the child, stared at it for a long moment, and then said, "I think the baby is hurt."

One hand clutching the boulder, she pulled herself into a sitting posture. "Bring him here."

Daugas crawled over to the child and lifted it. The small body lay limp in his grasp as he took it to Malgis.

She looked into her baby's ruined face. With a corner of one of her rags, she tried to wipe the blood away. Then she laid her ear against the tiny chest. Her head was still bent in that position when she said, "He's dead."

Daugas said, "Yes," and tried to take the corpse from her hands, but she would not allow that.

"I'll carry him," she said, "until we get hungry."

Alaric felt his gorge rise. "Bury it," he said. "I'll see that you're fed."

Daugas looked up then, cringing. "Go away!" he cried. "Leave us alone!"

"I'll take you out of the mountains now."

"Please," said Daugas. "Just leave us alone."

"I never meant to cause you harm."

For answer, Daugas touched the still form that lay in Malgis's embrace.

"Should I have stayed and let her kill me?" Alaric demanded. "She brought this on herself; will you tell me that I should have traded my life for your child's life?" His hands tightened into fists as the man and woman made no move, no reply. "Bury it," he said at last, harshly and loud in the mountain quiet, "and I'll take you to safety . . . by magic."

Daugas shook his head. "We want no part of your magic."

"There is no danger involved," said Alaric.

"No."

"You'll feel nothing. In the blink of an eye you'll be far from these mountains. I know a good land where you'll be able to make a new life for yourselves."

"No."

Alaric stepped one pace closer, and Daugas shrank back, his arm circling Malgis protectively. She, still hunched over the baby, seemed not to notice what was going on around her.

"Are you afraid of me?" asked the minstrel.

"Please leave us alone," said Daugas.

"I kept my vow to bring you food, did I not? Now I swear to you that I can take you to a better place as easily as I can breathe. Come along, Daugas."

He shook his head.

"But what will you do if you don't come with me?"

"We'll go back," said Daugas.

"You'll starve."

"We'll find food somehow."

Alaric sighed heavily. "I could take you against your will, you know."

"If you try, I'll gouge your eyes out, I swear it."

"I only want to help you, Daugas!"

"Liar!" he said. "Don't you think I know who you are?"

"I am your friend."

"Liar! What witch was ever a friend to anyone?"

Alaric looked down the slope, toward his knife, which gleamed in the morning sunshine. "All right," he said. "Be your own masters." He began a careful descent, giving a wide berth to the man and woman who remained motionless, one of them watching him. He picked up the blade and sheathed it. He glanced up, one last time. "Farewell, and good fortune to you both."

The dimness of the forest was welcome to him. He sat down in his bower, head in his hands. He felt cold, though the spring air was warm enough. There was a tightness in his chest when he thought of the gifts he had given the people of the mountains—a few meals of venison and a dead child. No matter that the death was partly caused by a woman's madness. *He* had made it possible: if he had not convinced Daugas to leave, if he had not squatted by the brink, if—above all—he did not possess a witch's power, then the image of the bloody child would not now be filling his heart.

After a time, he slipped the lute and pack from his shoulders and lay back among the boughs. He was not done with the mountains yet. Above him, he could see the sky through many layers of leaves; there was a full day ahead of him, a day for rest and planning. After dusk, he would return to the Red Lord's valley, and while human and animal slept the dark time away, he would steal goats. He did not relish the thought of traveling with kicking, bleating burdens: he would gain a few bruises, he knew, from this night's work. And he would have to dodge guardian dogs and the masters wakened by their barking. It would not be a simple matter, not like stealing chickens from a closed coop; this night would test his reflexes to their limits. He found his heart beating faster at the thought of the danger, but he did not let that weaken his resolve. He would gather a herd for the people of the mountains, tame goats that would not shy from men, that would eat the tough grasses of the heights and give milk and skins in return. He would gather the herd that they were afraid to gather for themselves, and bring it to their mountain fastness without leaving any trail that mortal men could follow. He would give them life and, with that gift, wipe the image of the dead child from his heart. And he would have some small vengeance on the Red Lord in the bargain, by helping his exiles to survive.

Of them all, Daugas might guess the source of the gift; Alaric hoped he would not be foolish enough to frighten the others into starving while a witch's goats thrived before their eyes. Then he thought of Malgis. She would eat. He nodded to himself. They would all eat, when they were hungry enough.

And Alaric would be free to travel on.

PART THREE

THE NOMADS OF THE NORTH

The air was thin and chill at the crest of the ridge, and Alaric the minstrel found his breath coming hard and fast even though he stood quite still. Far behind, in the lowlands of the south, spring was well begun, meadows lush with new greenery, tender buds on every tree; but here among the highest of the great northern mountains, the heavy hand of winter ruled. Though the sun was blinding bright, it gave no heat; beneath the frigid sky, snowfields glittered as if strewn with gemstones, and here and there naked boulders thrust up, too steep and jagged for snow to cling, but cold themselves as any ice.

Alaric shivered and pulled his cloak tighter. Slung against his chest, his lute shared the warmth of his body. On his back, his knapsack was light with just a change of clothes and a few scraps of meat tucked into it, and a seldom-used sword. He had traveled far with so few possessions; he expected to travel farther yet before the longest night closed his eyes, and so excised the canker of his dreams.

During his stay in the mountains, those dreams were grim and desolate. Within them, he saw himself running over a vast dark plain, but never gaining a stride on the gaunt shadow that loomed above the distant peaks. He knew that shadow, and its staring red eyes that pierced the hazy clouds. Eyes hot as coals, which burned into his neck when he averted his face. They were the eyes of a lord of misery, a Lord of Blood; and they held a bottomless hunger that gnawed at his bones.

He had more than his fill of such dreams, and of the somber mountains in which he suffered them; he was glad to see that this latest crest marked the last of the heights. Beyond, the land sloped downward ruggedly; in the distance, he could just make out the snowline, where frozen winter began at last to give way to hardy herbs and scrub. An ordinary human being—especially one with so little mountain-climbing experience as Alaric— would have labored at that descent, half scrambling, half sliding, clutching at frigid boulders, exhausting himself in the journey. An ordinary human would have taken two or three days to reach the end of the snow. But Alaric merely sighted on an outcropping far below, and in a single heartbeat, he was there. Four more such traverses brought him to the snowline. There, he brushed the clinging whiteness from his boots before moving on.

At last the land leveled itself into a rolling plain that stretched to the horizon, a plain where new grass was just beginning to show amid last year's dried and yellowed tussocks. Scattered trees, their branches barely touched with green, marked the sites of brooks and ponds, and a light, erratic wind blew as warm as spring should be. The young minstrel pushed his cloak back to let that breeze sweep the mountain chill from his body and from his heart.

Late in the afternoon, he caught his first glimpse of living creatures on the plain, a faint line of dots moving westward far ahead. With caution born of his wanderings, he dropped to the ground; wild or domesticated, whatever those creatures were, they might be trailed by men, and a stranger with a witch's mode of travel had need of caution when men were near. Lying on his belly, Alaric used his power to move closer, shielded by clumps of tufted grass.

The creatures were deer of a sort he had never seen before, with huge feet and slender legs that gave them a gawky, lumbering stride, as if they were never quite properly balanced. Their chunky bodies showed the tattered remnants of half-shed winter coats, like patches of thick pale fungus growing on their dark skins. Most of them were females, their brows not encumbered by antlers, their bellies bulging with unborn young; only a few were males, their massive, velvet-sheathed racks branching both forward over their noses and back past their ears.

Two of the largest males had riders.

Seated well forward on their mounts, elbows just touching the antlers which flanked them like curving armrests, the riders were men of middle years, their shoulders broad, their hands and faces weathered and hard. They wore leather jerkins and trews, and fur-trimmed, knee-high boots, and they had long dark hair clubbed behind with leather thongs. Each carried a bow slung over his shoulder, and a quiver of arrows fletched in white beside it; each bore a short sword at his waist. They did not speak to each other as they rode, nor did they seem to be in any hurry, lazing along beside the other deer, letting their mounts graze at will.

Herders, thought Alaric. That meant a village nearby, hot food cooked by another hand than his own, and ears to listen to his songs. He moved back to the place from which he had first sighted them and rose to his feet, dusting the dry grass from his tunic. Gauging the sun's height above the horizon, he judged he would spend a good part of the remaining daylight in approaching them as an ordinary traveler would. He tucked the lute under one arm and set off at a brisk pace.

They saw him, as he had presumed they would, long before he was close enough to hail them. One rode a short way toward him and then, obviously reluctant to leave the herd too far behind, stopped and waited, while his mount dipped its broad muzzle into the grass once more. Alaric's shadow was a long, thin companion at his side by the time he reached that rider.

"Good eve," said the minstrel, halting a few paces from man and beast, sweeping his hat off and making a deep bow. At that sudden movement, the deer started, taking three or four clumsy steps backward before its master could calm it, with one hand on the reins and the other gripping an antler. Though the creature wore a bridle, its rider sat bareback, without saddle or stirrups—a precarious perch, Alaric thought, on a skittish creature whose antlers could gash a rider as he fell. He backed off himself, not wanting to be injured by some accident. "Forgive me," he said quickly. "I did not mean to frighten your steed."

The herder peered down at him with pale greenish eyes

rimmed by countless fine creases. "Who are you?" he asked.

"I am Alaric, singer of songs." The minstrel curled both hands about the neck of his lute. "If you care for music, I have a good deal in me. Or if not, perhaps you can tell me of folk who do."

"I have not heard your name before," said the herder. He had a faint, lilting accent, pleasant to the ear in spite of the wariness in his words. "Where do you come from?"

Alaric tipped his head back toward the mountains. "The south."

The man glanced in that direction, his pale eyes seeming to measure the distance to those peaks before they turned to the minstrel again. "You crossed the mountains?"

Alaric nodded.

"The passes are open, then."

"Open enough, for a careful climber with very little baggage."

The man considered him a moment longer, and then the creases about his eyes deepened as his mouth broke into a smile. "I am Fowsh, of Nuriki's band. We've had no southern minstrel among us in my memory. Perhaps your songs will all be new to us."

Alaric bowed again, slowly this time. "Some of them at least, for I have written those myself and not yet taught them to any other singer."

"Come to our camp, then," said the herder. "The day is nearly gone, and we must return for supper. You can ride old White-ear over there." He waved toward the grazing animals.

Alaric looked at the herd uncertainly. "I have never ridden a deer before."

"Never at all?"

"I've ridden horses, but I don't think it is quite the same."

"Horses?" said the man. "Ah, yes, I've heard of them. Well, you won't find it difficult. My daughter has only known four summers, and she rides easily." He turned his animal about and led Alaric toward the rest of the creatures.

White-ear was docile enough, standing still in response to the herder's caressing hand on its neck. But though the deer was not so tall as a horse, it proved much more troublesome to mount. There was no saddle to clutch, no mane, and when the minstrel tried to lean his weight on an antler, White-ear ducked its head and shook him off. At last, with a helping hand from the second herder, he managed to scramble up gracelessly. Once astride the creature's back, he found his seat a bony one, and when the deer began to walk, he felt every step as an awkward shift in its shoulders, a shift that threatened to send him sliding down one side or the other at every moment. He clung to both antlers and quickly discovered that White-ear would veer to the right or left depending on which antler bore the greater weight. Fortunately, in spite of his varying signals, the deer was inclined to follow its mates, and so Alaric stayed with the herd, though on a path that wavered tipsily.

He had only just begun to gain a bit of control over his mount, clinging with knees and thighs, easing his grip on the antlers, when the herders' camp became visible in the distance. It was a cluster of perhaps a dozen tents arranged in a rough circle; outside this ring, in a series of enclosures formed by posts with ropes stretched between them, were groups of deer like the ones he accompanied. One of the pens was empty, and Alaric's companions led their charges to it, dismounted, and drew a pair of ropes aside to let their deer enter.

Alaric was glad enough to set his feet on the ground once more, and gladder still to follow the herders into the circle of tents, where a crowd of people bustled among a dozen cooking fires, and the smell of roasting meat filled the air. Here were more dark-haired men in leather, and as many women, dark-haired too, with their tresses unbound and splashing over their shoulders, and their eyes all pale shades of green or blue. The women wore leather, too, fur-trimmed boots showing beneath their fringed leather skirts, and sleeveless leather bodices above. Even the children wore finely cured hides, the same mellow brown as their elders, like the wood of the black walnut tree. And the tents were also made of hide stitched together with strong sinew.

Children were the first to notice Alaric's arrival. Three little ones happened to be nearby, and their great pale eyes became round as coins when they saw the stranger. Two of them stared a moment and then ran, shouting, to their mothers. The third stood her ground and merely looked up. Fowsh swung her up into his arms and gave her plump cheek a kiss, but the child did not take her eyes from the minstrel.

He smiled at her, and then he doffed his cap and gave her his deepest bow.

A moment later, the people at the nearest fires had turned their faces toward him, women with ladles in their hands, men kneeling at roasting spits. One of the latter stood as Fowsh led Alaric in his direction. He was gray-haired and gray-bearded, but his back was straight, and his bare arms were heavily muscled. A stocky, gray-haired woman stood at the other side of his fire, stirring the contents of a shallow pot, and close by her were a woman perhaps half her age and a beardless youth.

"We have a guest for supper," the herder said to them all. "A minstrel from the south. He calls himself Alaric."

"From the south?" said the older man. He looked Alaric up and down, his bushy eyebrows arching high above his pale eyes. "We don't see many travelers from the south."

"I don't wonder at that," Alaric said, still smiling. Thoughts of the Red Lord flashed through his mind, threatening that smile, but he swept them away, as a broom clears dusty cobwebs from a corner. "The mountains offer little hospitality. But I have traveled all my life, and a few mountains cannot daunt me."

The man stroked his short beard with thick, callused fingers. "And where are you bound, traveler, that mountains mean so little to you? On some quest for gold or gems? You will be disappointed if that is so, for we have none here in the north."

"I have no quest," said Alaric, "unless it be to view the great Northern Sea of legend. But I have no home, either, and an unquenchable wanderlust. I trade my songs for food and lodging. And the smell of your supper makes me hope that you will be generous with at least the first."

"Of course we shall," the gray-haired woman said sharply. "In the north we do not turn folk away from our fires."

"My thanks, good lady." Alaric bowed to her.

"You southern fools know nothing of life here. Why, when I was a girl a whole caravan of men froze to death on this very plain almost in sight of our own camp. We found them after a storm, all huddled together in a few flimsy tents. They'd not enough sense to slaughter their animals and wrap themselves in the carcasses. You'd find the Northern Sea, would you?" She shook the dripping ladle at him, her expression stern. "And you with no fur to cover you, nothing but a few thin woolens. What a fool you are!"

Alaric shrugged lightly. "Perhaps so, good lady. But I am willing to learn from you. I have no desire to die young."

She gave him a long, appraising look. "Anyone who travels alone and in a foreign land desires to die young."

"Ah, now, Mother," said Fowsh, "don't judge him so harshly. The young never think of death." Turning his face to Alaric, he said, "Our family had another son once. He went into the mountains, alone, and never returned. A mother does not forget the child she bore, even after twenty-five years."

"He was young and foolish, like you, minstrel," said the old woman.

Alaric wondered if she had lost him to the Red Lord, but that was not a question he would ever dare to ask. Instead, he said, "There are dangers in the mountains—I saw many while I was there, but I was fortunate enough to escape them. I sorrow that your son was not so fortunate, kind lady."

"It was long ago," the old man said gruffly. Of a sudden, he knelt at the spit once more and turned the brace of small birds that roasted over the flames. "Come," he said, glancing over his shoulder at Alaric, "if you be a minstrel, give us a song while supper finishes its cooking. Oren!" He waved at the beardless youth. "Bring a rug for our guest."

The boy ducked into the nearest tent and quickly returned with a cream-colored carpet, large enough for two or three people to sit upon in comfort. Its color, and its thick, felted texture, betrayed its origin in the shaggy hair of the deer. Oren spread it near the fire, and Alaric settled himself upon it, easing the pack and the lute down beside him.

At the first chords, the first few words that fell from his lips, heads turned in every part of the camp. People who had not given over watching the stranger since his arrival now moved toward him, ladles, knives, even bowls still in their hands. Others craned to see the source of the music, like hungry animals who, smelling food, sought it location. And they stilled themselves to listen, their silence flowing like ripples in a pond, outward from the minstrel till it washed against the tents.

> "Let yonder hill be my only guide
> Through storm and wind, through day and night,
> My love is there, in the crystal tree;
> A prisoner now, she waits for me."

It was an old tale of love and enchantment, of a princess captive, of an evil sorcerer, of a valiant knight; and like so many of Alaric's songs, it had a joyless ending. With the sorcerer's blood still marking his blade, the knight struck the crystal tree to break the spell, only to discover that enchantment could outlive the enchanter. The last verse found him dying of grief, his arms clasped about the tree. By the time the final melancholy words were sung, almost in a whisper, several of Alaric's listeners were weeping.

The evening breeze carried the last chord away, leaving only deep quiet for a moment, and then, as the leather-clad people realized the song was done and would not immediately yield to another, they began to talk again among themselves, but softly. And they turned once more to their suppers.

The younger woman at the graybeard's fire was one of those who wept. She dashed the tears away with the back of one wrist and gave a sigh. "Oh, it's a sad world where such things happen."

Alaric watched her for a moment, as she held a bowl for the gray-haired woman to fill from the bubbling pot.

And when she brought him that bowl, he smiled at her gently and said, "Fortunately, such things happen only rarely."

The stew was meaty, with fleshy roots sliced thickly into it. When Alaric finished his share, the graybeard pulled a bird off the spit for him. After they had all eaten, there were cups of blue-white liquid passed around, pungent as strong wine.

"If you've never drunk this before, take care," said Fowsh. "It goes to the head."

Alaric looked into his wooden cup. "What is it?"

"A wine we make from deer's milk."

The taste was odd, but not unpleasant. Having known some of the headiest wines of the south, Alaric limited himself to that cup, and to cold sweet water from a nearby brook.

They were a family group, the people at this fire. The young woman was Fowsh's wife, mother of the child; the youth was his brother; the elderly pair, his parents. They sat easily with each other, speaking about the small things of the day, the plans for the morrow. The whole camp would be packing up in the morning, moving north. To the calving grounds, they explained to Alaric, so that the does might drop their young.

"You are welcome to come along," said the graybeard, "if you'll sing for us again."

"I need little urging to sing," said Alaric, and he took up his lute. He gave them a cheerful song this time, the tale of the shepherd who fell asleep when he should have been guarding his flock, and who, on waking, found that the sheep had carried him home on their backs, and performed all of his evening duties to keep him from being punished. He had his hosts laughing—and a good many of their neighbors—at the antics of the sheep, who were so much more industrious than their keeper. After the song, a man from a neighboring fire came by to offer Alaric a cup of deer's-milk wine, but he refused it politely. He was already almost drunk on the reaction of his audience. But he did take more water, to keep his throat moist.

"You have a great skill," said the graybeard.

"I thank you, kind sir. I fear it is my only skill, though it has served me well so far."

"You have traveled much, you say. Tell us, pray, about life beyond the mountains."

Alaric shrugged. "To be honest, sir, I would rather sing. All of my life, every mile I have journeyed, every castle I have stayed in, every hovel, is somewhere in my songs. If I had to *speak* of it all, I would not know where to begin. Let me give you more music, for that fine supper was worth more than just a pair of songs."

And so he sang deep into the night, while the fires burned and burned and finally shrank to embers, while the children fell asleep in their parents' laps and even the parents began to nod. Little by little, as the needle-bright stars wheeled in the sky, his audience thinned, retiring to the circle of tents, until finally only Fowsh and his wife were left, barely visible in the fading ember-glow.

"Enough, minstrel," the herder said at last. "You will have no voice left for tomorrow."

But the songs had been low for some time, almost lullabies, and Alaric's throat was young and strong. He knew he would be able to sing in the morning. Still, his body was tired with the long walk of the day, and so he set aside his lute.

Fowsh brought a bearskin from his tent and held it out to Alaric.

"Thank you, but I have a good cloak to cover me," said Alaric.

"Dawn comes cold on the plain," said the man. "You may be glad of something heavier by then. Take it and welcome; we have others."

"You are most kind, sir."

Fowsh and his wife stood over him for a moment, arm in arm, their bodies faintly silhouetted against the stars. "Minstrel," the herder said at last, "the Northern Sea is no legend. I have never been there, but some among our people have. We will meet them at the calving grounds. If you wish to see it, you must go with them."

Alaric yawned. "Do they cook as well as you?"

The herder laughed softly. "So they claim."

"Then I will consider your suggestion."

Still laughing, Fowsh took his wife into their tent.

Alaric slept easy that night for the first time since leaving the Red Lord's domain, and he dreamed of rolling plains of soft herbs, and trees with pale fur pelts, and a sapphire brook; a gentle place where by law, nothing red could flow.

In the morning, Alaric's new traveling companions struck camp with a speed that amazed him. The tents came apart, each into three or four pieces, and were transformed into pouches for clothing, rugs, cooking utensils. Bound with ropes, these packs were lashed to the waiting deer. Atop them went bundles of posts that had tethered the herd or supported the deer-hide shelters. The sun had barely risen twice its breadth above the horizon when the whole encampment was mounted and ready to move northward.

Alaric bestrode his steed of the previous day, with a bridle this time and some small confidence. Around him, Fowsh's family was mounted as well, and in addition to their riding deer, they had six pack animals to carry their household goods. Not far away, Alaric saw his host's companion of yesterday with another such group.

Alaric neither saw nor heard any signal, but suddenly his group was in motion, the creature beneath him lumbering forward in its graceless fashion. The whole crowd, perhaps threescore people and twice that many animals, ambled northward, with the rising sun to their right and the mountains far behind. Looking back a few moments later, Alaric saw their camping place: the trampled grass, the dozen dark patches where fires had burned. A few moments more, and it had melted into the plain, as if it had never been. Alaric smiled and shook his head as he recalled how he had thought of their living place as a village. A village it was, of course; but a village on deer back.

The members of Fowsh's family shifted their positions here and there in the crowd, gossiping with friends, or swinging far to one side of the line for some time alone. At one point, the herder's wife caught up with Alaric.

"Minstrel," she said, after riding beside him in silence for a time, "was it very long ago?"

He glanced at her for just an instant; he needed most of his attention for the inequities of the ground, to anticipate his steed's clumsier movements. "Was *what* very long ago, lady?" he asked.

"Your song of last evening. The knight and the princess and the enchantment. Did it happen long ago?"

Alaric hesitated. Though most folk he met believed in magic, he did not. He had traveled much and yet never seen any real magic, save his own power, and that was just a natural thing, a gift of birth, no black art learned in the hush of darkness. His only concern with magic was that he not be taken, by the fearful, for a dabbler in that art. He had never given a thought to any truth that might lie in the tale of the crystal tree. "It is just a song, good lady," he said.

"Was it not founded on some true occurrence?"

For another moment he was silent, and then, slowly, he said to her, "In all truth, I do not know. It is a very old song."

"Oh." Disappointment colored that small sound. "And there was never anyone to help them?"

"Not that I have ever heard."

"Did he never search for help?"

Alaric had to shrug. "You ask questions that I cannot answer, lady."

"A witch could have broken the spell," she said firmly. "If only he had come to us, he would have gotten his princess back."

The young minstrel smiled slightly. "Have you a witch among you?"

"Of course. Do you think we could live here in the north without one?"

"Well . . . I'm sure I don't know. Just now, the north seems pleasant enough, but I recall last night there was some mention of terrible storms. . . ." He chanced another brief glance in her direction. "Who would this witch be? Yourself?"

"I?" There was startlement in her voice. "Do I look like a witch?"

"I have met a few witches in my day," he said. "I don't recall that they had any special appearance in common."

"Had they no amulets, no carven staves, no smell of sweet spice about them?"

"Are those the things that mark a witch among you?"

"Of course."

He shrugged once more. "Well, it is not so in other lands. The world is wide, and there are many customs in its many corners. But if you are not the witch, who is? I saw no amulets, no carven staves last night. Perhaps your witch does not care for music?"

"Kata is our witch," she said, "and she spends most of her time with the band of Simir, our high chief. I do not know if she likes music. You will see her at the calving grounds and may find out for yourself."

"She is a woman of great power, is she?"

"Very great power. She brings the good weather every year."

"Indeed?"

"And gives us hunting magic. You ate the fruits of her skill last night, that stewed rabbit and those roasted birds."

"I thought Fowsh's father shot them."

"Of course. Long ago Kata gave him hunting magic."

"Indeed?"

"And if my Fowsh ever needs it, she will give some to him."

"He is a successful hunter without any magic?"

"No, he never hunts. The deer are his work. But someday his father will grow too old for hunting, and then another member of the family will go out after game. Either Fowsh or Oren. And Kata will see to their success."

"A valuable woman," Alaric murmured.

He had seen witches before, both women and men, who said they knew potent spells, who chanted strange phrases and made passes in the air with their hands, who had the folk of the neighborhood convinced of their power. Such people were usually feared and hated, usually outcasts, often murdered in their sleep or when their backs were turned. In a few places, though, they were kept and even coddled by men whose armies gave them mastery over commoner folk, men who thought a few mystic powers could be useful. When he was younger, Alaric had feared witches, feared that their preternatural sensibilities would find him out, that they would expose him for the creature he was, and even destroy him out of jealousy or self-protection. Yet that had never happened. All the spell casters he had ever met had proved to be frauds: some of them merely poor old women, accused by neighbors seeking a cause for the failure of crops; some of them self-proclaimed but just as empty, deceiving folk for their own advantage. There were real witches in the world, Alaric knew, but they were all of his own blood, and their only mystic power was the one he possessed.

Is this Kata such a one? he wondered.

Alaric was an excellent hunter, in his own way. But his gift was not one that could be given away. And controlling the weather? *No, she is a fraud,* he thought, *tricking these people into believing she makes life in the north easier.* He shook his head slowly. *She must be quite a persuader, this Kata.*

And he found himself curious, most curious, to meet her.

Shortly after noon, the band stopped to make camp. As soon as the deer had been relieved of their burdens, they were taken out to graze, scattering to the west in groups of a dozen or two, each accompanied by a pair of herders. Other men and boys started northeastward on foot, some following the course of a slow-moving stream, some crossing it and drifting beyond, to search for small game. Alaric stayed at the camp with the women and small children, making himself useful to Fowsh's wife—laying out rugs, clearing a space for the fire, fetching water. Later he sang a little—gay and pretty songs—and the children gathered round him to listen, and to stretch shy fingers out to touch the lute. He even took a few of them on his knee in turns and let them pluck the strings.

Fowsh's father and brother returned with a bag of hares and a large fish, and by the time the herders had brought back their charges, a savory supper was ready. This time Alaric ate first and then sang, and once again, his listeners were silent, entranced. Late into the night he sang, and he could not help feeling that he had never sung so well in castle or manor house as within that circle of tents. But he stopped this night before he quite lost all his audience, and just as he was settling down for sleep,

Fowsh's neighbors came to ask if he would share supper with them the following night.

And so Alaric began to move among the nomads, from family to family, from fire to fire, as they all paid him in turn with the only coin they had. He ate well, he slept warm, and if rain came by night, there was always a corner for him in some dry, snug tent. The society of the nomads was a place of rare hospitality; it enclosed him like a bright cocoon, and it made the mountains seem very far away.

A month passed, and as the band traveled steadily northward, Alaric came to know them all, adults and children, graybeards and clean-shaven. They were a close-knit people, always ready to laugh and cry with each other, always ready to work together for the common good, to share in each other's cooking pots or to help in finding strayed livestock. Their leader, Nuriki, a man in his prime, a hunter and owner of many deer, was related in one way or another to virtually all of them. To Alaric he seemed less a commander than a gatherer of consensus, less a judge than a negotiator; certainly, no one treated him with the deference accorded even a minor noble in the south. There was no need for Alaric to please *him* especially, as he would have had to please a southern lord; Nuriki was happy just to be part of the audience. Alaric liked him for that. Indeed, he liked the whole band, every man and woman among them seemed his friend. He was comfortable with Nuriki's people as he had never been with other folk before.

Their northward movement seemed almost to keep pace with spring, and so when they finally arrived at the calving grounds, the season was still young, the grass still new underfoot. The calving grounds themselves seemed no different than any other part of the plain, save that they were occupied by so great a throng of people and deer—a chuffing, stamping sea of deer. There were no enclosures for the animals here; they roamed free in a vast, seething mass. It was the tent clusters, set on the fringes of that enormous herd, that were fenced, the ropes and posts now serving to keep the animals out.

A faint pall of smoke from a thousand cookfires overhung the area, and a constant hum, a wavering blend of human and animal voices, enveloped it. Alaric's companions selected an empty space at the southern edge of the herd for their campsite, and as soon as their deer had been stripped of all burdens, even before a single tent had been raised, Fowsh and the other herders escorted the animals into that milling, bawling mass.

"How will you ever find your own deer again?" Alaric wondered aloud. He was helping an elderly woman, his most recent host, to lace the pieces of a tent together with deer sinew.

She looked up at him with incomprehension in her eyes. "How not?" she said.

"There are so many."

She grinned, showing gaps among her front teeth. "Yes, more than when I was young. Many more." She nodded. "The north has been good to us, these years."

"So it seems," said Alaric, looking out upon the chaos of fur and antlers that had swallowed Fowsh and his beasts as a pond swallows pebbles. He put the question to Fowsh when the men reappeared.

"We know our deer and they know us," Fowsh replied. "Gathering them up will not be as hard as you think."

In his absence, the tents had all been set in their circle; now the campfires, fueled by deer droppings, were blazing heartily, and in a dozen pots, the midday meal was simmering.

Hunting had been poor these last few days, with band after band crossing the same territory, and so there were only roots and fragments of dried meat in the stew. But tomorrow, Alaric knew, deer would be slaughtered, and the nomads would begin to feast.

"I have passed the news that we have a minstrel among us," Fowsh said, watching his wife stir their pot with steady, graceful strokes.

His mother leaned out of her tent. "You could have waited," she said. "You could have held one more night of him for ourselves before you gave him away."

Fowsh laughed softly. "One more song, you mean, Mother. I doubt we could keep him secret longer than that."

"You have been kind to me," Alaric said. "I will not

forget that kindness. But I have consumed your substance long enough. It is time others knew the burden of feeding me.''

"It has not been a burden, minstrel." He shook his head. "Nuriki's daughter sings. Or calls it singing, anyway. But she has not opened her mouth since you came to us. After we lose you, I suppose she will take it up again." He shrugged his shoulders. "Well, there will be song and music in plenty while we are here in the calving grounds. There are other bands with singers and drums and flutes, and there will be dancing to all the old, familiar tunes." He grinned at Alaric, his pale eyes crinkling. "Mark me," he said, "Simir will claim you in the end.''

"Simir?"

"The high chief. He will offer the most comfort, the best food, the finest diversions. His band is the largest of all. And he goes north when the calving is done."

"To the Northern Sea?"

"Some of his hunters have seen it."

"And Nuriki's band?"

"No farther than this, minstrel. We are the soft southerners of this country. Life is too hard for us in the north." He laid a hand on Alaric's shoulder. "Take my advice, lad: if you must visit the Northern Sea, go in company. It is easy to die if you go alone."

"I shall not forget."

Fowsh grinned again. "Good. And now, if you will, give us a last song for Nuriki's people before someone spirits you away to another fire and a better midday meal."

And it was a last song because, before it was half-finished, folk from other camps had drifted near to listen to Alaric's clear, strong voice and the liquid coursing of his lute. It was a last song because, when it was done, a clamor of voices called out invitations, and Fowsh himself advised Alaric on which offer of food and drink was most worthy. It was a last song because the people that Fowsh indicated then surrounded the minstrel and swept him off, leaving Nuriki's circle to fade away in the distance, just one more group of tents among many.

His meal with the new band was as good as Fowsh had

promised, a hot thick stew of small game, a lucky hunter's bounty, well laced with aromatic herbs. Alaric sang after he ate a modest serving, and his new audience was just as entranced as the old.

Days passed, and the minstrel was shuttled from fire to fire and meal to meal, and he never lacked for praise. Yet he moved only on the fringes of the nomads' gathering. His was a small circle of entertainment, one of many in that vast company, circles of gossip and barter and matchmaking. When he was not singing, he wandered among the tents, listening to folk discussing their animals or trading news, or watching them barter rope, fine leatherwork, furs, and packets of herbs; he even saw a wedding, the bride and groom making their vows before a crowd of elders. And at night, sometimes, he went to the heart of the gathering, where tents stood shoulder to shoulder about a wide clearing with a huge blaze at its center. There by the roaring flames, the nomads danced to the steady beat of drums and the lively trill of flutes, and there they often sang, though to Alaric's ear the tunes were almost too monotonous to call music. Still, he listened sharply, in hopes of finding fresh material for his own verses, and sometimes he felt his own blood answering those steady pulses of sound.

When he sang at night, he took care to do it far from the dance ground, in places where the call of drum and flute was too distant to interfere with his quieter kind of music. And often, among his listeners, he saw the flushed and sweaty faces that marked folk who had left the dancing for softer diversion—for the tales of love and sorrow, of sorcery and death, and only rarely of laughter, that were his wares.

As the night deepened, the younger couples were usually the first to slip away, though not always the quickest, for they would dally at the edge of the crowd to hear the last lines of some sad song of love. And Alaric's gaze would follow them to where they lingered in the tent shadows, where sometimes they kissed before leaving his presence. And in that long moment, the frozen moment of embrace, they took on the semblance of graceful statues in some garden of ancient mystery; they became the emblem of something timeless and eternal, something that was a part of and also beyond simple desire. At last they would melt into the further darkness, and Alaric would find himself musing on his latest song, and on the one he might sing next. Now and again, his new choice would recount some greater sorrow than the one recounted before.

Alaric had been at the calving grounds no more than a week when the first of the deer dropped their young. Days were busy then, as men and boys from every band sought out the babes of their own animals and notched their ears in marks of ownership. Alaric marveled at the ease with which the nomads found their charges; to him, not only the animals but the ear notches all looked alike. He caught sight of Fowsh one day, throwing a calf to the ground, straddling it and cutting its ears while his father calmed the nervous doe. He waved to them and called a greeting, but in the tumult of the herd they did not notice, and Alaric thought better than to go out among all those skittish beasts to exchange pleasantries.

The deer had been calving for twelve days—and the nomads were saying that very soon the whole process would be done, and the bands would go their separate ways once more—when Simir the high chief sent for Alaric.

Simir's tents had been pointed out to Alaric more than once already. They stood on a rise at the northern edge of the herd, a few very large tents on the highest ground, surrounded by several circular tiers of smaller ones. Here the nomads went with disputes that could not be settled within their own bands, and here they paid their lord in kind for his judgment, in deer and leather and all manner of goods valued by the nomads. That, many told Alaric, was his only tax upon them.

Well, he builds no castles, no roads, no bridges, the minstrel thought. *What need has he for taxes?*

Alaric climbed the path of trampled grass that wound among the lower tiers of tents. Ahead of him walked the youth who had brought the high chief's summons. He was a tall lad, perhaps two or three years younger than Alaric, but already well muscled, and with a downy mustache just beginning to fringe his upper lip. His hair was much lighter than that of the other nomads, a chestnut brown to their black, and he wore it shorter, cut shaggy just below his ears. He had not given his name, but another man had called him Terevli, and Alaric's audience had parted to let him pass.

At the crest of the rise, seated on a thick pile of carpets before the largest tent and surrounded by chattering people, was a man of great physical presence. Had he been standing, he would have been taller than most of those about him, and he was broader of shoulder, and thicker of arm and thigh; he was surely a man who had swung a sword for the greater part of his life. And he was a blond, with high color showing in his cheeks, the only true blond in all that company of dark-haired folk.

Alaric's companion came to a halt in front of the man. "Father," he said, and he cocked a thumb toward Alaric.

The blond man had been nodding, his head turned to one side while an elderly woman spoke to him. Now, as she hurried away, he looked to Alaric, and his wide mouth curved in a smile. "Ah, the minstrel everyone has been talking about. Welcome to Simir's fire." At his gesture, the folk about him fell silent and made Alaric the center of their attention. "I trust you have been treated well among our people."

Alaric bowed low. "Very well, my lord. They are most hospitable."

The man's smile broadened. "*My lord,*" he murmured, and then he chuckled. "I can't recall ever being called so. It has a fine ring, minstrel, but I care not for its fit. Simir is my name; use that."

Alaric hesitated. "You are the high chief, sir?"

He nodded.

The minstrel bowed again. "My apologies, then. I am from the south, as you surely know, and it is a custom of the south to give such titles to those in high office."

"I know the custom," said Simir. "But we are in the north here, and no one will punish you for speaking my name. Now, I have been told that my cook is among the best of our people; and if you would consent to try her skill, I would ask you to sing for one who has spent a burdensome day in the judging of petty quarrels, and is

therefore twice as tired as those who have spent theirs
notching the ears of newborn deer.''

"I have heard some small word of your cook," Alaric
said. "But even were she the least of all the cooks at this
gathering, I would play for the high chief. It is, after all,
an honor."

"Have you sung for many high chiefs, young minstrel?"

"For kings and princes, and many a lesser noble, good
Simir. And for the poorest peasant, living in a hovel of
mud and thatch. I have sung for many, many people. And
if the food was bad . . ." He shrugged. "There was always another day, another hearth. One learns, when one
is a minstrel, to accept the good and the bad."

"A fair philosophy for one who travels in the north,"
said Simir. "Come, sit down." He gestured to the space
beside him. "Give me a song, that I may judge what
others have said of you. They tell me I am very good at
judgment." And he smiled again.

Alaric took a corner of the rug, the lute upon his thighs.
He strummed a note or two, then decided on an old song,
one well loved in the south, a tale of ancient and sorcer-
ous tragedy.

"The forest is deep and dark and still,
Round the cave where the ruby lies,
Yet once there was lightning within those walls,
And flame in an old man's eyes,
Though his heart was chill."

When the tale was done—the evil sorcerer vanquished,
the spells all rent to pieces, the lone survivor standing
with head bared and sword bloodied—the high chief and
all the folk about him clapped their hands and stamped
their feet on the trampled grass to show their pleasure.

"They did not lie when they said you were skilled,"
Simir declared. "We have none like you among us."

Alaric inclined his head. "I thank you, good Simir."

"They also said your store of songs appeared inex-
haustible."

"That is . . . a slight exaggeration. But I do have a
good supply."

Simir's eyes swept him up and down, head to toe, fingertip to fingertip, as a man might survey the lines of a horse or a dog. "Are you strong?"

"Strong? I fear I don't know what you mean, sir."

"I have heard that you seek the Northern Sea."

Alaric gave a small shrug. "I am a wanderer, good Simir; new sights and new folk are to me as gold and silver to other men. In the south, the Northern Sea is more than half legend; I thought to make it real for myself."

Simir tilted his head to one side, as if to see the young minstrel better from that angle. "It is a hard journey. I have made it, and I know. You do not look strong enough for it, minstrel, for all that you have crossed the great mountains to come here."

"We do not all have arms and shoulders like yours, Simir. Yet I can wield an ax and bend a bow and lift more than my own weight. And I have made a hard journey or two in my life. Such journeys are sometimes the stuff of good songs."

"If you survive them," said Simir. "What do you know of the north, minstrel? They say you've been here no more than a month."

Alaric nodded.

"Then you would do well to spend a few seasons among us, learning the northern way of life, before you decide to venture onward. Southerners have died on these plains through inexperience. I would not care to see so fine a minstrel as yourself join their number."

"Are you making me an invitation, good Simir?"

"To come with my band, to sing for us, I am indeed. We go north, minstrel. You will not find a band that travels closer to the Northern Sea than mine."

Alaric smiled. "Since you speak of an extended sojourn, first let me try your cook's skills. Then I'll give you my answer."

"Done," said Simir, and he beckoned to one of the men who stood nearby and gave orders for the evening meal to be served. He grinned to Alaric. "You'll be comfortable with us, minstrel, I promise that."

"I hope so, sir. I sing best when I am comfortable."

The group that gathered to eat at Simir's fire was large,

a retinue to match the high chief's rank, perhaps a score in all. Most of the men and women who had listened with him to Alaric's song were there, and others as well, old and young, who had arrived later. The boy Terevli was joined by two other sons of Simir—Gilo and Marak—both nearer to Alaric's own age; tall, muscular youths who carried themselves with easy assurance. All three took places close by their father as soon as the food was given out.

The meal was perhaps not quite as good as one or two that Alaric had enjoyed in great houses in the south, but it sufficed, the venison tender, the herbs pungent, the vegetables sweet and full-flavored. Of course, the season was spring; come winter, the fare might be thinner. Still, Alaric had never gone hungry since learning to hunt by his own methods; there would always be game from *somewhere* to put in his pot. More important to him, the company was lively, joking, laughing, talking with high animation, and including a wandering minstrel in that liveliness. That was much more important.

When the wooden dinner bowls had been collected, Simir called for silence, his voice big and booming. "Our guest has a decision to make now," he said, stretching one arm toward Alaric. "I ask him to make it here, though I already know, as surely as my heart beats, what it will be. What say you, young minstrel? Shall you give the cook a grateful kiss?"

Alaric rose to his feet. The cook, a stout matron with face reddened by the fire, stood beside the caldrons that had produced a meal for so many. She looked a trifle bewildered by the high chief's words, her gaze moving uncertainly from him to the minstrel and back again. Alaric grinned and made his way through the crowd to her.

"You are an excellent cook," he said, "and I look forward to eating your suppers for a long time." And taking her by the shoulders, he bussed her loudly on one rosy cheek.

"Here's to the minstrel who comes north with us," Simir called, raising his cup of milky spirits. "Here's to the nights when song will banish the sound of the cold wind, and our babes will rock to sleep to his lullaby."

They raised their cups and drank, and Alaric smiled at

them and took up his lute to give them a lively song to match their lively mood.

Simir's fire sank to embers, red in the darkness, with fitful flames licking upward now and again. Some people drifted away, to that other, brighter fire in the distance, where the drums and the flutes played steadily, and the dancers leaped. But some stayed to hear Alaric's music, so very different it was, the lone human voice and the pure notes of the lute. Simir stayed, and bade the minstrel play on and on, till even that other fire was dimmed, and that other sound faded away. The stars were bright and cold above their heads, and the human noises of the huge encampment were quieting for the night, when Alaric stopped at last.

"You shall have a place in my own tent, minstrel," Simir said. "You shall be my own personal guest."

"Thank you, sir. But if you have no objection, as long as the weather is fine, I enjoy sleeping in the open air."

Simir's shrug was just barely visible by ember-light. "As you will. There are carpets in plenty for your bed, and furs if you should become chilled." He rose from his seat, a bear of a man in the dimness. "I bid you good night."

An old woman helped the minstrel make a pallet by the embers and then scurried away into the darkness, the last of his listeners to vanish. Alaric wrapped his lute against the night damp and settled comfortably upon his carpets. Fingers interlaced behind his head, he gazed up at the stars and listened to the soft grunting of the vast herd of deer. He could smell them, just barely, a musky scent. Soon the herders would be gathering up their animals, the bands would part company, and he would move north, into the unknown.

He was just beginning to doze when he heard footsteps close by. He opened his eyes and saw a human shape looming over him. It knelt between him and the embers, a faceless shadow.

"Hello, minstrel," it said. A woman's voice, young, light, not one he recognized.

"Yes?" he murmured.

"I heard you last night and the night before. It was I who suggested Simir send for you."

Alaric peered into the darkness but could not make out her face. "Thank you, lady. I owe you much."

"So you do."

He felt her touch on his arm, felt her fingers slide up to his shoulder, to his neck. They were cool and smooth, the long nails like tiny daggers lightly scraping his skin. Then one hand slipped downward against the fabric of his tunic, against his chest, downward, till he caught it at his waist.

"Who are you?" he said.

"Ah," she whispered. "Does it matter?"

"Of course."

She laughed softly. "I doubt you even noticed me in the crowd." Her form blotted out the stars as she bent close, as she pressed her lips to his.

He pushed her back, firmly but not roughly. "This is not seemly behavior with a stranger, lady."

She laughed again, a deep, throaty laugh. "I am Zavia, and I make my own seemliness, minstrel." She took his hands in her own, then, and pressed them against the yielding softness of her breasts. When he tried to pull away, she let him go, laughing once more. "You think me ugly, don't you? You think some hag has come to you under cover of darkness. No, you never noticed me at all, though I stared at you well, minstrel. Oh, very well." She leaned away from him then, scrabbling at the fire, and a moment later he saw an ember flare as she blew it into fitful life. Laying a splint of wood against the flame, she lit a tiny torch and, turning back to him, held it close to her cheek. "You see," she said, "I am worth looking at."

Indeed, she was a strikingly pretty girl, with high cheekbones, a small, pointed chin, and eyes that seemed to dance in the flamelight. He did recall seeing her this evening, sitting with Simir's three sons. She had smiled at his songs. Gilo's arm had been about her shoulders.

She tossed the brand back into the fire and, lifting Alaric's coverlet, eased herself onto his pallet. Her hands touched him again, fingers curling, and he could feel the nails begin to bite into the flesh of his arms.

"I remember you," he said. "You sat with Gilo."

"So I did," she whispered, fitting her body to his side. "I would not wish to anger him. Your husband?"

"I have no husband," she said, moving against him slowly, insistently. Her lips found his throat. "I am my own, no one else's. Why do you lie so still, minstrel? Have you never known a woman before?"

"I do not know your customs, lady."

"Zavia. My name is Zavia."

The feel of her warm body against his, the touch of her mouth on his throat, was almost too much for him. With an effort of will, he gripped her shoulders with both hands and held her away from him. "There are many customs in many lands," he said huskily. "In some, this would marry me to you. In others, it would spur your brothers to hack off my head."

Zavia's laugh was light now, teasing. "I have no brothers, fair minstrel. Not a one."

"Even so, we travelers must be careful."

"There is nothing to be careful of here, pretty boy, except perhaps my tender bones. Your hands are strong. Does that come from playing the lute?"

He did not ease his grip. "And women lie sometimes, when passion strikes them."

She was able to touch his chest with one hand, just the fingertips, very softly. "You've had great experience of women, then?"

"Enough to know that the sweetheart of the high chief's son should not share a poor minstrel's bed."

She sat up suddenly, almost pulling him up with her. "I am not his sweetheart," she hissed.

"Shall I believe you, lady? Shall I believe that his arm about your shoulders meant nothing? That his way of looking at you meant nothing?"

"Nothing, and less than nothing. Just the same as yourself, minstrel!" With a sudden, sharp movement, she tore from his grasp and, flinging the covers aside, scrambled off into the darkness.

For a time, after the sound of her hurrying footsteps had faded away, Alaric lay on his back, arms pillowing his head. He could almost feel her warmth yet, her softness, the touch of her lips. A less cautious man would

have accepted her offer, he knew, even though they would
be lying where anyone who decided to stoke the fire
would see them. A less cautious man would not have
asked any questions, would not have driven her away with
his doubts. Alaric closed his eyes, relief and sharp regret
mingling within him, and he sighed more than once before rolling over and going to sleep.

Shortly after dawn, the chief's people emerged from
their tents to begin the new day. This morning, as they
ate a meal of cold venison, their talk was all of the coming dispersion. Already, they could point out early-rising
herders moving among the deer, singling out their own
animals and bridling them, and tying them to picket lines
near their tents. The chief's men agreed to put their own
efforts off another day or two, as a couple of their deer
had not yet calved.

Intermittently, Zavia walked among these men, col-
lecting empty bowls or filling cups from a large jug. She
did not have to do these things; Alaric had seen nomad
men serve themselves often enough. But she seemed restless. Terevli followed her here and there, like a calf trail-
ing its mother, occasionally catching up to speak in her
ear, but she would always shake her head and move away
from him. Once she even pushed him off with one hand.
She avoided looking at Alaric, except for one brief, sullen glance. She did not take his bowl or fill his cup.

During the morning, Simir busied himself with the
seemingly endless disputes of his people, leaving Alaric
free to do as he wished. He watched the process of judgment for a time, watched the high chief hear argument
after argument and dispense decisions based not so much
on right and wrong as on the need for members of a band
to live together in peace and harmony. Often, the dispu-
tants accepted his judgment, neither side completely satisfied, yet neither completely dissatisfied, both yielding
something and agreeing that the matter was finished. But
sometimes such compromise was impossible, and the
only way to settle the dispute was to separate the adver-
saries by sending one of them to some other band.

Alaric wearied of this wrangling before long and wondered how Simir could bear it day after day. The nomads
who seemed so cheerful, so cooperative, so easygoing at

their own fires became volatile, angry, and stubborn in dispute. And it was nearly all over deer, over their own-ership and their care.

More tiring indeed than notching a few ears, Alaric thought as he slipped away from the high chief's pres-ence. *They must save a whole year's quarrels up for him.*

The rest of the morning he spent wandering among the tents, watching the herders work. By midday, he found himself near the encampment of Nuriki's band; he rec-ognized Fowsh, who was tying a doe and a calf to a post beside one of the tents, and he waved. In a moment, he was surrounded by familiar faces, swept to the fire, and given food. Afterward, he sang for them. They would be leaving the next day, they said, going south. If he had changed his mind about seeking the Northern Sea, he was welcome to come with them, Fowsh said.

Alaric shook his head. "I have a place in Simir's band, just as you predicted."

Fowsh grinned and clapped him on the back.

Later, he returned to Simir's fire and found the high chief taking his ease with a few companions, all disputes put aside.

"Learning to cut the herd, are you, minstrel?" he asked with laughter in his big voice. "That's surely not a skill you'll ever need."

Alaric smiled at him. "I hope not. Still, it is an inter-esting sight. I marvel that anyone can find his own deer in that crowd."

"They are as different from each other as people are. Or so they tell me." He lowered his tone conspiratori-ally. "Truthfully, I can scarcely tell them apart myself. I am a hunter, not a herder. Perhaps you know a good song for a hunter?"

"Perhaps." With a flourish on the strings, Alaric be-gan a tale of eagles seeking their prey among the moun-tains, and of a boy who had vowed to take an eaglet for his own or die in the attempt. It had two endings, one tragic, one triumphant. For these listeners, he chose the latter.

"Where have you found so many tales?" Simir asked when the song was done and Alaric had been given a cup of milky wine.

The lute lay beside his hip, and Alaric plucked idly at its strings. "The world is wide and full of tales, Simir. I had a teacher, for a time, and I have met other singers over the years. I've even invented a few songs of my own." He shrugged. "I hope they are as good as the rest."

"I would hear one of those, good minstrel."

"You just did."

Simir shook his head slowly. "And I can hardly make a rhyme."

Alaric looked at him sidelong. "And I could not judge a dispute over deer to save my life."

The high chief laughed. "Do you always say the right thing, minstrel?"

Ruefully, Alaric replied, "I wish it were so, good Simir. I have said the wrong thing more often than I care to admit."

"But the music is always right, is it not?"

"I surely hope so."

"Then give us another song. Unless . . ." The sound of drums had just come to their ears, marking the start of the evening's dancing; the sun was low, and already the great fire had been lit, its flames visible in the middle distance. "You are young," Simir said. "You might want to be dancing instead of singing here. There won't be any dancing for my band when we leave this place; the drums and the flutes will not come with us. I won't keep you if you want to join the other young people."

"I have never been one for dancing," Alaric told him.

"My sons will show you the steps. Gilo! Terevli!"

The two youths approached their father. They looked remarkably alike, though the age difference was obvious. Gilo, the elder, was well filled out, broad-shouldered and tall; Terevli was like an immature version of him, more lightly built, with softer features.

"Yes, Father," said Gilo. He stood spraddle-legged, his fists resting on his hips, an impatient posture.

"Take the minstrel with you to the dancing," said Simir.

Gilo swung his gaze to Alaric, an arrogant gaze, one that seemed to evaluate the minstrel's slender frame and find it lacking.

Alaric looked doubtfully at Simir.

"Go, go," the high chief said, waving his hand sharply. "You'll enjoy yourself. I'll look after your lute myself. No one else shall touch it."

With some reluctance, Alaric rose to his feet. Then he bowed to Simir, and to Gilo and Terevli, and followed the youths as they walked silently away from Simir's fire.

Does he know about last night? Alaric wondered, watching Gilo's back.

They met Marak and Zavia at the last row of tents belonging to Simir's band, and the five of them moved on together, toward the drums. Zavia walked as far away from Alaric as possible, as far away as Marak's arm about her waist would allow.

The dancing had already begun before they arrived. A dozen couples were leaping to the raucous music, sometimes clapping and stamping, sometimes swinging round each other with clasped hands. The steps seemed less complex than merely strenuous. Marak took Zavia out among the dancers and soon had her kicking and whirling like the rest.

Gilo clutched Alaric's right arm above the elbow, and his grip was like the grip of a wounded wolf's jaws. He gestured, open-handed, to the dancers. "Can you do that, minstrel?"

"I am not a very good dancer," Alaric said, and then he had to repeat the words more loudly, to be heard above the drums.

"Here," said Gilo, and he pulled Alaric over to a young woman who stood in the front row of onlookers. She was very plump and plain, and her eyes watched the dancers as a starving man watches meat being sliced. "This is our new minstrel," he said to her. "He would like to dance with you."

She looked from one youth to the other, then smiled hesitantly. "Yes," she said. "Oh, yes."

Gilo let Alaric's arm go at that. "My father's orders," he said, and slipped away into the crowd.

Alaric bowed stiffly to the young woman. "I don't know how well I'll do, but I'll try."

She knew the dance, and she was remarkably light on her feet for one so plump. Alaric muddled through the steps, mostly by imitating her, and he whirled and leaped and swung her till his sweat was flowing freely and the breath began to burn in his lungs. But the music never stopped, nor did his partner, who smiled more broadly the longer she danced. At last, Alaric had to call a halt, apologetically, when a cramp in his side threatened to double him over.

"Are you ill?" the young woman said, her eyes round.

He shook his head, one hand pressed to his waist. "Just unused to dancing. But thank you. For being such a good partner." And he bowed, a bit awkwardly, and smiled.

"Oh, thank *you*," she cooed.

He could almost feel her eyes on his back as he limped away from the throng. He looked over his shoulder only once, and she was watching him as she clapped time, and he had to smile. He did not see Simir's sons or Zavia anywhere, but he felt sure they had watched him dance. *Well, let them have their joke,* he thought. *I've survived worse.*

He walked slowly, and by the time he began to climb the rise to Simir's fire, the pain in his side was gone and his breath was easy. But the cool evening breeze, which had been so pleasant on other nights, was making him shiver in his sweat-drenched tunic. When he reached Simir's fire, he nodded briefly to the people gathered there then sought out the knapsack that contained everything he owned. Inside was another tunic, dry and clean. He stripped off the wet, clammy garment and shrugged into the other.

Supper was cooking over Simir's fire. Alaric moved close to the flames, held his hands out to them; he was still chilled in spite of dry clothing. The cook grinned at him and scooped a ladleful of hot stew from the pot, filled a bowl, and passed it to him. As he took it and smiled his thanks to her, he saw Zavia standing on the other side of the fire, staring at him. Her expression was not unlike the one that had been on the plump young woman's face as she watched the dancers. He turned away and walked toward his pallet to eat, but Simir beckoned to him, offering a place on his carpet, and he went there instead. The lute was waiting exactly where he had left it.

Simir was eating his own meal, and when Alaric sat down, he waved to the folk about him to move off a bit and leave the two of them to talk together. "You enjoyed the dancing?" he asked.

Alaric gave him a small smile. "Not as much as you would have at my age, I think. But I did manage not to trip over my own feet."

"Did you dance with her?" Simir's voice was low, and only with his eyes did he indicate that he meant Zavia.

Alaric shook his head.

"No? Well, I suppose the boys kept her busy."

"I suppose so. I was a bit too busy myself to notice, thanks to your eldest. He found me a very lively partner."

"Did he?" Simir pursed his lips thoughtfully. "That was good of him."

Alaric bent his attention to his bowl; yet from the corner of his eye, he could see Zavia turn her back on the fire and move off into the darkness between the tents.

"She's been watching you, minstrel," Simir said softly. "Or haven't you noticed that, either?"

Alaric shrugged. "Everyone watches a minstrel."

The high chief was silent a moment, then he said, "You hurt her pride, last night, by saying she was Gilo's."

Alaric looked up at him sharply.

"Don't be surprised at what I know, minstrel. There are few secrets in a nomad band; we live too close to each other, with our eyes and ears open. She is a pretty girl, don't you think?"

"Yes. She is."

"She is much pursued by the young men, my sons and their friends. Some have even caught her, now and again, whenever she wanted to be caught. But none has ever set a bridle on her. Not Gilo, not Marak, none." He smiled slightly. "She'll forgive you, minstrel. You are new and different, and she wants you very much."

Setting his empty bowl on the edge of the carpet, Alaric picked up the lute, and with three fingers, he plucked a chord from it. "And what of those pursuing young men? What will they say to that?"

"What can they say?" said Simir. "The choice is hers."

"They can make the stranger's life unpleasant."

Simir smiled again. "The stranger is a friend of Simir, the high chief. They make his life unpleasant at their peril."

"Even his own sons?"

"I do not shrink from punishing my sons."

Alaric looked toward the shadows where Zavia had disappeared.

"Go on," said Simir, and he nudged Alaric's knee with the back of one hand. "Don't waste your youth, minstrel. It will be gone soon enough, believe me."

The shadows were empty, the space between tents merely a narrow corridor leading to another circle of dwellings, another fire. In the flamelight there, beyond the laughing, chattering company that clustered at the cooking pots, he saw her. She stood with Gilo.

She faced away; she could not see him. Almost, he stepped back into the darkness, to let her be, however pretty she was, however much she fancied him. There had been other girls for him, there would be others yet. What need was there to meddle with one so much pursued? Almost, almost, he let the shadows claim him. But he recalled the sharpness of his regret, and as he hesitated, the moment for that backward step passed. Gilo noticed him, and Zavia, seeing her companion's face change and his eyes focused on something behind her, turned and saw him as well.

She smiled then, slowly, a small, triumphant smile. But Alaric scarcely noticed it; his eyes were held by Gilo's, by the proud, hard anger he saw there, the anger of a young man whom time had not yet resigned to being crossed.

He hates me, Alaric thought. *I've done nothing. I refused her. And still he hates me.*

And when at last he looked at Zavia's smile, he understood that she was just as proud as the high chief's son. *What is it like,* he wondered, *to feel that way?*

At her first step toward Alaric, Gilo caught her arm. But she threw him off with a rough word and a rougher gesture.

"You owe me a dance, Zavia!" he called as he followed her around the fire. "You haven't danced with me at all this night!"

"Leave off!" she shouted over one shoulder. "I've danced with you enough all year!" She halted a pace or two from Alaric. Her smile was wider now as she looked up into his face with eyes that were pale as the winter sky. The firelight glimmered on her cheeks, seemed to make her skin glow. Softly, she said, "I would rather dance with the minstrel."

"Dance?" Gilo edged halfway between them, one bare, muscular shoulder almost thrust into Alaric's face. "Stagger, you mean. *Stumble.*" His voice was heavy with contempt.

She didn't look at him. Instead, she touched Alaric's arm with just the tips of her fingers, and by that delicate pressure drew him a few steps away from the high chief's son.

He took her hand in both his own. Her skin was smooth and warm, and immediately her fingers curled about his, claiming him, marking him, speaking to him, youth to youth, Simir's selfsame message. *I am not young anymore,* he thought. *Not with what I have seen, what I have done. But I would be.* "You would be disappointed in my dancing, I fear," he told her, smiling to her smile. "But perhaps you would accept a song instead."

She tilted her head to one side, as if already listening for it. "What sort of song?"

"A special one, sung only in the finest halls of the south, where the cups are made of gold and the walls are hung with silk. A song to make great ladies weep into their jewel-encrusted hands."

"I have no wish to weep," she said in a low voice.

"Then I shall make you laugh instead."

Her fingers tightened on his. "I believe I would trade a dance for that."

"Come then; we must claim my lute from Simir's custody."

In the dark passage between the tents, he looked back only once, to Gilo, still standing in the firelight. His bare arms were crossed upon his broad, leather-clad chest, and hate was like a mask on his strong young face. *You will have to learn to hide that when you are high chief,*

Alaric thought. *But for now, better that I know how things stand between us*.

A sudden chill climbed his spine, but it was dispelled just as suddenly by the pressure of Zavia's hand in his.

They had not quite reached the light of Simir's circle when she stayed him. "Minstrel."

"Yes?"

"The song is for me. For me alone."

"It is."

"Then come to my tent and sing it there."

He did not hesitate. "As you wish," he said.

He heard her sigh in the darkness, and after a moment, her hand dropped away from his. "Why don't you fetch your lute from Simir? I'll wait for you here."

They reached Zavia's tent through the shadows, a winding route that would have bewildered any man without Alaric's unerring sense of direction. Set well back from the fire, shielded from that light by the bulk of half a dozen other tents, it was a small shelter, the smallest he had yet seen among the nomads. Within its open entry was utter blackness.

Zavia slipped off for just a moment and returned with a burning splint; it lit their way inside, where she transferred the flame to an oil lamp. The light revealed a cozy space, floored with a fine thick carpet and scattered with plump cushions. It seemed perfect for one person, but there was room enough for two to stand in its center, room enough to sit down cross-legged side by side, even to lean back on the cushions. Zavia closed the entry with leather laces.

"No one will disturb us now," she said.

Alaric set the lute on his knee. He plucked a chord, and another. Then he laid his hand flat against the strings, silencing them. He looked up at her. "Last night," he said. "I was . . . harsh. I hope you'll forgive me."

Her eyes were steady, locked with his for a long moment before she whispered, "Surely you know I do."

He put the lute aside then and reached for her, and she came into his arms eagerly, hungrily, as if she had been waiting for him a long, long time. Was it just one day that he had known her, just one night since she had slipped into his bed? It seemed like more; it seemed that he had waited half a lifetime to kiss this mouth, to feel this smooth flesh under his hands, to press these hips against his own. And if some vagrant memories of other women tried to intrude on him—other women far behind, lost forever—he pushed them away. In the life of the wanderer, only this moment was real. Only this.

Afterward, as he lay dozing, his arms still curved about her, his cheek against her breast, she stroked his hair. "My minstrel," she murmured. "My Alaric." She kissed his forehead. "Alaric. What a strange name that is."

"Common enough some places," he muttered sleepily.

"In the south I suppose."

"Yes." He yawned and settled himself even closer to her. "There's a song about him. The original Alaric. Very old song. He was a great conqueror. Sacker of cities. Not much like me."

She kissed his forehead again. "You've conquered me."

He looked up at her and smiled. "I rather thought it was the other way round, Zavia."

She spread her fingers across the curve of his cheek. "If you hadn't come to me tonight, my Alaric, I would have used magic to compel you tomorrow."

"Ah . . . magic." He stroked her arm, her shoulder, her naked back. "Well, perhaps it was well then, that I came to you tonight. I've always been . . . resistant to the effects of magic."

"How weak the magic of the south must be. You would never have resisted ours."

"Has it worked so often for you?"

"Of course. For me most of all, because it's in my blood."

He laughed softly. "I would believe it was in your lips," he said, and he pulled her head down to his. "They've cast a spell on me." Her mouth was like warm silk against his own.

"A different sort of spell," she whispered.

"The best sort."

She kissed him yet again. "But you would have come to me. You would have wanted me. Perhaps more, even, than you do now. Perhaps I shall use the magic anyway, to make you want me more."

He slid his hand down her arm and twined his fingers in hers. "As you wish, sweet Zavia. Bring on your magical chains. I will wear them, so long as they give me freedom to play the lute. So long as they don't jangle against the strings."

Her pale eyes gazed down into his. "You jest."

He smiled at her. "A habit of mine, sweet Zavia—jesting."

"You don't believe me."

He raised her hand to his lips and kissed the fingers. "What must I believe? That there is magic in your blood? Do you mean to say that you're a witch, fair Zavia? You are very young, I think, to call the weather and command the hunt. I have heard that is what the witch of this land does."

"She does indeed."

"And her name, I have heard, is Kata."

Zavia lifted her chin. "She is my mother. And I will be a witch after her. Already I am her acolyte."

Alaric stroked the edge of her jaw with one finger. "And do you call the weather or command the hunt in her name?"

"Not yet. But someday I will. In my own name."

"You are very proud," he said softly. "It must be a fine thing, here in the north, to be a witch."

"Of course."

He slipped his fingers into her hair, to comb the glossy tresses, to let them slide like silken ribbons across the back of his hand. "Did you know, fair Zavia, that in the south, witches are feared, and even hated? That sometimes they are hunted down and killed because folk cannot rest easy feeling their power?"

She frowned a trifle. "You know songs that tell of such things?"

"I have seen it myself."

The frown deepened, and she shook her head, but not so hard as to shake his hand away. "But why? Magic is so precious, so . . . useful."

"Useful for good, and for evil. In the south they fear the evil more than they desire the good."

"What fools they are."

"I've often thought so myself." He curled a lock of hair about one finger and brushed her cheek with it. "And what magic do you know, O acolyte?"

She lowered her eyes. "If truth be told, not really so much. But if I needed it, my mother would help. I don't doubt that."

"Even to win me?"

"An easy thing for her."

"I've not seen this mother of yours yet, I think. Someone would have pointed her out to me, surely."

"At calving time she visits all the fires, to heal the sick and cure the unlucky. You'll meet her when Simir's band is ready to start north."

"I look forward to it."

She cupped his chin in her hand and tipped his head back. "Will I need her help, my minstrel?"

"Not you," he whispered, and pulled her tight to him once more.

PART FOUR

THE ELIXIR OF LIFE

The next morning, the first of the nomad bands left the calving grounds, though Alaric never saw them go. He spent most of the day in Zavia's tent, only leaving it for a brief, cold meal and a call or two of nature. Some of the time, in that leather-bound closeness, with the sun blotted out by the tight-laced hides and only the glow of the oil lamp to show him Zavia's face, he sang. Sad songs and merry ones he sang, softly, sweetly. But some of the time, most of the time, there was need for more than music between him and Zavia, and he pushed the lute aside. Daughter and acolyte to the witch, she had few duties during calving season, and no one to look after. No one but him.

Each time he went out, he saw Gilo sitting by his father's fire. Once, their eyes met, just for an instant, across the whole breadth of the tent circle. Gilo dropped his first.

Toward sunset, the smell of cooking venison, and Alaric's own sense of debt to the high chief, lured the new lovers out to the fire. The judging was obviously done for the day; Simir was laughing and casting knucklebones with half a dozen companions. When he saw Alaric, he gestured for some of them to move aside and make room on his carpet for the minstrel. They made room and to spare for two, and Zavia sat close beside him.

No secrets in a nomad band, thought Alaric, and he answered Simir's welcoming smile with one of his own.

Gilo was there, in the tight cluster of his brothers, on the far side of the flames. Their backs were turned.

"A long day," Simir was saying as Alaric settled the lute on his knees. "Sometimes I think the calving makes my nomads as nervous as it does their deer. They fight at the slightest excuse, and every one expects me to side with him in his dispute. But tomorrow it ends, and I return to the lesser task of leading my own small band. Tomorrow, minstrel, we start north.'' He gave Alaric a long, piercing look. "You have not changed your mind about coming along?''

Alaric glanced at Zavia, who was watching him with that small triumphant smile on her lips. "No, good Simir,'' he said firmly. "I have not changed my mind.''

Simir clapped him on the knee. "Then give us a song about travel, to give us spirit for the journey and to make the morning seem closer.''

Alaric obliged with a tale of merchant caravans crossing the great desert, and another of a voyage to a land of silver palaces under the sea. Both were fanciful stories, with as much of fable to them as of truth.

When the last chord had died away, Simir said, "Well done, well done. And yet . . . I must complain, young minstrel. These are strange songs for the nomads of the north. What do we know of endless sand and blazing sun, or tropic oceans? Have you nothing suited to our winter snows? To our rootless life?''

Alaric shook his head apologetically. "I fear not, sir. It is all so new to me. But I do hope to invent something soon.''

"Then sing another song of the mountains, like the one of yesterday, with the eaglet. Some of us, at least, know the mountains well.''

There were murmurs in the company at that.

Alaric hesitated.

"Surely you have such a song,'' said Simir, his voice coaxing. "You came to us out of the mountains. Surely you were inspired by the heights, the beauties, the dangers. Who could travel the mountains without feeling them speak to his heart? If I were a singer, I know they would inspire me.''

"You say you know them well,'' said Alaric.

"I do. And so do some of these others.''

"I,'' said one graybeard. "I've been in the mountains.'' And a few other men nodded to his words.

"The mountains are harsh,'' Alaric said.

"Yes," said Simir. "Harsher even than the plains. Few here doubt that, minstrel."

He took a deep breath. "I have a song for you, then. Of the beauties and the dangers of your mountains." And he closed his eyes as he bent to the lute.

"The land is fair where the Red Lord reigns;
My love is there, her heart in chains;
Sometimes she sleeps, sometimes she weeps,
Sometimes she drinks the wine of pain."

It was not an easy song to sing, nor had it been easy to devise. It was a simple tale of a mother's loss, a father's grief, a daughter's death. A simple tale of people trapped, by their own resignation, in the power of a madman. In detail, a fiction, with no minstrel playing any part. Yet behind the words lay horrors real as the fire that reddened his eyelids; the very melody seemed to conjure up the Red Lord's evil smile, the smile that fed on human pain. Whether his eyes were closed or no, the song made Alaric see again the woman, his fellow prisoner, tortured so near to death by her lord that she had begged for the mercy of oblivion. The lute strings sang under his fingers, but he felt again the yielding of her breastbone as he plunged his sword into her heart. And the greatest horror of all was that the Red Lord paid, and his people accepted that payment; in exchange for the blood of their own, he gave them security, and wine.

It was a fearful song to sing, but they had asked for something of the mountains, and he had always known, since the first words had come to him among the heights, that he would have to sing it for someone, someday. By the final verse he was weeping, and no matter how deep he breathed, how hard he swallowed, his voice was unsteady.

"If you would sleep in the Red Lord's reach,
To raise your grain and lambs in peace,
Give life for life, come pay the price,
And you will find his wine is sweet."

The company was very quiet when the song was done. There was no shuffling of bodies, no coughing, no whispering. Alaric opened his eyes, and his vision was blurred by tears. He swept them away with one hand. Someone was holding a cup of deer's-milk wine in front of him. Simir. He took it gratefully and drank.

"So you know him," Simir said quietly.

Alaric nodded.

"Some of us wondered if you had passed that way. It's the easiest route through the mountains. The caravans always used to take it. Since he became their lord, of course, none have gotten farther than the valley."

There were murmurs about the circle, nodding heads.

"I was the lucky traveler," Alaric said, his voice steadying slowly. "I escaped. But not before I saw and heard . . . too much perhaps." He looked at Simir. "You are the bandits he protects them from?"

"We were. Or rather, some of these men you see here were." He waved to include some who had nodded and were nodding again. "I was not. No. I was something quite different. I was a soldier of the Red Lord." He nodded slowly. "A long time ago."

Alaric stared at him, speechless.

"You are not the only one to escape the valley. There have been others. But you and I, we are the only ones to come north out of the mountains." He picked up his own cup and drank deep. Then he held it out to be refilled. "Your tale could almost be my own. Except that the one I lost was my wife. I was his man, heart and soul, until then. He was a great leader, he could wring the last dram of strength from a man, and he was wily to put the fox to shame. I was there the last time we had to turn the bandits back. The last time we took so many foreign prisoners." He drank again and then held the cup between his two big hands. "He had a way of making them last, minstrel. He could spin a prisoner's agony out for weeks. But when they were all gone, he would be restless, and eventually he would need to choose . . . a prisoner from among his own." He looked down into the cup. "As his man, I never thought about their little lives. They never mattered to me. Until he chose my darling."

Like the barest breath of wind, Alaric sighed, "Simir." He glanced at the other listeners gathered round; they were rapt, though there was no surprise on any face. They had heard this tale before.

"I tried to kill him, minstrel. He'll bear the mark of my knife on his throat forever. But he was the stronger. And I would have been his prisoner, too, except for my friends among the men. Perhaps they paid the price after I was gone." He shook his head. "When the youngsters offer themselves for the journey to the valley, I always warn them. I know he is still there. If he were dead, we would see the caravans again." He shook his head once more. "I would that none of them ever had to go."

Alaric saw the pressure of Simir's hands on the cup, the whitening of the fingertips. And he felt a great kinship with the man, and with all of the others who sat so silent and near, who had gone to the valley of the Red Lord and understood the horror. But he could not help wondering, "Why do they go, Simir? To steal a few goats?"

Simir looked at Alaric. "In the Red Lord's valley, we feared witches. We had none, but we feared them just the same. Here in the north, we have one, and we value her above all our other possessions. She is a woman of great wisdom, our Kata, and her greatest wisdom is a potion we call the Elixir of Life. It cures the uncurable. It prolongs health and strength. It has even been known to raise the dead."

"A great potion indeed!"

"But one of the herbs from which it is made grows only in the Red Lord's valley. And so someone must go there to harvest it."

Alaric brushed one string of the lute with a finger, and the sound was low and sweet. "Life for life," he murmured.

"It was not so before the Red Lord."

"And that was . . . the whole of your banditry?"

Simir set his cup down at last and flexed his fingers. "I won't say there have not been a few goats taken along the way. The young are . . . subject to temptation."

"Then why not send someone older and wiser?"

"The old and wise have families to look after."

"The old and wise are overcautious!" That was Gilo's voice, loud and sudden enough to make all eyes turn to him. He stepped between his father and the fire and stood with his fists on his hips. He seemed very tall there, standing while so many others sat, and very straight. "Only the young have the courage to cross the mountains and steal from the Red Lord. The old and wise—are afraid."

"For good reason," his father said mildly.

"If they were not, they would strike at the Red Lord's valley. The time is right. Can he still be on his guard against us after all these years? No, we have lulled him with our restraint, and now we can pluck him like an overripe apricot. I would lead the fight, gladly. I would take him in my own hands, and I would not be satisfied with a scar on his neck, not I!" And he clenched his fists as if the Red Lord's throat were already between them.

Simir looked up at his son, and then at the seated company. "It is good, I think, that the young do not make our decisions for us."

"You think too highly of him, Father," Gilo said. "No man can stand undefeated forever."

Simir nodded. "I hope you will remember that when you are high chief."

Gilo looked from one face to another in the gathering. "How many years has it been since we last lost a harvester? Nine years. Nine long years since last the Red Lord heard of us. He doesn't know our strength. He doesn't know how hard we could strike." Then he glared down at Alaric. "Unless this one goes back to tell him."

An indrawn breath, soft as the crackle of the fire, swept the company, though not all turned their eyes to Alaric.

"What do we know of him?" Gilo demanded. "He could be the Red Lord's spy. He could go back the way he came some night, and then we would not carry surprise with us to the valley. He has seen us all, he has counted us. What do we know of him? Nothing!"

Zavia sprang to her feet. "Gilo! You do this because of me! But if you would ever see me smile at you again, you'll stop now!"

Gilo pointed at Alaric. "How has he passed through the valley when no one else has? He's the Red Lord's man, I tell you, come to spy on us!"

"Gilo!" With a single stride she reached him, and with

a backhand blow across the mouth, she rocked him. He caught her arms then, as the blood began to trickle from his lower lip, and his face was hard, the white teeth showing.

"Enough!" cried Simir, and at his voice half a dozen men leaped up to separate the two. When they were well apart, though still glaring at each other, the high chief rose from his carpet. He was taller than his son, broader of shoulder, thicker of arm, and Gilo took a step back as his father came to him. "I will have no fighting at my fire," said Simir.

"And no lies, either!" cried Zavia.

Simir silenced her with a glance.

Gilo straightened, lifting his head defiantly. "He is a stranger, Father. Why should we trust him?"

Simir looked into his son's face. "You heard the song, but you did not *listen*. This is not the Red Lord's man. He understands the pain too well."

"He could have left a hostage behind to guarantee his loyalty." He glanced at Zavia. "Someone he loved."

"Then he is more a fool than you," said Simir, "not to realize there would be no hostage at his return."

Gilo's mouth twisted sullenly. Blood was flowing freely from it now, and he wiped it with the back of one wrist. "Father, you like this minstrel too much."

"I like whom I choose, and to what extent pleases me. We are all free to do that. It would be well for you to remember that, my son."

Without replying, Gilo turned and stalked off, and his brothers hurried to follow him.

After a moment, the high chief looked back at Alaric. "I think we could do with a happier song now, minstrel. And please, not one that tells of quarreling."

Alaric brushed the lute strings lightly. Then his fingers hesitated. "Thank you for defending me, Simir," he said. "I swear to you, I am not a spy."

Simir smiled. "Zavia's was the more vigorous defense, I thought," and he gestured for her to sit down again as he settled back in his own place. "He is young. Before he can be high chief after me, he will have to learn to judge folk by their hearts, and not by his own desires." He shrugged lightly. "But I was a fool at his age, so

there is time.'' Picking up his cup once more, he toyed
with it between his two big hands. ''You know, minstrel,
there is a part of me that wants what he wants—to lead
a nomad army back to the valley, to break my old master,
no matter what the cost. Yes.'' He looked into the fire,
nodding, as if seeing the deed in those flames. ''But there
is the cost, you see. It would be far from easy. And they
are my people, my care. I could not ask them for that
price.'' Then he held his cup out and called for wine.
''A happy song, minstrel,'' he said when he had drunk
again. ''Something to make us laugh.''

After the song there was venison stew to be passed
around, and then more songs, while the sun sank below
the horizon and the dance fire was kindled. It was the
last night of dancing for the season, the last chance for
young people of different bands to visit and to pair, and
it was wilder and louder than ever before. Zavia teased
Alaric into dancing with her for a little while, but soon
enough they returned to Simir's circle. He sang again,
then, but not for long.

Gilo and his brothers had not returned to their father's
fire by the time Zavia took Alaric's hand and led him
back to her tent.

In the morning, he helped her strike her tent and pack
up her few belongings. All around them, others were doing the same; the nomad throng, barely thinned by early
departures, was seething like a simmering pot, men
shouting, women scurrying, children underfoot everywhere, no one still for a moment. Even the deer, now
picketed in small groups, were moving restlessly, tug-
ging at their tethers, as if eager to begin the northward
march.

Out of this ferment stepped a figure of immense dignity: a tall woman, moving slowly, purposefully, leading
a string of four heavily laden deer. The chaos parted before her, flowed around her, like a river meeting a rock
in its bed. She climbed the gentle rise to Simir's circle,
now a circle no longer, and she halted where the fire had
been before it was dashed to cold black ashes. Alaric,
who had seen her approach from his place with Zavia,

watched her raise an arm, a graceful, beckoning gesture, that brought Simir himself to her side.

Zavia, lacing up the last of the bags that had been her tent, saw where he looked. She tossed her work down and moved to stand beside him, hooking one arm about his waist. She nodded at the woman. "My mother," she said.

Kata was nearly as tall as Simir, tall and slender and handsome, her face much like Zavia's, but refined with age, the cheeks hollowed out, the chin chiseled free of youth's softness. She wore her hair in two thick braids, each bound with leather, and on her arms were wide leather bracelets inlaid with polished pebbles. In the crook of her left arm she carried a staff taller than herself and carved into fanciful shapes, thick as a man's arm here, narrow enough to clasp with one hand there. She spoke quietly to the high chief, and he nodded several times.

"You must meet her," said Zavia. "She will expect it." Taking his hand, she started up the rise.

It was a changed Zavia who introduced them. Gone was the boldness, the self-possession, the pride. She lowered her gaze to speak to her mother.

Like all the nomads, Kata had pale eyes, and looking into them, Alaric had the sensation that they could see deep inside him, deeper than anyone he had ever met before. Perhaps it was because they were so steady, perhaps because around them her face bore no expression.

"I have heard much about you, minstrel," she said, "but I have had no time to come and listen for myself." Her voice was lower than Zavia's, smoother. "You must be a fine singer, though. I see nothing else about you to attract my daughter."

Zavia's hand tightened on his, but she made no sound.

"Ah, Kata," said Simir, "you are unkind." He smiled at Alaric. "He is no bad choice. He has a good heart."

"A strong man is best for a nomad woman," Kata said, "and I see no great strength here. Wait till winter tests him. If he stays with us that long."

"I will stay," said Alaric, and he returned Zavia's pressure.

"He says he wishes to see the Northern Sea," Simir said.

"Oh?" Kata looked into his eyes again. "Well, that can be arranged, if his courage is equal to it."

Alaric tried to smile, but under that unwavering stare it was far from easy. "I will try to be an adequate nomad, good lady. I promise you."

"Oh, don't promise that, minstrel!" said Simir. "Just promise to sing, and we will see to your comfort. You must hear him, Kata, and you will think better of him."

"Perhaps," she said. "For now I have other things to consider. Will we be traveling soon? I must speak to you of one of the men in Donril's band. . . ."

She had turned away from Alaric by then, and he had experience enough of great houses and great ladies to know that he had been dismissed. He pulled Zavia away, down to her tent site, where a little boy had brought up a pair of deer for her use in the journey north. Silently, they lashed her goods to the creatures' backs. But now and then Alaric looked toward Kata, still in deep conversation with Simir, pointing sometimes here or there as the high chief nodded. And he wondered if perhaps this day he had not met the true lord of the north.

When the deer were laden, one more lightly than the other, Zavia mounted the former and looked out over the nomad throng. Already a few groups had begun to move outward, spreading toward the horizon in a slow, dark wave. Barren ground, grazed clear by the animals, showed behind them.

Alaric leaned against the second deer and watched the folk around him complete their own packing. Up on his rise, Simir was directing activities from deer back, and Kata sat beside him on her own mount.

"Is your mother the only one who knows how to make the Elixir of Life?" he wondered.

"Yes," said Zavia. "But she will teach me soon."

"It must be wonderful stuff."

"It is."

"You've seen it used, I suppose."

"I've drunk it myself."

"Have you? And what were you cured of? Or were you raised from the dead?"

"I drank it when I became a woman. All our children drink it when they leave childhood behind. It makes us strong." She hesitated, then looked down at him. "But it doesn't always succeed at raising the dead."

"No? Well, there are always failures in the world. But I would see it raise the dead. I truly would." He smiled at her. "You know, my Zavia, in the south there are lands where grain rules, or gold, or the sword. The longer I am here, the more the north intrigues me."

One of Simir's graybeard companions brought Alaric a riding deer, and shortly afterward the high chief's band, near eightscore in all, began its own journey northward on the broad rolling plain of new spring grass.

They made camp in midafternoon, on the bank of a north-meandering river. The calving grounds and all trace of the other nomad bands had vanished in the distance behind them. Around them, the earth seemed empty, the game frightened off by the bustle of the approaching herd, the only trees those that grew by the watercourse. As women and children set up the tents and started their fires of dead wood and dried deer droppings, men took their bows and fanned out north, east, and even across the river in search of wild meat for the stew pots. A few youngsters set hooks in the stream, in hopes of fish; others scoured the verge in search of edible plants. The days of feasting on the deer were over; from now on just a few slaughtered animals would be eked out by every possible form of hunting.

Their burdens removed, the deer spread out, grazing avidly under scanty guard. Their masters, however, clustered together, ranging their tents as if there were still a vast multitude surrounding them. Alaric helped Zavia pitch her own tent beside her mother's.

"I have to be here if she needs me," she told him. "At the calving grounds, she always works alone, but now there will be herbs to grind and salves to compound and potions to mix, to replenish her stores. We'll be busy, I know. And then there are my lessons. There is so much to learn!"

Whatever need Kata may have had for her daughter, she displayed none of it that afternoon. She did not speak to the girl, nor even look at her. She went to her tent as soon as three of Simir's graybeard comrades set it up for her, and she did not come out, not even for supper. Before eating his own meal, Simir himself took her a bowl of braised fish, the best caught that day.

Kata's tent was the largest of that gathering save for Simir's own; but in his slept a dozen and more, including his sons, while hers was for one person alone. Yet hers was crowded, for Alaric saw the burdens of her four packdeer passed through the entry. And it was an unusual tent in other ways, with a curious pattern of hexagons, like a loose honeycomb, inscribed upon its roof, and the ancient six-pointed symbol of the Pole Star, heart of the north, limned in white above its entry flaps; and beneath the star, to either side of that entry, Kata's carven staff and its identical twin were set hard into the ground, like stern wooden sentinels guarding her privacy. Within the tent, unlike the rest of the nomads, she kept a fire—Alaric spied its glow when Simir delivered her meal—and its steady smoke trickled upward through a roof vent to waft across the encampment, bringing with it a sweet, spicy odor.

Alaric sang that night, and if Kata the witch listened, she did not come out to watch as well.

The next few days passed peacefully, mornings of leisurely northward travel, afternoons by the river, evenings of laughter and music by the fire. The food continued good, the high chief's cook able to turn anything the hunters brought her into a savory meal. The sun was warm by day, and Zavia was warm by night. If Kata rarely spoke to him, that hardly mattered; she treated everyone else the same. Simir was the only one who truly conversed with her. The high chief himself was friendly as ever, and his company welcomed every song Alaric offered; they never asked him for more than that, never asked him to go with the hunters or to lend a hand with the common labor, and everywhere he went among them, there was always a pleasant word for him.

Only the boys, Gilo, Marak, Terevli, looked on him

with sullen eyes and turned their backs when he came near.

"They can stay away," said Zavia. "their time with me is finished."

Alaric smiled, stroking her glossy hair. Outside her tent, he could hear the faint grunting of deer and the quiet sounds of people disposing themselves for the night. Inside, the oil lamp threw the dim shadow of his hand against the nearest slanting leather wall. "Did all three of them have time with you, sweet Zavia?" he whispered.

She stretched her arms above her head and yawned and then settled more closely against him. "They've all seen the inside of this tent."

He slid his fingers between her naked breasts. "Like this?"

She covered his hand with her own. "Yes."

He laughed softly. "Surely not all three at once."

"I never thought the tent was large enough for that." She kissed the tip of his nose. "And I prefer to give all my attention to one man at a time."

"Sweet Zavia," he sighed. "My life here would be quite perfect if not for their jealousy. They make me feel like I have stolen the fairest flower of the north." He kissed her lips, her yielding, parted lips. "And perhaps I have."

"Once there were others jealous of them," she murmured. "Now they know how it feels to lose something precious. A healthy lesson, I think." And she smiled that triumphant little smile.

"Were there many others, my Zavia?"

"A few." She kissed him again, long and lingeringly. "But none like you, my minstrel. None like you."

Seven days they moved north with the river, seven nights Alaric slept with Zavia. On the eighth afternoon, it was clear to him that Gilo and his brothers had had enough of the stranger.

The herd had dispersed with its guards, the hooks had been set in the water, the hunters had disappeared in the distance. But the chief's three sons, who often went out on the hunt, lingered behind. They found Alaric by the stream, where he and Zavia were trying their luck with a pair of lines. They wore swords at their belts, all three of them, though the nomads rarely wore their blades so near to camp.

"Battling a fish, eh?" said Gilo. "The only creature you're fit to battle, I'd say."

Zavia shifted so that her back was squarely to him. But the other boys fanned out so that no matter which way she turned, one of them could see her profile. She cast black looks at the two younger ones.

Alaric said nothing.

"I know you're afraid of me," Gilo said. "I'll wager you're afraid of my brothers, too. Even little Terevli." And when Alaric still said nothing, he added, "I'm tempted to let Terevli teach you a lesson, minstrel. He wants to. He's begged me for the chance."

Terevli made an affirmative noise.

"If you wish to live in the north, you'll have to be strong. Show us your strength, minstrel." Gilo's voice was a trifle harder now, a trifle impatient. "We've even brought your sword; you won't have to go back to Zavia's tent for it."

The small, slick sound of a blade being drawn from its sheath made Alaric turn toward the youngest boy. He saw Terevli holding the finely worked scabbard in one hand and the bright steel sword in the other—the sword that Alaric had carried long but never drawn in anger.

"It's a fine blade," Gilo said. "The one who bests you will keep it, I think. Choose one of us, minstrel. We're waiting."

Alaric looked from one youth to the next. "I have no desire to fight any of you."

"You think we care about your desires?"

"I am a minstrel, not a fighter."

"A coward, then!"

Alaric smiled slightly. "To some men, that would be a deadly insult. But not to me. I know my limitations."

Gilo strode to Terevli and took the sword from him, sheathed it. "Then you have no need of this weapon, have you? I can't think why you keep it at all, if you fear so much to use it. *I'll* use it, though, and many thanks."

"So you're a thief, are you, Gilo?" Alaric said softly.

Gilo's mouth twisted in malice. "Do you insult me, stranger?"

"The truth is no insult."

"Then fight me for it!" He threw the sword down on the grass between them. "I'll give you a fair chance to draw it."

Alaric made no move to touch the sword.

"Take it!" Gilo shouted. One hand was on the hilt of his own weapon.

"You're a fool, Gilo," said Zavia. She glared at him over one shoulder. "His death won't win me back to you."

"Quiet, woman. This has nothing to do with you."

"No? The minstrel is mine; harm him and you'll never drink the Elixir of Life again."

Gilo's lips pressed hard together for an instant. Then he said, "That would be your mother's choice, not yours. You'll not protect him this time. Fight me, minstrel, or I claim the sword as your default!"

Alaric looked at Zavia, at the proud anger in her face. *Why does this wild creature still choose me?* he wondered. But he knew the answer to that—it stood before him, strong and virile, surely; but hotheaded, arrogant, insufferably imperious to a spirit like Zavia's. She needed a softer mate, one who would ask, but never command. *There are few softer than a minstrel,* he thought, *who lives on the sufferance of others, and trades nothing but his songs for food and shelter and love.*

"I will not fight you, Gilo," he said quietly. "The sword belongs to me. If you take it, I will tell your father. Let him judge if you have done right."

Gilo growled deep in his throat, then looked to his brothers and signaled sharply with a toss of his head. The three strode away, leaving Alaric's sword lying on the ground.

Zavia threw her line aside and reached for the sword herself, drawing it close by the tip of the scabbard. She pressed the sheathed blade against her bosom for a moment as she glared at the brothers' retreating backs, and then she held it out to Alaric, hilt first. "This is a fine weapon," she said. "Not for an oaf like him. Or any of them."

Alaric took the sword by the scabbard, never touching the hilt. "Too fine for me, also, but it was a gift, and so I keep it. Sometimes, though, I wish he had given me something other than a sword. Something . . . innocent."

She closed both hands about his arm. "It was proper that you didn't fight for me. I am no man's prize."

He set the sword down in the grass. "That's as well, sweet Zavia, for if you were, I would lose you in an instant."

"You shall not lose me, my Alaric, until I choose to be lost." And she linked her hands behind his neck and kissed him softly on the mouth.

But oh my Zavia, he thought, with her breath warm on his lips, *you have chosen to be lost before. How long shall this last, I wonder?*

A fish tugged at his line then and, laughing, they broke apart to pull it in.

In the deepest part of the night, when Alaric and Zavia lay curled together beneath his cloak, the oil lamp dark, the tent close and warm, he woke suddenly. For an instant, he did not know what had wakened him. Then he realized he had felt the tent flap opening, felt the faint cool draft of the night enter. Yet Zavia lay still on the curve of his arm. Instinctively, he rolled away from her, over the mounded cushions, to the skirts of the tent, which were pegged firmly to the ground. The tiny shelter was suddenly filled with struggling bodies, with thrashing and panting and whispered curses.

Just as suddenly, Alaric was gone.

He appeared by the riverbank, and for just a moment he felt bewildered. Under the cool stars was no herd, no nomad camp, just a patch of bare and trampled grass. Then he recognized the contour of the river and realized that in his urgency he had traveled to last night's camping place. He stumbled to his feet, wiping the sleep from his eyes. He would have been naked, save that when he had rolled away from Zavia he had taken the cloak with him, and it was still wrapped about him now.

He knew what had happened, of course. Who else but the three brothers would be paying Zavia's tent such a nocturnal visit? To frighten him, perhaps. More likely to kill him, and rid themselves of his troublesome presence. If not in a fair fight, then in a final one.

I should give it over. I should just go away, he thought. The night air was too cool for comfort; he clutched the cloak about his shoulders. His hands shook a little, but he knew it wasn't from the chill. *Even Zavia isn't worth my life.* And then he felt his heart sink. What if they had hurt her in the confusion?

His reason told him to leave the nomads behind him, to go back to the south, where the great houses would welcome him and the kitchen maids would be willing enough. The south, where the forests were lush and the deer were skittish of human beings. He could be there in a heartbeat, and he could find clothing and even another lute with the help of his special talent.

What if they had killed her?

He was at the other riverbank then, the one where Simir's band was camped, because he had to know.

The camp was in an uproar. He had been gone no longer than it would take a man to run a hundred paces, but in that time someone had stirred a fire to flickering life, and lit torches, too, and people were coming out of every tent and milling about in the light, talking excitedly.

Somewhere in all the confusion, someone was screaming.

Twisting the cloak about his middle, Alaric ran toward Zavia's tent.

Half the camp was there before him, blocking his path. He began to elbow his way through the throng, then caught sight of Simir's blond head, surrounded by torches, off to the right. Alaric pressed sideways to reach him.

"Simir!"

"Minstrel." The high chief took in his bare shoulders and legs with a single inquiring glance. "What's going on?"

"I don't know. I went out for a call of nature, and suddenly there was all this."

With Simir leading the way, Alaric reached the tent. Or what had been the tent, for the whole structure had collapsed, and among the jumbled hides and carpets and cushions were thrashing bodies, though how many was difficult to say. Several voices came from the struggling mass, and one of them was Zavia's, screaming curses.

"Stop this!" Simir shouted, and his voice was so loud that it stilled the gawking crowd. "Clear this away," he said, waving to those nearest him, and he set the example by pulling a carpet free of the jumble and tossing it behind him. Willing hands took over the task then, and in moments Zavia and Simir's three sons were revealed. Zavia sat astride Gilo, punching, kicking, and gouging him while Marak and Terevli tried to pull her away. Onlookers had trouble separating the four.

Three knives were found lying loose among the ruins of the tent.

"What is this?" Simir demanded when the four young people were standing before him, panting and disheveled. The boys were bruised and bleeding, Gilo's nose smashed, Marak's left eye closed and beginning to swell, Terevli with a knife slash on his right arm. Zavia, naked, stood straight and proud and disdainful, though scrapes across her shoulder, breast, and thigh were oozing blood and her cheek was dark with a blow; she hardly seemed to notice when someone wrapped a fur about her.

Then she saw Alaric and lifted a hand to him, and he went to her and closed her in his arms.

"Gilo," said Simir, pointing at the youth. "Speak."

Blood was streaming down Gilo's face and over the hand he held up to it. "A mistake," he mumbled. "Just a mistake."

"I see that clearly enough," Simir replied. "But how did you make this mistake?"

Gilo coughed and spat blood and shook his head.

"We were just visiting Zavia," said Marak. "Nothing more."

"And she attacked us," added the youngest boy.

"Visit? Bah!" snapped Zavia. "They came to kill the minstrel."

"It was a friendly visit," said Marak. "We didn't know the minstrel was there."

"And your knives were friendly, too," said Zavia. "Do you take us all for fools?"

"You forced us to draw—"

"Shut up!" roared Gilo. He coughed again then, and droplets of blood scattered from his nose. "We wanted to frighten him. To make him think again about staying with her." He choked on the last word and sprayed crimson once more with a fit of coughing.

The crowd swayed back suddenly. Kata had emerged from her tent. She strode the few paces to Simir's side. "Whatever has happened here, this boy needs care." She stretched a hand out to Gilo, and he stepped forward. "Come," she said, curling her fingers about his arm. Without a backward glance, he went with her into her tent.

Simir glared at the remaining boys, and the cold anger on his face seemed more menacing than hot fury could ever have been. "You think because he is not one of us that you can do as you please to him? You think because you are my sons that I won't lift a finger? Do you know me so little? Very well. I have not beaten you in some years, but I have not forgotten how. Those little wounds that Zavia gave you will seem like nothing when I am done. And afterward you will remember to tell your brother what your *mistake* has brought you." Half turning, he tapped the man beside him with the back of his hand. "Bring my rod."

"It was Gilo pressed us to do it!" cried Terevli.

"I shall not forget him. Now, while we wait for the rod, the two of you will put Zavia's tent back together. And if anything is damaged, you will be responsible for it."

"I'm bleeding, Father," said Terevli, holding up his slashed arm. It was a shallow cut but long, and the blood trickled over his fingers. "I need Kata's help."

"Try not to bleed on Zavia's leather," Simir said coldly.

Someone tossed the boy a thong to bind the wound.

While they set up the tent, the crowd dispersed, yawning people more concerned with the remainder of a night's sleep than with the beating of the chief's sons. By the time Zavia's shelter was ready, the chief had been holding his rod—actually a length of leather cured almost to the stiffness of wood—for some time, slapping it lightly against one palm in a slow cadence.

"Thank you, Simir," said Zavia.

He nodded to her, and then with a curt gesture he directed the boys to the fire, where they began to strip off their clothing. Naked, they took their blows in alternation, and the sound of the rod on flesh was sharp and rhythmic in the night air. Once only, Terevli cried out.

Alaric tried to urge Zavia into her tent, but she would not go until the punishment was over, until Simir had stalked back to his tent and the boys had crept back into their clothes and followed him. Then she pulled the tent flap back.

"Get a brand from the fire," she whispered, and she slipped inside.

They kindled the oil lamp, and by its flame she inspected her wounds. One seemed to have been made by a knife skittering across the skin, the others by fingernails; all were broad rather than deep. Zavia pulled one of the cushions to her, unlaced its edge and raked through its contents. She found a small ceramic pot, a pot such as Alaric had seen often enough in the south, holding a lady's unguents or a cook's spices, but never yet among the nomads. Inside the pot was a salve which she smeared on her wounds, wincing at its touch.

"I should have killed him," she murmured.

He cupped her cheek in his hand. "He could have killed *you.*"

She shook her head. "I wasn't his quarry."

"Still, in the dark, he might have taken you for me."

She looked at him levelly. "If you had stayed, we would have been two against three in the dark. We might have killed *him* at least. Without him, the others would have run."

"Perhaps it's as well that I wasn't here, then. I don't care for killing."

"You were here," she said, her eyes steady on his. "But you went away."

He shrugged. "When nature calls, we can't deny her. They must not have seen me leave."

"You went away after they were in the tent, my Alaric."

"No, I was already gone when they arrived. I was by the river when I heard the commotion."

She sighed. "I woke when they started unlacing the entrance. I felt you beside me. Then they leaped in and suddenly you and your cloak were gone. And you didn't get out past them, my minstrel. I won't believe that."

"I wasn't here, Zavia."

"You were here, and then you *weren't* here. You didn't run away. That just wasn't possible. No, you . . . vanished."

"You were dreaming, Zavia."

"I know the difference between dreaming and waking, Alaric."

"But this is absurd." He kept his eyes steady. "I wasn't here. I don't deny that I would have run from them, given the chance. But I didn't have to." The lie was beginning to seem lame to him now, but he couldn't go back on it. That would mean too many explanations—why did he go to the river, why didn't he raise the alarm himself, why didn't he fetch Simir? And wouldn't changing the tale just make her more suspicious? "No one can just . . . vanish."

She touched his naked arm with the flat of her hand, ran her palm down to his elbow. "What a potent skill it is. Little wonder you escaped the Red Lord. How far can you go, my minstrel? Can you cross the mountains? Or is it just a little thing, a leap, a short run, a bowshot?"

"Zavia, this is your imagination playing tricks. I don't know anything about vanishing."

Her hand moved upward, to his shoulder, to the back of his neck. "I would learn this skill. I'll be a witch someday; it's a thing a witch should know. You'll teach me, won't you, my Alaric?"

"Zavia, I don't know—"

"You'll teach me, surely," she whispered, moving closer to him. Her free hand slid to his waist and tugged the cloak loose. "You'll teach your Zavia, my sweet minstrel." And then she pulled him down on the cushions, down on her smooth, warm flesh.

"He denies it, Mother." Zavia sat on her knees in the dimness of her mother's tent, her hands folded meekly before her, her eyes downcast. "For two days he has denied it. He even laughs sometimes when I ask him. But I know what happened."

Kata sat beyond her fire, her hands busy with something her daughter could not quite see, dared not look at too closely. "You are a foolish child," she said. "Perhaps he was right. Perhaps you dreamed it. This is a strange and potent skill you speak of. Why would he wander the world as a minstrel when he could use it to live in luxury? He could steal anything, he could cow anyone, and yet he is nothing and no one."

"Mother, I have thought back on that time. I swear to you, I was awake. He was touching me, and then he rolled away and was gone. The tent was pegged fast to the ground. There was no way out but where the boys were coming in, not until they brought the tent down." She raised her eyes just a trifle. "Ask them if he was there when they burst in. I know what they'll say."

Kata was silent a moment. Then she said, "Perhaps I will."

Zavia rose a little on her knees and dared to look across the flames. "Mother, this would be such a valuable skill. To travel without needing to walk or ride. You can pry it from him, I know you can."

"Possibly."

"And I brought it to you, Mother. I could have kept silent, but I brought it to you instead. Surely that shows I'm worthy of your trust. Worthy to do more than grind a few herbs." Her voice became plaintive. "I will work hard, Mother, I promise you. Only teach me. Please."

For just an instant, Kata looked up from her task, meeting her daughter's eyes above the fire, and Zavia flinched. "You are too young and too angry, child," said the nomads' witch. Her voice was as firm and emotionless as when she spoke to anyone else, no special warmth for the flesh of her own flesh, no hint of intimacy. "When I judge you are ready, you will begin to learn."

Zavia bowed her head. "Yes, Mother," she whispered.

"Now fetch Gilo to me, and we shall see how matters stand with your minstrel."

* * *

Much to Alaric's relief, Zavia finally gave over asking him to teach her his witch's skill. He could see by her eyes, though, that she still didn't accept his denials. Perhaps that was because she was a witch herself, he thought, or would be one day, and was accustomed to the idea of magical things—of magical hunting, magical weather, magical cures. Almost, because she seemed so approving, he told her the truth. Almost. But he stopped himself, because nothing good had ever come of revealing himself. Nothing but danger and death. In time, Zavia's memory of that night would fade, and eventually she might even come to believe that she had really dreamed his disappearance. What had she to prove it, after all? Feelings, guesses, deductions. But she hadn't *seen* him. No one had seen him.

He was at the fire singing for Simir when he saw Gilo slip into Kata's tent, and still singing when the youth came out some time later. As the afternoon wore on, Marak and Terevli visited her also, one by one. He supposed they were seeking treatment for their injuries. Gilo's was the worst, of course. He walked about holding a huge poultice to his nose, a soggy wad of herbs that covered most of his face, and over the top of it, his eyes peered out, rimmed in black bruise. He spoke to no one, not even his brothers, and he stayed far away from Zavia. The other boys trailed him like a pair of dogs, but moving gingerly, obviously feeling their father's beating. Occasionally one would look at Alaric, but mostly they kept their backs to him.

That night, as he and Zavia walked toward her tent arm in arm, he heard a quiet voice call his name.

It was Kata. She stood at the entry of her own tent, between the carven staves. "Come, Alaric," she said. "I wish to speak to you."

Zavia's hands tightened on his arm for just a moment. Then she let him go; she even seemed to give him a little push in her mother's direction.

He looked back at her, but she said nothing.

Kata held the flap of her tent aside and waved him in.

He had only glimpsed this place before, when Kata's goods were being passed through the entrance, and once or twice when someone went inside. Now he was enveloped by it, and he felt as if he had stepped into a world far beyond that of the nomads. It was a rich tent, richer by far than Simir's, its leathern walls hidden behind patterned hangings, its floor covered with thick carpets as plush as velvet, and high-piled with cushions of crimson, ocher, and citron. The fire, which blazed in a shallow bronze bowl, crackled with strange colors, now blue, now green, now red as the sunset sky, and it gave off a thin plume of smoke that seemed to fill the tent with the thick sweet smell of spices. Kata let the entry flap close on the last cool breath of the evening and, sliding past him, beckoned him to a place by the fire.

"You are a strange one, Alaric the minstrel," she said, sitting down quite near him. Behind her, the cushions were mounded especially high; she tossed two of them aside to reveal a small wooden chest, its dark, polished surfaces inlaid again and again with the six-pointed symbol of the Pole Star. Tipping back the lid, she drew a ceramic flask from the mossy padding within, and two cups so small they could scarcely hold a single mouthful each. Cups and flask were a set, near white in color, and thin-walled. Kata pulled the stopper from the flask and poured pale liquid into the cups. She offered one to Alaric.

"Thank you," he murmured, looking down into it. The liquid was transparent, faintly pink, clearly not deer's-milk wine. "What is this?"

"An herbal distillation," said Kata, and she drank her own share in one swallow. When he hesitated still, she added. "Not poison, minstrel. I promise you that."

"Oh, I never thought it, lady. What reason would you have to poison me?"

Her gaze was steady. "My daughter's life is her own, minstrel. I would not poison her choice merely because I would have chosen differently."

As when they had met, he found himself unable to smile properly before her pale, expressionless eyes. He raised the cup to her health and then, cautiously, sipped. To his surprise, the liquid had hardly any taste, and less substance; indeed, it seemed to evaporate on the tongue and never reach the throat at all. Yet a moment later there was a tartness upon his lips, an aftertaste, spreading gradually to every part of his mouth, and it was not unpleasant. And now the cup was empty—that single cautious taste, he realized, had drained it.

"You are a strange one," Kata repeated, taking the cup from him and setting it aside. "You are a skilled singer, with many fine songs. You could be living softly in the south, in a grand house, with a grand patron. You could wear jewels and gold and eat the finest of delicacies. Oh yes, we of the north know what such things are, though we have no need of them. We know what the south counts as wealth. And you are from the south. Yet here you are among us, some say on a quest for the Northern Sea."

He shrugged. "As good a goal as any, Lady Kata."

"A foolish goal. There is nothing in the Northern Sea but ice and death. I know. I have been there."

He held a hand out to her fire, disrupting the rise of the smoke, making it eddy and swirl. "I am a wanderer, lady," he said. "The Northern Sea or the southern desert—they are all one to me. I travel, I see new sights, I invent new songs. I have never found a place that held me for long." He watched the firelight play on his palm, flushing the skin now blue, now green, now red as the sunset sky. "It seems I am a nomad in my heart."

"A nomad follows the same trail year after year, minstrel. He knows what lies ahead of him as well he knows what lies behind."

Alaric shook his head. "Not I. I never go back. Not to the castles, not to great houses, not to the people." The varicolored flames were beautiful, he thought, like bright draperies rippling in a draft, like skirts swaying with their wearer's walk. They seemed to pull at him, to promise him, as if within their light he could find some truth he had long been searching for. He leaned closer to them, and closer still, till their heat licked at his face.

Kata caught his shoulders and pulled him back from the fire. He tore his eyes from the flames and looked at her. He saw her wreathed in smoke, he saw a thick pall of smoke filling the whole tent, blotting out the walls and the plush carpets and the thick cushions. And he felt the smoke inside himself, as if he were made of it, as if the slightest breeze would blow him away. He reached for her, and she was solid between his hands, solid in a world made of smoke.

"Look at my eyes," she said in a smooth, low voice, and her eyes were like pools of water from whose surface fog was rising. "What are you running from?" she asked him, and yet it was not a question. It was a command.

"Running?" he murmured. And then he could almost feel himself running, running through the smoke, and far behind lay all the places, all the people he had ever known, calling to him, calling, though he never looked back. Dall the minstrel, his friend and teacher, calling from the grave; Solinde, his first love, from her tower window; friends and enemies, highborn and low; all of them, even the woman whose name he had never known, whose blood would always be on his hands, though she had begged him to spill it. But he never looked back, because he knew that close behind him followed death— death to the witch who could travel with a wish, death by the arrow, the knife, silent and sudden. And so he ran, hiding his witch's power, ever onward, ever homeless.

"But you use it," Kata whispered.

Had he spoken? Had he said so much aloud? Time passed, but he could not reckon it. The smoke was thick around him, and he felt as though he were floating on a sea of fog.

"Even though you would hide your power," Kata whispered, "even though the south fears witches so, you use it sometimes when others are watching."

"To save my life," he said. "As a startled man would raise his hand to ward off a blow, I use it."

"As you used it to escape the high chief's sons."

"Yes."

He felt her hands on his face. "You are just a boy," she whispered. "You are nothing. Less than nothing." Her hands slid downward, over his throat, his chest, to his thighs. He shivered under that sweeping touch. He knew indeed that he was nothing, that for all the years of wandering, for all the places and people he had seen, he had learned nothing. *She* was wisdom; he could see it in her eyes, he could feel it in her touch. She was the infinite wisdom of the north.

She was pushing him back now, back against the mounded cushions, and her cool hands were unlacing his trews, stripping them away. He tried to shrink from her, but could not. She was the cold north, the wind from the ice, the winter darkness. Her naked flesh was frost against his own, but it claimed him, he could not help himself. He shuddered as she moved upon him, and the sea of fog became a sea of ice, the Northern Sea itself, and he was drowning in it, helpless, helpless.

"You are mine, now, Alaric," she whispered as the sea closed over him. "Mine."

He woke groggily. He lay on his back, and above him, rainbows danced wildly. He rubbed his eyes with the backs of both hands and, with an effort, focused his vision. The rainbows coalesced into the gleam of multi-colored flames on the smooth leathern surface over his head. He rolled to his side and pushed himself up on one elbow. His naked body seemed twice its natural weight, or perhaps three times.

Kata sat on the other side of the fire, fully dressed, busy with some small task he could not quite see. In a moment, she looked up.

"Drink from that flask," she said, gesturing toward his feet. "You'll feel better."

He glanced downward, saw a leather bottle such as all the nomads carried. But he shrank from it, pulling his feet away as if it would burn them.

"It's only deer's-milk wine," she murmured.

His clothes lay tumbled on the cushions beside him. He dressed hurriedly, tying the laces tight, as if that could shut the woman, and the memory of her cold, cold flesh, away. But even with his clothes on he could feel her touch, though she herself sat far beyond his reach.

"Yesterday you did not believe in magic," she said, and catching his gaze with her own, holding it as a predator holds the gaze of its prey, made him shudder. "You were a witch yourself, but you scoffed at every other form of magic." She smiled slowly, and it was a terrible smile of triumph and possession. Beside it, Zavia's smile had been nothing, less than nothing.

He knew the tent flap was behind him, knew he could

reach it and be outside in the clean, fresh air in a moment, and yet he could not move, could not even look at it over his shoulder. His voice was hoarse when he spoke. "I would not scoff now, lady."

The smile faded at last, replaced by that careful lack of expression, that cool, steady dignity that did not betray the mind behind it. "You have no secrets from me now, Alaric the minstrel. I know your whole life. Your loves. Your fears. Your shames. You are even less fit than I thought to be my daughter's love. But if you would stay with us, I will find some use for you."

"Some use . . . ?" he echoed.

"Are you afraid to serve another witch?"

He clenched his fists; the flesh of his palms was clammy. "I am a minstrel, lady. I will sing for you. . . ."

"They all serve me," she said, "in one way or another. And I serve them. Don't be afraid, boy. I will not ask for more than you can give. It is a pity, though, that you cannot teach me your special skill. I could wish to travel by a thought instead of by deer."

"My lady—"

"Don't bother denying it, minstrel. I told you, I know everything. From your little love Solinde to your coward's fear of the Red Lord. You could have killed him— you, of all people. But you were afraid of death. That's not an unnatural fear. Do you think anyone breathes who doesn't know it? Some show it less, that's all. But you could have killed him, I think, and escaped with your life. There's where your cowardice showed. You were afraid to chance it. You let your fear keep you from acting for the good of the many."

He swallowed thickly. "They wouldn't have wanted it, lady. They needed him to keep them safe. They were willing to pay his price for that."

"So the deer needs the herder," said Kata, "even though he may slaughter it someday. A perverse exchange, wouldn't you say?"

"Lady, who am I to turn their lives upside down—"

"Who are you to do justice? Indeed, you are only a minstrel. And will you run from me now, Alaric, so ill named?"

He wrenched his gaze from her at last and looked down at the carpet beneath his feet. "Lady, I fear you."

"That is as it should be."

"You hold my life in your hands."

She said nothing to that.

"Will you tell the others about me?"

"Do you wish me to?"

He shook his head. "I am not a witch."

"You cannot deny the name, Alaric."

"I *do* deny it. I want to live my life as an ordinary man. I want no power over others, no magic laid to my name. If I must serve you lady, let it be with ordinary skills, with the strength of my arms or with my songs. Let be the rest."

"Look at me, minstrel."

Almost against his will, his head lifted and turned toward her, and he looked into her pale eyes, their pupils like dark pits leading deep into her skull. Smoke drifted about her—thin blue smoke, translucent this time, like a nimbus of dawn mist over a river. The fire played a shifting light over her skin, seemed to caress her with its colors, like a living creature.

"You can run if you wish," she whispered, and her voice was like a breath of wind fanning the flames. "But if you stay with us, you are mine."

He felt her cold again, as if it moved out from her body in waves and enveloped him, making him shudder in spite of the fire. As if the multicolored flames themselves gave out cold instead of heat. He wanted to leave. He wanted to vanish and find refuge in the forests of the south. There were a thousand places he could go, bowers where the green leaves would hide him away, or lonely roads where no man walked by day or night. He wanted to run from her certainty, from her power. But he could not. She held him, with her eyes, her will, her word.

"Go now," she said, "and make your choice."

As if a chain had snapped between them, he staggered back and, groping blindly behind himself, found the tent flap. He nearly fell outside.

Daylight.

The camp was awake and bustling, some tents already down, pack-deer standing ready for the day's loads. Alaric squinted against the sunlight. He still felt woozy. Someone caught his arm. Zavia.

He flinched at her touch. For just an instant, he saw that her eyes were like her mother's, and he felt the cold sweep over him again.

"Are you ill?" she said.

He shook his head. The feeling was passing. Yes, her eyes were like her mother's, but still young, still innocent. The acolyte, he thought. No, here was no acolyte, not of *that* master. Here was simply a passionate young woman with grand dreams. He wondered if she even understood what she aspired to. He closed his arms about her, kissed her there in the bright morning sunlight. Her mouth was soft and clinging and flooded him with warmth.

What shall I do? he wondered, holding her fast against him.

"We have to pack up," she whispered.

A dozen people spoke to him as he and Zavia took the tent down. A dozen smiling, friendly people. They joked as the nomads always joked, and they laughed easily. Some of them were helping Kata to load her deer.

He stayed away from her, stayed at the tail of the line as the nomads moved north, while she rode near the front with Simir. And though Zavia tried to converse with him as they ambled along through the greening grass, he would not speak. He would not tell her what had happened in her mother's tent, or how it made him feel. He would not tell her that he still didn't know whether to stay or go, to love or to fear, to serve or to fly free. *Cold or warm,* he thought; *is it possible to be both at once?*

He sat by Simir's fire for a long time that night. Till the embers dulled to red and ceased giving warmth, till the last of the graybeards went to bed. Till even Zavia, sensing his mood, retired to her tent without him. Only he and Simir were left at last, alone among the silent tents, under the distant stars. Alaric had set the lute aside some time since, and he sat with his arms about his knees, his eyes seeing the embers, the past, and nothing at all.

"Your songs were very sad tonight," said Simir.

"Were they?" Alaric put his head down on his knee.

"A minstrel always knows more sad songs than any other kind. Perhaps someone should have asked for something brighter."

"They were fine songs, though. And well sung."

"Thank you, Simir."

They sat in silence for a time, and then the high chief said, in a soft voice, "Do you plan to stay by the fire all night, minstrel?"

"I don't know. Perhaps."

Simir laid a hand on his shoulder. "Did you and Zavia . . . quarrel?"

Alaric shook his head.

"I thought . . . perhaps . . . because of her mother. It was soon to call you to her tent."

Alaric turned his face toward Simir; he could barely see the man, by starlight and ember-glow. "Soon?"

"Soon after you and Zavia became lovers. She usually waits till a man's first child is born."

"Waits? To do what?"

Simir paused. "Didn't she give you hunting magic?"

Alaric raised his head. "And how would she do that?"

"Didn't she take you to her bed?"

"Is that how it's done? Body to body?"

"She kept you all night. Everyone assumed . . ."

Alaric glanced toward the place where her tent stood, a shadow among shadows. "She didn't mention hunting magic. But perhaps it was included. We spoke of other things. She was curious about my past. She said . . . she might have certain tasks for me. I don't know what they would be."

Simir's hand tightened on his shoulder. "If she wants you to go back to the valley, I won't allow it. We have hunters, and brave young men in plenty, but only one minstrel."

Alaric sighed. "She thought . . . I might be leaving soon."

Simir's arm dropped away. The night was very quiet for a moment. At last he said, "Why would she think that?"

"I've thought it myself."

He heard Simir climb to his feet, saw the big silhouette

loom above him, felt the big hand on his arm, urging him to rise, too.

"Come, minstrel, walk with me. These are not things we should speak of while others are close enough to hear. Come walk by the river."

The reflected stars were like drops of silver scattered over the surface of the water, their images shimmering now and then with the breath of the wind or the movement of some fish. *Like my life,* Alaric thought, *placid for a time, and then suddenly convulsed by some outside force.*

Simir was a large shadow beside him, walking, while the river flowed deep and sluggish to one side and the tents receded in the distance behind. "Something is wrong, minstrel," said the high chief.

Alaric had to laugh ruefully. "Aside from your sons hating me, what could be wrong?"

"They'll stay away from you now."

"And your witch thinks I am her personal property."

"She thinks that of everyone, Alaric. It's nothing."

"To you, perhaps."

"Are you restless, minstrel? Are you . . . sorry that you took up with us?"

"No, Simir, no. You've been good to me. You're good, kind people, and I find it difficult to imagine you swooping down on the Red Lord's valley to lay waste and leave carnage behind you." He smiled slightly, into the darkness. "All except your sons. I can see them doing it easily."

"It was long ago," said Simir.

"I like you people. Most of you. And Zavia—perhaps I love her. But I fear her mother."

"She is a fearsome woman."

Alaric sighed. "Has she ever given you hunting magic, Simir?"

"Why, yes."

"And . . . what was the experience like?"

Simir hesitated. "It was very pleasant."

"And afterward . . . did you ever want to go back for more?"

The high chief's laugh was deep. "I have. Many times."

Alaric shook his head. No, Simir had not had the same experience. Her magic had been something more familiar for him. *Go back for more?* he thought. *No, not in a thousand years.* "I am not used to witches," he said aloud. "We fear them in the south. It is a hard habit to break." There was no way to explain his feelings to Simir, no way short of telling the tale that Kata now knew. He could almost feel her looking over his shoulder at this very moment. Would he always feel that, here in the north? Would he always wonder what way she would find to use her knowledge? To hold him hostage with it, as she had held him with her eyes?"

"You have been very kind to me, Simir. I like you very much."

"Are you trying to say good-bye, minstrel?"

Alaric felt an ache begin, deep inside him. He had never had a home, never. And yet, with the nomads, he had known a kinship, of one wanderer for others, and a sense of comfort that transcended the petty hatreds of Gilo and his brothers. "I don't know, Simir, I don't know. I want to stay. Truly, I do."

"Then stay. Kata won't harm you, I promise."

"Ah, Simir, what is harm?"

"She has our good at heart, Alaric. She takes care of us. We don't fear her, and you—"

His voice cut off suddenly in a half-stifled cry of surprise, and then someone had seized Alaric from behind, an arm about his throat, choking his breath away. Alaric twisted, staggered, and felt the flat of a knife blade skitter along his shoulder. And then the riverbank gave way beneath his feet, and he and his assailant tumbled, struggling, into the placid water. The shock of the fall made his attacker loose his grip and, kicking wildly, Alaric thrust away, diving, diving for the gravel bed of the stream.

An eyeblink later, he was crawling up the bank, coughing, gasping, elsewhere. Clutching at the rank grass, he vomited river water. The sound was loud and ugly in the vast emptiness that surrounded him.

He lurched to his feet. He was safe. He had run, as he always ran, and once again his power had saved him. He took a deep and ragged breath. He was safe.

But Simir was back there, at that other spot beside the river. Struggling, alone, in the dark. *He has been good to me,* Alaric thought.

A heartbeat later, he was there.

It was a quiet fight, two slim shadows against a bigger one, the only sounds those of hard breathing and scuffling feet, and a distant splashing from the river. They hung on Simir's arms like dogs on a bear. Alaric leaped at the nearest, tore him away from the high chief, and instantly slipped out of reach in his special fashion. The darkness was his friend. He was a wraith, here, there, never where his quarry clutched. The one from the river stumbled into the fight, but Alaric took him on as well, dodging, landing a kick from behind, a punch from beside, then ducking away so that the two of them struck one another, not knowing where their target stood.

Then Simir came to him, and with a pair of mighty blows knocked his assailants to the ground.

"Minstrel," he said, his breath coming hard, "are you hurt?"

Alaric bent over, bracing his hands on his thighs. He felt a little dizzy, and his shoulder was beginning to throb. "I don't think so," he gasped.

"Ho, a torch for Simir!" the high chief shouted, and his voice boomed toward the camp. "A torch!"

Sounds of movement came from the tents, and then a brand flared, and another and another. Holding them high, half a dozen of Simir's men followed the trail of his voice.

The light revealed Gilo, Marak, and Terevli lying on the riverbank. All seemed senseless until, with the torch blazing just above him, Gilo raised his head. His still-swollen face was bleeding, and in his bruise-rimmed eyes was a deep and defiant ugliness.

Simir kicked him in the side, not too hard, but hard enough to make him grunt. "So you would be high chief now, would you? No need to wait till I'm too old. No need to wait till I say you're ready." He kicked the youth again. "You think they would follow you? As those two dolts do?" He stared down at his eldest son, and his face was grim. "I told myself that time would give you wisdom. I told myself that you were not really a fool. You

have shown me how mistaken I was." He turned to one
of the torchbearers. "Bind them. Guard them well. In
the morning I will give my judgment. Come, minstrel; a
cup of wine would not be amiss now."

Alaric found himself walking a trifle unsteadily, and
his wet clothes made him shiver.

"You're wounded," said Simir, reaching out to him
with both big hands.

Alaric looked to where Simir's eyes were focused and
found that the collar of his tunic had been ripped across,
and a ragged cut on his shoulder welled blood. He felt
dizzier than ever, seeing it.

"Kata must bind this up," said the high chief.

"No! No, it's nothing, I'll see to it myself. But what
of you, Simir?"

"A leather jerkin turns aside a poorly used blade. You
should have been wearing one yourself instead of this
thin stuff."

Alaric smiled feebly. "I'm too fast for a knife."

"Fast indeed," said Simir, and he slung Alaric's good
arm over his shoulder and helped him toward the fire.
"But for your courage and quickness, I would be dead."

Alaric shook his head. "You were a match for all of
them."

"I think not."

"Well, remembering all that courage is making me
very weak now, Simir." He sank gratefully to the carpet
in front of Simir's tent.

A few people were looking out of their own tents cu-
riously; Simir beckoned to one of them and sent him for
Zavia. "This wound needs care," he said, "and if you
won't have the mother, then the daughter must serve."

Zavia was livid. "I'll kill him for this," she hissed as
she peeled Alaric's torn, wet tunic away from his skin.

"It wasn't Gilo," said Alaric.

"He planned it."

"The other two aren't innocent, my Zavia." The salve
stung sharply as she spread it over the cut. "He couldn't
have moved without them."

"And they wouldn't have moved without him. Not
those two. They don't even breathe unless he tells
them—"

"I'll deal with all three," Simir said firmly. "And you won't kill him, Zavia. You won't have to."

The next day, the nomads did not take up their northward journey. Instead, they gathered in conclave, eightscore men, women, and children, all their attention focused on the three bound youths who sat cross-legged by Simir's fire. Even Kata came out of her tent, to stand between her carven staves and watch the proceedings with pale, expressionless eyes.

Simir stood, tall and impassive, his thick arms crossed over his broad chest, waiting till the murmuring of the crowd should cease. His closest companions surrounded his sons, penning them in, returning their black looks with cool ones. Simir himself ignored them. At last he spoke, and the few whispers that remained died away at his first word.

"You know my sons," he said, not shouting, but with a carrying voice. "My sons Gilo, Marak, and Terevli. Last night they tried to kill me. As you see, they failed."

There was some muttering in the crowd, but not much. The word had spread quickly with the sunrise, and few were surprised to hear it spoken now.

"They were proper sons once," Simir said. "Though they have not pleased me much in recent years, I have tried to be lenient with them, because they are my flesh and blood. Now there must be an end to leniency. If any of them would speak his mind before I pass judgment on them, let him do so."

"Father, you misunderstand completely!" said Marak. "It was the stranger attacked you, the minstrel." With a thrust of his chin, he signed toward Alaric, who stood near the front of the crowd, beside Zavia. "We were only trying to beat him off!"

Simir did not even glance at him. "Marak is always ready with a lie," he said. "He thinks I didn't notice that his blows were aimed at me. And poor Terevli—surely he will blame everything on Gilo; he always does." He looked at the boy, the youngest of the three, but Terevli's sullen face was downcast. "Perhaps only Gilo will have the courage to admit his crime. Gilo, whom his mother loved better than the others. It is well that she did not live to see this day. She would be ashamed of him.''

Gilo stared up at his father, his back very straight in spite of the ropes that bound him. His battered face would have been pitiable had the eyes not been so defiant.

''Gilo?'' said Simir.

Gilo's mouth twisted. ''Do what you will with me, Father. You have found another to take my place.''

Simir gazed down on him for a long moment. Then he said, ''You are the ringleader. Yours must be the greater punishment.''

''Will you kill me yourself, Father?''

Slowly, Simir shook his head. ''No, Gilo, someone else shall have that pleasure.''

Zavia's hand tightened on Alaric's. He glanced at her and saw that little smile of triumph on her lips; he felt a shiver climb his back. *No,* he thought, *he wouldn't do that.*

Simir went on. ''You have told us many times how you yearn to meet the Red Lord. Now you shall have your wish. You shall be taken to his valley and left there naked and weaponless, bound fast to a tree. You shall see what the Red Lord considers proper treatment of a stranger.'' He turned to the other boys. ''And you two shall leave Simir's band, and if any of us ever sees you again, on the plain or at the calving grounds, I will count your lives forfeit. From this moment, you are no longer my sons.''

The crowd exhaled a collective breath, and Alaric wondered if they had expected to see an execution or three that day. Beside him, Zavia was clearly disappointed, her shoulders slumping.

''But I will have another son,'' Simir said, ''if he wishes it.'' He turned to face Alaric, and he stretched out his hand. ''I owe my life to the minstrel, to his courage and his quickness. I would have *him* as my son.''

Alaric saw all eyes look to him. The nomads murmured. Zavia turned to him, smiling, and then she threw her arms about him and hugged him tight.

''Me?'' His shoulder throbbed, and he felt very tired; he had hardly slept at all that night. He tried to shrink back into the crowd, but people behind him pushed him forward. Simir's hand was beckoning. "I am not worthy to be your son, Simir."

"Worthier than these," Simir replied, indicating the boys with the merest tilt of his head. "Stay with us, Alaric. Make your home with us. We will be your family."

Alaric's mouth was suddenly very dry. "This is a kind offer, Simir," he said. "But you would be disappointed in me as a son. I am only a minstrel. Nothing more."

"You have a special strength, Alaric. I owe it my life. We may have more need of it someday."

Alaric looked up into his face. *Does he know? Did he see, last night? No, I was a shadow among shadows. What could he possibly have seen?*

He had not noticed Kata glide up, but there she was, at his elbow, holding a shallow bronze cup in her two hands.

"Alaric," said Simir, taking the cup, "this is the Elixir of Life. We of the north drink it when we enter the adult life of the band. I drank it when they took me in, so many years ago. Now you shall drink, and become our brother."

Alaric glanced from Kata to Simir. *Has she told him?* The liquid in the cup was dark and oily and gave off a pungent smell, though not unpleasant.

"I have never had a home," he said.

"We welcome you," said Simir.

"We welcome you," said Kata.

He looked over his shoulder, at Zavia, who stood in the crowd and smiled; so proud was she of him, so proud. He looked to the three bound youths, who stared back with hatred in their eyes. He looked at Simir and saw . . . pleading. He was a man who had lost so much he held dear. *Would this have happened if I hadn't come?* Alaric had no answer for that, or none that eased his conscience. He closed his eyes and thought of a forest glen in the south. He could be there in an instant. Or he could walk away, out of their lives, and never be seen in the north again. *What do I care for him, after all? I could say good-bye and wander on. As I always have.* He opened his eyes and looked at the cup, at the oily dark liquid. *Or I could stay, for him, for Zavia.* He looked at Simir again, and remembered all his kindness, his friendship. Perhaps he did know. And still he offered welcome. And Kata . . . Kata, whose magic lay in herbal distillations and in her compelling eyes—Kata stood beside him in the bright day, and without her smoke and her fire and her potions she was not so terrible, save in his memory; she was, instead, a creature of the natural world just as he was, just as a bear or a snake was, and no more or less frightening than either of those; and he knew, glancing at her, that he could run from her now, that nothing would hold him back. He could run. If he wanted to.

Alaric's shoulder throbbed, and he was very tired, in his body, in his mind—tired of saying good-bye, tired of wandering alone, tired of having no one and nothing. *Not for them*, he thought at last. *For me.*

Gravely, he took the cup and drank. The taste was pungent as cloves and faintly sweet. It seemed to flood through him, filling him up, stomach, heart, head, to the very tips of his fingers. The throbbing in his shoulder faded away. And the weariness seemed to go with it. He stood a little straighter, breathed a little deeper. As if he had never noticed it before, he suddenly felt the sunlight on his face, spring sunlight, fresh and warm. He felt as if he had drunk it along with the Elixir. A new day, a new spring, a new life.

"I have been raised from the dead," he whispered.

Kata took the cup. "You will heal quickly now."

Simir smiled at Alaric and said, "And you have healed me already."

Then Zavia was beside him, kissing his cheek, and all the rest of the band pressed forward with congratulations and good wishes for their new member. And everyone seemed to have forgotten completely the three boys who waited sullenly for their fates.

PART FIVE

THE ARCTIC WASTE

"I must do this myself," said Simir. "It would be wrong to leave it to another." He was lashing a small pack to the back of his riding deer, no more than the bare necessities of life. The men who would ride south with him were waiting, men with sternly set faces and bleak eyes, a hard and unforgiving escort for the three youths who sat trussed and silent in their midst.

"But you are the high chief," Alaric said. "The people need you."

Simir shook his head. "They know the way north without me. And Kata will be here, if some dispute needs settling."

"But it's dangerous." He gripped Simir's thick arm, as if to hold him back. "What if something happens to you? What will we do?"

The high chief clapped Alaric's hand with his own and then slid away from it, mounting the deer with the grace of a man half his size. From his new height, he gave Alaric a grim smile. "*We*," he said, and he reached down to tousle the minstrel's dark hair. "It's good to hear you say that. My son." He looked over the camp, the tents, the fires, the people all gathered to watch him and his companions. "If I have not returned by the time the snows come, you shall choose a new leader." Then he turned his face to Alaric once more. "But I don't doubt that I shall be back long before that. I have not reached this age without learning to deal with danger."

"Simir," said Alaric. He could not bring himself to call the man *father;* adoption felt too strange to him yet. "Let me go with you. I'll beguile your evenings with song. The journey won't seem so long that way."

The high chief shook his head. "We ride hard and fast,

lad. We'll have no time for music. Besides, how do you
think Zavia would feel if I took you away from her?''

Alaric glanced over his shoulder; she was some distance off, standing with a few other women at the nearest
fire, but watching him, and smiling. The thought of leaving her made his heart ache, but the thought of letting
Simir enter the Red Lord's valley with only these few
followers made it race with foreboding. No outsider was
safe in that valley, not unless he had a witch's power to
slip from the very clutches of the enemy. Or a witch to
help him do it. Simir was tall and broad, with the strength
of two ordinary men. But in the Red Lord's valley, how
much would strength tell against numbers?

''I could be useful. . . .'' he began.

Simir silenced him with a raised hand. ''If you would
please me, go north with my people. Beguile *their* evenings with song.''

''Simir—''

''And there's an end to the matter.''

Alaric sighed. *Does he know?* he wondered, for the
dozenth time. Events had moved so fast, the judgment,
the adoption, the readying for the journey—there had been
no moment to take him aside and discover, by indirec-
tion, if he knew Alaric's secret. And no moment to ask
Kata, either, if she had revealed it. *Shall I follow, in case
he needs me?*

''Don't worry so hard, lad,'' Simir said. ''We know
what we're about.'' And with that, he turned his mount
toward the south and led his little caravan out of camp.

Alaric walked half a hundred paces after them, past
the last cluster of tents, the last picketed animals. Hard
and fast they rode indeed, and none of them looked back
. . . none but Gilo. Bound up tight, stiff and straight on
his deer, he turned his head to cast a final glance at the
stranger who was his downfall. A hate-filled and defiant
glare it was, and it made Alaric flinch but did not make
him look away. Rather, he found his gaze held fast by
that receding figure, trussed and helpless and doomed,
and yet so far from any sign of repentance. Before long,
men and deer were like bobbing dolls in the distance;
soon, very soon, they would vanish into the flat immen-
sity of the plain.

"Don't go."

The voice at Alaric's elbow made him start, half ready to vanish in his own way, but he stifled the impulse. It was Kata.

"You must not help him, minstrel," she said. "You, of all people, must let him do this in his own fashion."

It came home to Alaric that she was speaking of the high chief. He looked after the dwindling figures again. "This is my fault," he said. "I owe him help."

"You don't understand, my Alaric. This has been coming for a long time. You were merely the excuse. The boys were spoiled and insolent. Simir thought they would gain wisdom and steadiness with age, but I think not. The people did not trust them. Gilo would never have been high chief, nor the others, not unless time changed them out of all recognition. But time rarely does such things; we are what we are, from an early age." She caught hold of Alaric's chin with one hand and forced him to look at her. "You, for example, my Alaric—you are a coward. You will never be more, no matter that you sprang to Simir's aid last night, no matter that you want to go with him now. Your first thought always is to run. You even fight by running, by dodging, never by standing your ground to face the enemy. You should throw your sword away, my Alaric, or put it to use cutting your meat."

Alaric met her cold gaze steadily. "I won't deny I'm a coward, lady. But we are what we are, as you say, and we must all make the best of it."

"You will never be high chief."

Startled, he stepped back, pulling away from her. "I? High chief?"

"He wants it. Don't you know, minstrel? He sees wisdom in your songs."

"Not *my* wisdom. Not most of it."

"He sees . . . you in twenty years, ready to take his place."

"Oh, surely one of your own people would be the proper choice. . . ."

"He was not of our people, once."

Alaric looked toward the southern horizon. The riders were mere dots now, against the pale green of the plain.

"Is that why he adopted me? For this dream of a son as high chief?"

"That was part of it."

Alaric shook his head. "He is blinded by grief now, lady. But he'll see me clearly when a little time has passed." He turned back to her. "And you'll be here to tell him the truth."

"Always."

He studied her face, so expressionless yet so knowing, as if all the world were transparent to her. How many of the nomads, he wondered, had yielded their hidden depths—their desires, their fears, their shames—to her? As he had. "Have you told him about me?"

She looked toward the horizon then. "He knows."

They stood together for some small time after that, silent, each gazing southward, till there was nothing left to see but the rolling plain and a few clouds in the morning sky. At last she said, "You will not follow, will you?"

Alaric sighed. "No."

"I did not think you would."

He doesn't want me along, Alaric thought. But he could not help wondering, in some small corner of his mind, if his real reason was not that, with time to think about the venture, fear had begun to creep upon him. In the valley of the Red Lord, even a man with a witch's power could die.

Behind him, he could hear the nomads striking their tents. It was time to resume the long trek north.

With Simir gone, Kata took a more active part in the life of the band. Instead of shutting herself away in her tent as soon as camp was made, she sat by the fire on Simir's own rugs for much of the afternoon, speaking quietly to his old companions, and sometimes asking for songs from Alaric. She was like some pale reflection of the high chief, carrying out his role, but without his joy and spirit. No one complained, but everyone seemed subdued, and even Alaric's most amusing songs could not provoke the laughter that Simir would have offered them.

And with Simir gone, people found fewer excuses to visit his fire, and spent less time there when they did come. Instead, they moved about a good deal, from fire to fire, from task to task. A restlessness pervaded the camp, a feeling of tension and unnecessary busyness. The children played harder, the hunters ranged farther, the herders used their switches of woven grass more often. Yet in all this disquiet there were few disputes, as if Simir's people would not allow themselves to quarrel while he was not there to judge.

Some of the nomads' restlessness was channeled into archery and swordplay. Alaric had seen the men pair off for competition before, and coach their sons as well, but never so assiduously. Now they sent their arrows at man-shaped targets and clashed their blades one against another as if preparing for some invasion, though everyone he asked assured him that there was no enemy on the plains, and none expected. But it was good, they said with equal certainty, to keep one's skills honed. And after saying so, they would look to the south, where only grass was visible to the horizon.

After observing for some days, Alaric asked if he might join their sport, just as a novice. For a small space, then, each afternoon, he set his lute aside and gave himself over to the interplay of steel and steel, with a borrowed shield of wood and hard-cured leather on his left arm, with sweat prickling his body under borrowed leather armor. Though he was not without grace, from practice long ago, he found himself a novice indeed compared to nomad youths of his age, and rarely did any onlooker cheer a stroke from his arm. But that didn't matter to him. He hadn't joined in to pretend to be something he was not, but to make his days fly faster. For he, too, was restless, and all his songs, and all of Zavia's sweet distraction, could not prevent him from turning to the south half a dozen times a day.

At last, one morning when the nomad camp lay silent in sleep, and dawn twilight had yet to give way before the rising disk of the sun, Alaric's restlessness overcame him. He could guess how far each day's hard ride would take Simir's company, and he thought they must be in the mountains by now, they must be near that terrible valley. Softly, he crept from Zavia's tent and stole away through the tall grass. When he was a hundred paces from the camp, he dropped to the ground and vanished.

He appeared on a slope high above the valley. He did not know what route Simir had planned through the mountains, but he was sure the high chief's goal must be a place visible to the goatherds that visited these heights. He made a sweep of the likeliest-looking approaches, flitting from tree to boulder to tree, but he saw and heard no token of man or deer.

He returned, lying on his belly, to a spot nearly a mile from camp, and he walked the rest of the way in, as an ordinary person would. The nomads were waking by then; Zavia was waking, and he told her that he had been answering a call of nature.

The next morning he made another fruitless search, and the next. On the fourth trip, he found what he was seeking.

He saw nothing of Simir and his bleak-eyed men; he supposed they had arrived by night and gone away as soon as their work was done. They were probably well to the north already, and safe. But true to Simir's word, they had left Gilo tied fast to a tree, in full view of the valley.

It was a lightning-blasted stump, thick and gray and broken off jaggedly two man-heights above the ground, like a clutching fist half-buried in the earth. Gilo stood against it like a statue, his head back, his eyes staring, a fingerlike root separating his knees. On his face, hatred mingled with fear in an expression that was at once ugly and pathetic. The brightening twilight showed dark smears of blood around the rawhide binding his arms, signs of the struggle he had given over.

Hidden by thick brush, Alaric watched him—watched his eyes that looked straight at the Red Lord's castle, watched his lips that, from time to time, whispered curses. There was agony in those eyes and on those lips; Gilo's torment had begun already, before the Red Lord could touch him. And despite everything, Alaric felt a stab of pity for him.

He heard the sound of footsteps then—hard boots crunching on loose pebbles. Some distance down the hillside, a dozen of the Red Lord's men were climbing toward the blasted tree.

There was time, Alaric knew, for him to reach Gilo and carry him away. Time and to spare, before the soldiers finished their climb, to deliver him to a new life in the south, far from the nomads and his father, and safe from appetite of the Red Lord. A new life, another chance, all in the space of a heartbeat. Several heartbeats passed, along with the steady crunch of gravel.

He jumped then, but only to the cover of a more distant thicket. *A terrible punishment, Simir,* he thought, *but it is not for me to counter your judgment.*

The soldiers approached the tree warily, their swords drawn. Soon, though, they realized that Gilo was no bait for an ambush, only a sacrifice, and they slashed his bonds and marched him down the slope. Surrounded by the heralds of his future, Gilo walked stiff-legged, but without hesitating, without stumbling, and with his head held high.

Alaric looked away at last, a shudder coursing through him. And then he was in the north once more, and in the distance lay the nomad camp, bustling with morning activity. He ran toward the tents, and the people, as fast as his legs could carry him.

He made no more southward journeys. But that did not keep him from looking in that direction often, as often as all of Simir's people did.

"Too soon, too soon," a woman would say to him, though she would be scanning the southern horizon herself, with a long-handled spoon in her fist and a pot steaming under her hands. She knew how long the high chief's journey should take; all the nomads did. They gauged the time not just by the days that passed, but by the miles they traveled and by the changes in their deer. While Simir's company was gone, the new calves grew long-legged and sturdy; the bucks' antlers spread and lengthened like strange, naked branches reaching for the sun; and even the does—to Alaric's amazement—sprouted antlers, nubs welling from their foreheads into slender fingers pointing forward and back. For the deer, the warm season moved at a smooth and steady pace; they never had reason to look anxiously to the south.

"Too soon, too soon," someone would say. And then, late one afternoon, when the cookfires were blazing and the scent of stewing game seemed to envelope the whole camp, it was no longer too soon.

A sharp-eyed lad on watch with the herd saw them first, and he shouted the news so wildly that the deer started and snorted and tossed their heads. Word passed like a storm wind through the camp, creating a great noise and bustle. Like a song, the name leaped from mouth to mouth: Simir, Simir! Only later, when someone thought to count the approaching figures, did the high chief's people realize that more deer than had gone south were returning, and every one bore a rider.

The nomads streamed out to welcome their leader, who rode straight and hard as only a man coming home would ride. They scarcely let him dismount before they mobbed him, crying out his name, grasping at him as if they needed the touch of his flesh to be sure he was real. He pressed hands all among the crowd, bellowing greetings in every direction. But Alaric's was the hand he clasped most firmly.

"You did stay," he said, his voice barely audible in the tumult.

"I said I would," Alaric replied.

Simir waved toward the other riders, who had followed in a cluster some distance behind him and were just now reining in their deer. The people who had greeted him so warmly were less forward with them, for among the men who had gone south with Simir were nine strangers.

Alaric recognized them.

They did not look as they had when last he had seen them. Gone were the linen tatters that had passed as their clothing, gone the mangy goatskin cloaks. Instead, they wore the nomads' leather garments, and good boots on their feet. And they sat their steeds with confidence, they who had once scrambled barefoot and starveling in the mountains. Their hair betrayed them, though; blond as Simir's own, it marked them as born in the Red Lord's valley.

The pale-haired newcomers remained mounted after their nomad companions had joined the welcoming crowd. Seven men and two women, they looked about nervously, eyes ever returning to one another, seeking reassurance. Even their leader, Berown, whom Alaric remembered as a hard man clinging to the remnants of an old pride, seemed cowed.

There had been eleven of them, back in the mountains. Missing were the two who knew Alaric's secret.

Simir raised an arm for silence, and when his people had hushed, he made a broad gesture toward the strangers. "These are exiles from the Red Lord's land," he said in a loud, carrying voice, "just as I was. We found them in the mountains, near death, and we brought them with us out of pity. I hope that you will take them to your hearts, and that the north will be good to them, as it has been to me."

At that, people pressed forward to help the newcomers down, to clasp their hands and offer them food, and to give them the smiles that Simir's return had prompted.

"And a troublesome bundle they've been," the high chief muttered as he turned once more to Alaric. Taking the minstrel's arm, he pushed through the throng toward his own tent, answering with nods and a lifted hand the greetings that still assailed him from every side. At last he reached his fire, and beckoning to Kata, who had stayed there while so many others had rushed away, he slipped into his shelter.

Inside, he set his hands on his hips and looked from Kata to Alaric. "Has all been well since I left?"

"Quite well," said Kata.

"Good. And with you, my son?"

"Well enough. Though I missed you. I missed your laugh."

Simir smiled. "I missed your songs. It was a long journey." The smile faded. "But a successful one."

Alaric looked down at the rug beneath his feet.

The high chief set his big hand on Alaric's shoulder. "They are all far away," he said firmly, "and we will not speak of them again."

Alaric raised his head. "As you will, Simir."

"You had other success, I hope," said Kata.

Simir nodded to her. "Four bags of the plants. We gathered all we could find. And not a Red Lord's man did we see the whole time." His fingers tightened on Alaric's shoulder a moment and then let go. "Just this ragtag bunch, half dead of hunger."

"You could have left them to the other half," Kata said. "We have enough of our own mouths to feed, and there's a hard winter coming, Simir. I've told you that before."

"We couldn't leave them; they might have set him free." He shook his head. "They didn't want to come; we had to be a bit rough about persuading them. But when they're used to us, they'll be content enough. And what do nine more mouths mean? We'll manage."

"No hunters among them, I'll warrant."

"They'll learn."

"They gathered roots and berries in the mountains," said Alaric. "They had no bows for hunting."

Both Simir and Kata looked to him.

"I met them there. I offered to guide them to the south, where life would be softer, but they wouldn't go. They were eleven then, at the end of last winter."

"They swore they were only nine," said Simir. "If we left two hiding in the mountains . . ." He frowned deeply.

As much for his own sake as for Simir's, Alaric said, "I'll find out."

Berown was crouching by one of the more distant fires, taking a bowl of stew from the hands of a stout matron. When he noticed Alaric standing on the other side of the flames, he almost dropped the bowl. "You!" He scrambled to his feet, one arm curled protectively about the food.

"Good eve," said Alaric.

"So *this* is where you came from." And he glanced down at the bowl, as if suddenly afraid of its contents.

"No, I am a guest among them, as you are."

"Guest! Is that what you call it?" His eyes darted to the two men who stood some paces off, swords buckled to their waists, watching him.

"Better to live here than to die in the mountains," said Alaric. "At any rate, they tell me you were dying. You don't look so bad, Berown, none of you do. I suppose they fed you on the journey north."

He nodded hesitantly.

"They're good people, my friend. You'll be happy among them. Malgis and Daugas would have been happy, too. Why aren't they with you?"

Berown's lips pressed together whitely. "Don't you know? You drove them to it."

Alaric frowned, a chill of foreboding touching the back of his neck. "What do you mean?"

"You tricked them into following you. Where were you leading them? To death, or to something worse? Some foul witch's place, wasn't it, where you'd drain their blood and use it in your brews?"

The words seemed to freeze his very marrow. Spoken here in the open, where anyone could hear, that name—*witch*—made him want to shrink away, to use that witch's power to escape. He fought the impulse with all his strength. "Berown—"

"They told us about you! A minstrel you said you were, a simple traveler, when all the time you wanted to carry us all off with you, to serve your evil purposes."

"No! That isn't—"

"They told us! They saw you use your witch's power. Deny it if you like, but I know the truth when I hear it. Before their eyes, you melted away like mist. Daugas said so, and he was no fool!"

Alaric took a step toward him, and Berown backed off twice as far, the bowl still clutched in his hands. Beside him, the woman who had given him the food looked on, her face suffused with puzzlement. A few other people were drifting near, drawn by the raised voices.

"Daugas was hungry," Alaric said firmly. "Hunger can make the mind play strange tricks. Whatever he thought he saw was in his imagination, nothing more. I'm no witch!"

Berown spat on the ground. "Malgis was mad before you found us; but she was madder still after running from you. She wouldn't stay in the mountains any longer; she said she wanted to go home. So she went down into the valley, in full daylight, and no one could keep Daugas from going after her. We never saw either of them again.''

''Berown—''

''Your fault, witch! You lured them, and when they realized your lure was evil, they lost all hope.'' He backed off yet another pace. ''And here we all are, in your clutches.'' Abruptly, he threw the bowl to the ground, and its contents splashed the fire. ''Have I lived so long as an exile just to come to this?''

''Berown, listen to me!'' Alaric raised a pleading hand toward the man and then, seeing him retreat again, curled it into a fist and dropped it to his side. ''I am not a witch, Berown. I don't know what Malgis and Daugas thought they saw, or dreamed they saw. I only tried to lead them to safety. But she was afraid. *She* turned back. Not from fear of *me*, Berown, but from fear of the outside world. That was her madness, and finally, *it* made her go home.'' He felt an ache behind his eyes as he remembered her pathetic, emaciated face. ''I tried to help you, Berown. You know that. I never meant you any harm.''

''They died because of you.''

Alaric shook his head. ''Because of themselves.''

He saw the man waver, saw the clash of fear and anger in his face give way to uncertainty. Malgis had been mad, that was sure. And he must know, perhaps even from his own experience, that starvation could bring visions in its wake, and raving. He had seen nothing with his *own* eyes, that was the most important thing. He wavered.

''I am sorry about them, Berown,'' Alaric said. ''Truly sorry. I would have it otherwise, I swear. But the nine of you, at least, are safe now.''

Berown straightened his back at that and looked around, wariness in his eyes. ''Safe?'' he said. ''Safe among our enemies?''

''Not yours. Not anymore.'' He backed off a few steps, and when Berown just stood his ground, he turned and walked away.

Halfway to Simir's fire, he felt a tug at his sleeve: the woman who had served Berown his dinner. ''Are you truly not a witch, minstrel?'' she asked.

He tried to smile at her, and thought he succeeded partly. "No, kind lady, I am not."

"What a shame," she murmured, and let him go.

That evening, at a small fire kindled some hundred paces from Simir's tent, where the two of them could sit alone with no listeners but the stars in the sky, he told the high chief about himself—about the long road behind him and the many people left along the way; about the troubles that his witch's power had brought him, and saved him from; about the doubts and fears that had driven him. It was a long chronicle, for one not yet twenty summers old, and the tale of Malgis and Daugas was only a small part of it; still, in spite of all that he had said to Berown, he felt the weight of their deaths on his shoulders.

"Kata was right," he murmured, toying with a cup of deer's-milk wine. "I am a coward. I could have saved them both in spite of their fear. I had only to take them away, kicking and struggling as they might, and then they could never have gone back to the valley."

"It isn't easy to make other people's decisions for them," said Simir. "One learns that, as high chief."

"I wanted to help. At the end, all I could do was steal a few goats for them. Oh, I thought it was a good herd for just eleven men and women, but even so, you found them starving."

"I remember they spoke of goats. They had eaten the last one sometime before we arrived."

Alaric shook his head. "So even there, I failed them."

Simir set a hand on his ankle. "You didn't fail them, my son. You helped them to live longer than they would have without you."

"But I could have done more."

Simir refilled both their cups from a small flask. Then he looked at Alaric thoughtfully. "Tell me," he said, "what is it that you really wish you had done for these people?"

Alaric took a deep breath. "I wish that I had killed the Red Lord."

The high chief nodded.

"But I was afraid. And the longer I put it off, the more

afraid I became. After a time, I convinced myself that there were good reasons not to kill him. His people needed him, with a terrible, twisted need. I told myself that folk who felt that way even deserved him, and that, at any rate, they would never thank me for the deed. So I turned my back on it. And on them.''

"You could have done it, I suppose," Simir murmured.

"I think so. But there was danger, of course. And I have always tried to avoid danger." He turned the cup in his hands. "So I gave them goats instead." He felt the pain behind his eyes again, the heat of tears that would not come. In his mind's eye, Malgis's face was overlaid with that other woman's, that victim of artful damage whose pain he had ended with his sword. "Only goats."

Simir sighed. "I have no answer for you, my son."

Softly, Alaric said, "I could still do it. I could be there before you could blink your eyes, hunt him down in his own castle, stab him to the heart." He looked down into the cup. "But I won't. Because I'm still afraid."

Simir gripped the hand that held that cup, gripped it firmly with his own big paw. "You're one of us now. Your concerns are here, not in the valley. *This* life is what matters to you, just as it does to me."

Alaric looked into his face. *Yes*, he thought, *this is a man who knows what failure is. Not cowardice, but at least failure.* "I suppose you are right."

"You'll understand when winter comes. You won't have time to worry about the past then. The northern winter takes all a man has in him, and more."

"So I've heard."

"And this may be a harder one than usual, if Kata is right."

"Is she generally right?"

Simir nodded. "But we'll manage, together. We always do. These are strong and determined people, these nomads of the north."

Alaric smiled a little. "You love them very much, don't you?"

"They've been good to me. It's easy to love goodness."

Alaric leaned forward, elbows on his knees. "Tell me,

did you know any of our new arrivals . . . before? Berown was one of the Red Lord's men. . . .''

'I knew him, a little. He was just a boy then, a fresh recruit, but already a bully. Like the rest of us. His years as a fugitive have beaten him down.''

"Not entirely," said Alaric.

"No, not entirely. But he'll be watched, he and the others."

"He'll cause trouble, I think."

"He caused trouble on the way north. I expect more before he settles down." He finished his wine, refilled the cup. "I think perhaps you should stay out of his way for now. I doubt that a few words from your mouth truly convinced him that you're not a witch, and he needs some time in the north before he understands our feelings toward witches. Kata must work on him, on all of them."

Alaric nodded, though he suspected that Kata was more likely to add to their fear than allay it.

"I won't say I didn't think of leaving them somewhere along the way north, somewhere like Nuriki's band, where we borrowed the extra deer. But it was my idea to bring them along, and so they are my responsibility." He pointed to Alaric. "As you are."

"I'll stay away from him."

"Well, you'll be with me a good part of the time, so you won't have much chance to fall afoul of him. I missed your songs, Alaric; I missed them mightily on that long journey. And I hear that you sang very little while I was gone."

Alaric shrugged. "You are my best audience, Simir. Without you, the songs seemed . . . flavorless."

"And I hear, too, that you kept yourself busy with other things. With learning some warrior's skills."

"It was just exercise. I am no warrior."

"Still, I'd like to see what you've learned."

With a short, dry laugh, Alaric said, "See what I haven't learned, you mean. I'm a poor swordsman, Simir. Every time I try, I prove it over again."

Simir smiled at him, then. "You don't need your sword to be one of us," he said. "All you need is your music. You haven't sung for me yet today, my Alaric. My ears thirst for the sound of your lute as a dying man thirsts for water on the endless desert sands.''

"What do you know of desert sands?" Alaric said, smiling too.

"Only what you've told me in your songs. Come, we'll go back to the camp and show everyone that you sing your best when Simir listens.''

"Yes," said Alaric, scrambling up and dashing out the fire with one swipe of his foot. "Yes."

For the next few days, he was too busy singing to join the weapons practice, which, though it had slacked off since Simir's return, was still more common than before his departure—as if, in his absence, the nomad men had rediscovered some old fascination with sword and bow. Through all the daylight hours they spent encamped—and the summer days were long now—some bowman would always be sighting on his target, some pair of feinting, slashing, thrusting swordsmen would be testing each other's endurance. Several times, one of his regular sparring partners came to Alaric, trying to lure him to that afternoon's practice field. When he demurred, Zavia would tease him that he'd given up the sword because he kept stumbling over his own feet; and he would laugh and say she wasn't far wrong. Finally, though, he did go back, just for a short bout, because Simir wanted to watch him.

"You're not as bad as you think," Simir said afterward. "You're not clumsy."

"And sometimes I even hit my mark," replied Alaric.

"That comes with time."

"And discipline."

The high chief nodded. "It's an exercise that brings strength. Not a bad thing to have, come winter."

Not so much because he cared to spend his time so, but because Simir seemed to want it, Alaric took his sword up regularly once more. The other swordsmen were all glad to see him return, but he thought that was hardly because he was a promising student. Rather it was because, with him in their contests, every one of them could be assured of defeating *someone*.

"I can feel the muscles of your arms and chest growing, my Alaric,'' Zavia whispered as she snuggled against him.

He smiled at her in the darkness. "That pleases you, does it?''

"Everything about you pleases me,'' she purred.

He kissed her hair. "Then I am pleased as well.''

For all its value as exercise, the weapons practice was a measured business, almost stately in its movements, the movements of men who had no wish to harm each other. The best of them, paired off, contested most swiftly, sure of each other's skills, but even this was mere sport; when they wanted to show their fighting blood, they set up a wooden post and took turns hacking pieces from it.

Berown watched their practice for some afternoons, his eyes following the arcing blades at first with indifference and then, at last, with hunger. When he asked to join, finally, there was some discussion of the matter, and a compromise was reached: no sword for him, but if he cared to spar with a wooden blade, they could carve a few, and several youngsters were willing to try his skill.

He was awkward in the beginning, but that soon passed. He had been the Red Lord's man, and he knew something of sword and shield. He was, indeed, a good, middling swordsman, better than some but yielding to others. And though he took praise proudly, he also yielded with some grace—Alaric noticed that particularly, and it heartened him. It was a sign that the man was feeling easier in his new life. His companions had all begun to settle in, to learn new ways, to smile again, even to laugh; they had shut the past behind them. For Berown, though, Alaric had thought it would be harder, for he had been a leader back in the mountains, if only of a handful of ragged fugitives; and now . . . now he was nothing. But a wooden sword, it seemed, was giving him a place among strangers.

They had not spoke to each other since that first day; they only nodded now and then on the afternoon's practice field. In the evening, in the long slow twilight that preceded the northern summer night, Berown stood at the edge of Simir's circle sometimes, as other people did, and listened to Alaric sing. There had been no trouble, no trouble at all.

Afterward, though, Alaric thought that perhaps Berown had watched him a little too hard on those long evenings, with eyes that forgot to blink.

How it began, he never quite understood—what particular thing provoked it, what he might have said or done. Later, witnesses said that Berown had been sparring steadily with his wooden sword, but not doing quite so well as usual, and reddening a little in the face. His assigned watchers were lax, had been so for some time, seeing nothing much worth watching in him, and caring more for the archery a few paces away than for a contest of wood against wood. Not far off, Alaric stood talking to another man, his sword point against the ground, his back to the wooden combat.

He never knew whether he heard Berown's rush or just *felt* it somehow, a vibration in the ground, like the pounding hooves of a warhorse. He turned, and the man was there, looming, steel in his hand and rage in his face. There was no time to call for help, no time even to raise the sword and block the falling blow. Death looked into Alaric's eyes, and instinct claimed him. He vanished.

He found himself far to the south, beyond the mountains, in the forest where he sometimes hunted, where the trees were close-set, and the game was scarcely shy of men. Safe. As he had always managed to be safe.

He shook his head sharply and gripped the sword with rigid hands. They had all seen, a dozen and more of them, there was no escaping it. No darkness had been his shield, no smooth talk of delusion would cloud their memories. In an instant, Berown had stripped him naked to their eyes. *Then let it be so,* he thought, his teeth clenched so hard they ached. He would not run away this time.

He willed himself back to the north, but a short space from the practice field, where the grass was high and no men stood.

He saw them all before anyone saw him. They had fallen back from Berown, a ragged, wary circle in whose center the fugitive from the Red Lord's valley swung his stolen sword with vicious swiftness, and turned, turned, so that no one could strike him from behind. Then someone caught sight of Alaric and shouted and pointed, and a great commotion arose.

They were cheering.

They had seen, and they were cheering.

Alaric felt a great love well up inside him for every man on that practice field, and just for a moment his vision blurred. They were not like other people, these nomads, not anything like them. He dashed the tears away with the back of one arm and straightened his spine. He raised his sword, and the hilt felt slick with sweat.

"Stand aside, all of you!" he shouted. "He is mine!"

They obeyed instantly. Berown was left alone, still slashing at air, but turning no longer. "Face me, witch!" he roared.

Alaric did face him, in his own special way, appearing behind him, before him, to his left, his right, flickering like a flame, hardly there before he was gone again. Never had he used his power so completely, with such flexibility, not even the night he fought at Simir's side. Berown slashed a dozen times, twisting, turning, shouting hoarsely, but he wounded only empty air. Alaric's sword flickered with him, feinting, teasing, tantalizing, till at last it struck with a loud slap—not the edge but the flat of the blade, a stinging blow to Berown's calf. Another to his buttocks, a third to his belly, almost doubling him over with its force. Another to his head, to knock him over, and then Alaric's boot stamped on his sword hand and scuffed hard, and the blade went spinning free.

"Yield!" Alaric shouted, the point of his own blade against Berown's throat. He saw that throat work as Berown tried to speak and failed. He eased the blade back a finger's-breadth, enough to let the man nod.

Alaric stepped back, then prudently sidled to the fallen sword and picked it up. Berown made no move to rise. For a long moment he stared up at the sky, and then, very slowly, he turned on his side and curled his body, drawing his knees up, hugging his crossed arms to his chest. He began to weep.

Alaric turned away from him, holding the second sword high. "Does this belong to someone?"

A man came forward to claim it, and then the circle of onlookers broke, and the nomad men surrounded Alaric, shouting and laughing, every one of them trying to grip his arm or clap him on the back. He laughed himself, leaning on his sword in the midst of the hubbub, loving them all. He laughed, wild and free and joyous. Around him, the crowd grew and grew, till nearly all of Simir's band had enveloped him, and he felt his heart expanding to encompass them all. Zavia shouldered her way through the throng to throw her arms around him, and he kissed her soundly, loving her even more than the rest.

"I knew it was true!" She had to shout to be heard above the clamor.

"Yes, it's true," he shouted back.

"The strangers spread the story; everyone must have heard it by now. You could have told *me.*"

"Are you angry with me?"

"Only a little." And she hugged him again.

The crowd parted to let Simir through. His face was anxious at first, but when he saw Alaric smiling, with Zavia in his arms and all the other people pressed close about him, he smiled, too. "So it's out in the open, now," he said. "And you see how empty your worries were! This is the north, Alaric. Everything is different here!"

"I believe that now," said the minstrel. "I hope Berown may come to believe it, too." He hesitated. "He's not well, I think. Perhaps I hit his head too hard."

Simir's smile turned crooked. "Anyone else would have killed him. *I* would have."

Alaric shook his head.

"Still, you have your victory," said Simir, "and one these folk won't soon forget. Come," and he raised his voice to the crowd, "let us toast Alaric's triumph with wine all around. Let us drink to the skills of our new-found witch." He put his big arm around Alaric, and around Zavia as well. "Simir's band is so rich in magic—how lucky we are here in the north!"

Berown would not rise from the ground, would not even uncurl his arms and legs to let himself be carried easily, and in the end they had to bring a litter to transport him to Kata's tent. Two days and a night she kept him, and when he left her at last, he was a different man, walking silent and slow and slope-shouldered, as if he carried a heavy rock on his back. He was no longer interested in weapons practice. Instead, he spent his days in camp doing simple tasks for the cooks, carrying water, fetching fuel. He avoided Alaric, but if by chance the two of them met, his eyes did not linger, and they were dull.

"She has soothed his soul," Simir told the minstrel.

Alaric nodded. "But at what price?"

"You're concerned, my son?"

"He was a leader once, even if his people were ragged and starving. Now he has nothing, perhaps not even himself. I pity him, Simir. Don't you?"

"He tried to kill you."

"Even so."

Simir smiled. "I do pity him. He's lived a tragic time. Will you make a song of him?"

"I don't know. I'm not in the mood for tragic times just now."

He could not remember being happier—not, at least, since his childhood with his teacher Dall. The endless trek north beneath the bright summer sky, the long pale evenings of song and laughter, the nights with Zavia in his arms—he could not think of what more he might ask of life. And since learning his secret, the nomads looked at him with new respect, new fascination, new friendship.

He thought nothing of it when a woman who had served him a few meals, a woman of middle years, a trifle plump but still handsome enough, caught his arm one evening and whispered an invitation in his ear. A minstrel grew accustomed to such invitations; the lure of the stranger was strong, and a good voice, charm, and youth enhanced it. He smiled at her but shook his head. Zavia, he said, was enough for him.

Some nights later, a second woman asked, and later still, a third. It was the third who told him bluntly what she wanted of him: not his body for its own sake, but his magic for her hunter husband. As Kata could give a man hunting magic, so—she thought—could Alaric transmit his power to a man through her.

"I'm sorry," he told her, "but this power is mine alone; I have no way of passing it to someone else."

She went away disappointed, but her disappointment did not keep other women from asking for their own husbands. Nearly every night, he had to give the same answer to someone else. Knowing magic as they did, he realized, they could not believe that he might be unable to grant their wish.

"Yes, a male witch could have his pick of the women, once each at least," Simir said when Alaric told him about the invitations. "It might be a pleasant time, as well as a duty."

"But how can I make them believe that it won't help them?"

And Simir smiled and said, "Perhaps you can't."

Alaric knew that Zavia had noticed the whisperings, but she said nothing; indeed, she smiled more broadly when he came away from them, and she linked her arm in his as soon as he was beside her.

Kata was the one who called him to account.

"So we have a new witch practicing among us," she said when he had entered her spice-scented tent after a peremptory summons. There was a glint in her eye at odds with her usual cool expression, and not a pleasant glint. "I hear you're much in demand, my Alaric."

He looked down at the carpet. "They may demand, lady, but I have nothing to give. Perhaps . . . you could explain that to them; they don't seem to believe me."

"Why should they? It was a pretty display you put on, with your sword and your nimbleness. How could it fail to impress them? Now they ask of you what they would ask of any witch."

Alaric shook his head. "Lady, I meant only to save my life."

"You could have accomplished *that* by vanishing and never returning."

He looked up sharply. "No. That would have saved my skin, but not the life I've found here in the north."

"And what life would that be, my Alaric?" Her cold, pale eyes narrowed. "Not the minstrel's life, no, not anymore. Your name is in every mouth, but not as a minstrel. They speak of you as they speak of me, as if we two were equals. As if this paltry power you were born with could be as great as the wisdom I have spent my life uncovering.'' Her voice deepened, became almost harsh. "And yet, my Alaric, I hold you"—she raised a hand toward him, empty palm upward, and she closed the fingers tight on that emptiness—"here.''

For a moment, he could not tear his gaze from her fist. The smell of sweet spice seemed to swirl about him, and he felt, for just an instant, that he had shrunk to a mite and was standing inside those caging fingers, struggling. Then he shook himself and realized that she had dropped her hand, and he lifted his eyes to hers. "What can I do, lady? I've told them. . . .''

"Then you must show them.''

"In what way could I—''

"You must serve me on my next journey to the Great Waste. You must carry my goods and obey my orders and put my life before your own. Only so will they understand that you are no better than they.''

"The Great Waste?''

"You wished to visit the Northern Sea, did you not? We'll pass it on our way.''

"Pass it? In the south, they say the Northern Sea is the end of the world.''

"They are fools in the south.'' Then a slight smile curved her lips. "Or perhaps not such fools after all, for it is not *this* world that lies beyond, but a different one.''

"Different? In what way, different?''

"That, only those who have gone there know. Well?''

Alaric bowed to her. There was only one possible answer. "I am yours to command, lady. If you wish it, I'll go.''

"The journey is hard and dangerous.''

"I've known hardship and danger before.''

"You think your witch's power will protect you. But you must swear to me that you will not use it.''

"Lady—''

"You must swear. We go to gather magic on this journey, and it must be done properly. Using your power may destroy what we seek; we dare not chance it. I know what the journey requires; all else, we leave behind. I will protect you, my Alaric. Look to me, and you will be safe.''

He hesitated. Not to use his power, to face danger exactly as other people did—that was a hard promise to keep. He had made it to himself often enough, as he tried to pass for an ordinary man, and broken it again and again. He wasn't sure he *could* keep it, for his instincts, his reflexes seemed beyond the control of his will, preserving him when conscious thought would have been too slow. And yet he saw that this time he must keep it, must obey Kata in every particular, or lose her goodwill forever. ''How many others go with you?''

''Four, all men who have made the trip before.''

''And how long will you be gone?''

''We return before the first snow flies.''

''A long journey, then.''

''Farther than back to the mountains. But summer is short here in the north, and the first snow comes sooner than you might think. Well, my Alaric, will you come, or are you too much afraid of doing without your magic?''

He took a deep breath. ''I *am* afraid,'' he said. ''But I am curious, too. I would see this different world you speak of. Perhaps there's a song or two in it. When do we leave?''

''As soon as supplies can be made ready.''

Simir's face showed his displeasure at the news of the minstrel's coming departure, but he said nothing. Instead, he ordered one of his own deer slaughtered and the meat smoke-dried for the journey. And he gave Alaric his best fur cloak to take along, ''Because I have been to the Waste, and I know how cold the nights are.''

Zavia was furious, though she only showed that fury when they were alone in her tent: and even there she kept her voice low, whispering her anger, for her mother was near enough to hear a shout. ''What have I done to her?'' she demanded. She sat on her heels, with both fists raised to the blank wall beyond which her mother's tent was pitched. ''Why must she take you away from me?''

''I doubt she was thinking of you, my Zavia,'' Alaric murmured.

''She never thinks of me! I don't mean anything to her,

I'm just a servant. Her own daughter, her heir, but my happiness is meaningless.''

He put his arms around her. "Dear Zavia, we won't be gone very long.''

She looked into his eyes, and her own were wide and wild, like some mountain cat's. "I won't let you go. I won't!''

He shook his head. "This is important to her. She must be sure of me. I don't want her to look on me as a rival.''

"Why not? A little competition might do her good. She's been the most important person in the north long enough!''

He smiled and kissed her cheek. "You're the one who'll be her competition someday. You have the fire for it. But I am just a minstrel.'' And when she would have answered that, he set two hushing fingers against her lips. "No, don't say I'm more. I won't be more.'' He kissed her again. "And I'll have peace between myself and your mother so that you and I can be happy.''

She clung to him. "You'll be careful, won't you? I've heard stories about the Waste. They say the rocks reach out and seize you as you pass. They say the very ground can open and swallow you up.''

"I'll be careful. After all, I value myself even more than you do.''

"That can't be possible,'' she said fiercely.

When the meat was dried nearly as hard as wood, Kata's small company made ready to leave the band. The four who had made the journey with her before were strong men, hunters all. The youngest, Grem, was nearly old enough to be Alaric's father; the others, Lanri, Velet, and Oltavin, had grandchildren already. None bore sole responsibility for a family, in case, Kata said, they never came back.

They had two tents among them, one for the men and a smaller one for Kata alone—special tents, marked on their sides and roofs with the symbol of the Pole Star, guardian of their journey. These, and food and hooded furs and the many well-wrapped bundles that belonged to Kata, were enough to load all of their riding deer and three pack animals besides. They were leaving behind all metal save for their short knives, the men even trading their fine barbed hunting arrows for stone-tipped shafts fashioned by Kata herself; metal, Grem said, could not be trusted in the far north. And though it was not metal save for its strings, Alaric had to leave the lute behind as well, for Kata insisted there would be neither time nor strength for song on their journey. He doubted that, but he said nothing, understanding that she would be jealous of everything about him on this trip, everything that might detract, however little, from her own importance.

They set out just past noon, when the band had stopped for the day and the midday meal was finished. Once more, as when Simir himself had ridden south, the nomads clustered to bid farewell to their far travelers. But this time there was cheer among them, loud good wishes for a swift journey, and kisses for the men. And this time it was Alaric who was leaving, and Simir and Zavia who walked out onto the plain after him as if they would follow. He saw them still standing there every time he turned to wave, and he turned a dozen times and more, till they had dwindled to a pair of dots on the landscape, and he could no longer make out their lifted arms. Only then did the last small pang in his heart give way to a buoyant curiosity as he set his eyes firmly on the north.

They rode silent and steady, the six of them, with Kata in the lead. They rode through the whole long summer day, eating their dried meat on deer-back, stopping only for water and to answer nature's calls, and by dusk they had traveled farther than in three or four days of nomad wandering. After tethering their deer by long ropes that would let the animals graze, they set up their tents, their two tiny shelters upon that vast rolling plain of grass; they did not bother making a fire. But before they curled up to sleep the brief darkness away, Kata made them all bow to the north, and she took off the large brooch she had donned for the journey, a brooch with the symbol of the Pole Star worked in gold wire within its circle, and she held it out to the sky as they bowed, as if offering it to the first faint glimmer of its namesake.

The next day they set off at dawn and rode till twilight, and the next, and the next, and the next, and soon the days began to blend together for Alaric. One stretch of rolling plain seemed like another, one meandering watercourse, with its accompanying double file of trees, twin to the last. And yet one day—it might have been ten days after they left the band, or eleven—they crossed a stream where the trees were unusually short. That was also the day Alaric realized that, bright and hot as the summer sun might be, the wind—when it blew from the north—was chill. At the next stream, the trees were not merely short, but sparse and weirdly stunted, their trunks growing sideways, almost hard against the ground, their boughs gnarled and twisted, like thick, exposed roots with a scanty covering of leafy twigs. If Grem had not told him these strange plants were trees, Alaric would scarcely have guessed it.

"And that's the last of them," Grem said, and it was true. Beyond, the river made a long, sweeping northward curve, and its banks were open, covered with short grass, wild flowers, and herbs; there was not a tree in sight to the horizon.

The plain grew boggy after that, and the grass thinned, exposing great open patches of sandy soil, ridges of gravel, and boulders marked by growing things as if by daubs of paint. A thousand ponds dotted the landscape, and by night the wind from the north, blowing ever stronger, ever colder, would rime them with ice. The daylight that thawed the ice now lasted longer than Alaric could ever remember, the sun easing to its rest at such a shallow angle to the horizon that it seemed reluctant to leave the sky; and in its wake, twilight seemed nearly endless. The travelers began camping before sunset and sleeping well past dawn, else they would have been too tired to ride through the day.

At last, mountains appeared in the distance.

Kata called a halt as soon as the peaks were plain to see—jagged peaks, steep and dark and forbidding, stretching far to the east and west, like a vast line of spears draped loosely with black canvas.

"This is the first magical region on our journey," she said to Alaric. "Be sure your knife is well secured."

He glanced down at the blade, which sat firmly in its sheath, as always. But that was not enough for Kata. She motioned to Grem, who helped Alaric lash it fast with thongs so that he could not draw it without untying them. Grem's own knife was already bound in the same fashion.

"Don't try to use it till I give you leave," Kata said.

"Is this the place where metal can't be trusted?" Alaric asked.

She nodded. Then, reaching into the bundle that hung behind her right leg, she pulled out a small metal box. It was a cunningly made container, a trifle larger than her fingers could span, its sides polished mirror-bright, its top chased with the symbol of the Pole Star. Tilting back the lid revealed that the metal walls were thick, leaving only a tiny space inside, which, save for a lining of dark velvet, was empty. Kata unpinned the brooch she wore upon her bosom, set it in the velvet, and shut the lid over it. Then she slipped the box into its bundle.

"Is gold even less trustworthy than steel?" Alaric wondered.

She cast him a cold glance. "The Pole Star looks after its own," she said. "Be it metal or flesh." Then she gave him a longer look. "Perhaps we would both do well to remember that."

He smiled slightly, thinking of the symbols on their tents. "I remember it every night."

At his smile, her lips had tightened, but she said no more, only raised her arm to signal the resumption of their journey.

The mountains looked high at first, and very far away, but Alaric soon realized that was just an illusion. Rugged they were, as if some enormous ax had hewn them out, but they were neither distant nor lofty. They were, in fact, mountains in miniature; he had seen man-built towers taller, and castle keeps with as much girth. He and his companions rode like giants through the narrow passes, and they could have shot their arrows over the peaks.

But the strangest aspect of those mountains was not their size, but their particular form. They were barren, with not a tuft of grass, not a leaf, clinging to their slopes; and everywhere the naked rocks were split and broken into countless points and serrations, like myriad fingers reaching for the sky. Streaked with shades of red and rust and brown and a steely gray so dark it was almost black, those stony ramparts showed a single texture everywhere, a striated surface, a grain that looked almost to be carved upon them by a sculptor's tool. And all the striations, all the shards and all the ridges, were precisely aligned, all of them tilted from the vertical, so that the whole range of miniature mountains was tipped to the south, bristling toward the travelers like an irregular palisade of sharpened stakes.

Alaric rode through them wide-eyed and wondering, and once he brushed so close to an outcropping that he could not resist reaching out to touch it. He caught at a needlelike shard, intending to break it off, but fragile though it seemed, it would not come loose. Then Grem, riding behind him, called to him to leave it be, and Kata turned and said the same, but sharper.

"This magic we don't take away with us," she told him.

"Is it magic?" he wondered. "Yes, if there is any true magic in the world, it must be here. But of what sort?"

Kata's mouth made the smallest of smiles. "There is more true magic in the world than you can guess, my Alaric, and this is the least of it." From one of her bundles, she drew an arrow, not a stone-tipped one, but one of the ordinary arrows the nomads made, with a point of steel. She tossed the shaft to Lanri, saying, "Here, show him the faithlessness of metal."

Lanri fitted the arrow to his bow and, pointing to a spot of reddish stone, an easy target not far off, loosed it. But the shaft never reached its goal; instead, it swerved in midflight and struck dark stone much nearer. Struck and clung to the rock face as if glued there, barbed tip and shaft both hard against the stone and nearly horizontal.

Alaric rode up to the arrow and, wrapping his fingers about the shaft, gave it a sharp tug. But all his strength merely cracked the wood just behind the barbs; the steel tip was caught fast, though nothing visible was holding it.

"Lodestone," said Alaric. He turned to the others. "Are all these mountains lodestones?"

"So you know something of lodestones, do you?" Kata said, the smile gone from her lips.

"I've seen small ones that would fit in my hand. Children's toys, they are in the south. Except in one place, where a man I met once, who called himself a witch, ground them up and used them for spell casting."

"Spell casting?" She leaned forward between her deer's antlers. "What sort of spell casting?"

"Several different sorts." He shrugged. "But as far as I could see, none of them ever came to anything, except in his mind."

She straightened abruptly. "Bah. The witches of the south are fools."

"I've long thought that, lady."

"We have the true magic here in the north, my Alaric. Don't think otherwise. These"—she waved to encompass all the harsh, low mountains—"these are the guardians of that magic. Beyond lies a land such as you have never dreamed."

"I look forward to it."

Her frown was as small as her smile. "It pleases me," she said, "that you are not afraid."

He bowed to her.

They passed through the miniature mountains in a single long day's ride, but beyond, at least for a time, lay no strange and frightening land but merely more of the boggy plain. When the mountains were well behind them, Kata brought out her brooch once more, offering it with open hands to the north before fastening it to her jerkin. Then the long dull journey resumed, interrupted only by sleep and, once, by Grem's deer getting stuck in a muddy pond.

Alaric scarcely noticed the whiteness in the distance. He thought it was a cloud bank, like so many others in the pale northern sky. But he noticed the wind, which was now bitter by night, and so chill even during the day that the travelers had begun to wear their furs. He did not think of the whiteness as a source of that cold, even though it loomed larger ahead of them day by day, never moving, as if waiting for them. Only when they were almost upon it did he realize that the whiteness was an enormous wall of ice.

Higher than the lodestone mountains, higher than any

human-built rampart, the wall swept eastward to the limit
of vision. Its face was a slope of icy rubble, of tumbled,
broken blocks as big as a peasant's hut, part melted by
the summer sun and refrozen by the cold wind into fan-
tastical shapes. To the west, the barrier thrust abruptly
into a great gray sea whose steep and rugged verge then
angled away southwestwardly; and upon that sullen surface floated fallen icy chunks of every size, like gobbets
of bread in a vast dish of soup. As the travelers watched,
standing a hundred paces back from the shore, a huge
white slab broke free of the wall of ice and slid with a
great thundering crash into the water, raising a wave that
washed up almost to their feet.

"The Northern Sea," said Kata. "Well, my Alaric,
your wish is granted at last."

He looked up, up at the white barrier. "There is no
song to describe this, lady. No minstrel has ever seen this
sight. Or none that thought anyone would believe him."
He glanced sidelong at her. "Do we turn east now?"

"No," she said, and she pointed to the broken face of
the wall. "We climb."

Only five of them went, with furs wrapped snug about
them, and no baggage but some coils of rope. Had Alaric
not given his promise, he would have flashed to the top
of that icy rampart in a heartbeat. Still, it was not a bad
climb, not after Kata had lashed wooden cleats to their
boots and passed around tent pegs to be hammered into
the ice for support. The surface was well compacted,
almost as firm underfoot as stone and soil, and in most
places no more treacherous than many a mountain slope.
Only where meltwater had gathered in a hollow or spread
in a thin layer across some level space was there real
danger of slipping; but Lanri, in the lead, warned of every
such place, and they reached their goal with nothing
worse to show for the climb than a few bruised shins.

Atop the wall, Alaric found himself at the edge of a
new world. To the south stretched the pond-dotted plain,
to the west the ice-scattered sea; and to the north the ice
beneath his feet was the beginning of a landscape flatter
than any grassland, and of a white so intense, so brilliant
beneath the afternoon sun, that it pained the eyes to look
upon. The wall had been no barrier to the farther north

at all; rather, it *was* the farther north, with not a blade of grass, not a flower, on its bosom to the horizon.

"The Great Waste," said Kata, encompassing it with a hand.

Oltavin had stayed below with the supplies; now the others tied their ropes end to end and let the line down so that he could send packs up to them for the final leg of their journey. He would be remaining behind, where the deer could graze, while they continued north.

Well prepared for this new world, Kata had stiff muslin masks, darkly translucent, to shield their eyes against the glare; and strange wooden hoops, webbed with thongs, to lash to their boots for walking across the crusty frozen surface. Alaric was grateful for the mask, less so for the new footgear; the hoops tripped him again and again before he learned the knack of widening his stride to accommodate them. It seemed a tiring way to walk, till he tried without them and found himself sinking ankle-deep into the treacherous surface, or turning a foot painfully against unexpected solidity. Tiring, too, was the heavy pack he carried; and now he was glad that Kata had made him leave the lute behind, because he knew, as much as he loved that instrument, he would have begrudged its extra burden.

They walked late that day, later than they had ever ridden on their deer, Alaric thought, though he could only gauge the time by the exhaustion in his legs. Darkness no longer marked an end to the day; the sun, after sinking and sinking toward the ice, barely touched the horizon and then began to rise again, as if repelled by the cold. The travelers stopped at last, set up their tents, and slept till Kata woke them; and the sun stood high and bright for the beginning of their next march. Thereafter, it was always above the horizon, riding an enormous circular path in the sky; and it seemed to Alaric that on the Great Waste, he and his companions were walking, sleeping, walking on, all in a single endless day.

Kata led the way steadily northward. Most people, Alaric knew, would have lost all sense of direction by now, with no stars to guide them, and the sun behaving so strangely, and not a landmark anywhere. He had not; his sense of direction did not depend on external guideposts, but on an instinctive awareness of his own movements, of every step, every turn, every measure traversed in his special way; it was of a piece with his witch's power, born to him. For a time, he thought Kata must have it, too, and then, walking close beside her, he watched her hold her brooch out to the north . . . and he saw what had escaped him till now. At the touch of her thumb, a tiny post thrust up from the center of the ornament, bringing with it a flattened needle that had been resting nearly invisible upon the device of the Pole Star. Pierced midway along its length by the post, the needle swung freely on that pivot, and no matter how Kata turned the brooch, the needle's point always bore to the north.

She noticed him staring at it, or at least noticed his mask turned in the direction of her hand. "Do you think you can read this better than I, minstrel?" she said sharply.

He shook his head. "I would not presume so, lady, since I've never seen its like before. But tell me, does it point north permanently, or is there some way to change its bearing?"

She curled her fingers about the brooch. "Have they no north-seeking needles where you come from?"

"I've seen none. Of course, I am only a minstrel, and there are many things I do not know. Still, a contrivance like that would be useful to travelers, and I've met many a traveler in my time, and none that carried one."

At a flick of her thumb, the needle sank back flush with the gold device. She refastened the brooch to her bosom. "So they know lodestones in the south, but not the needle that seeks the Pole Star." Her mouth curved with the faintest hint of contempt. "This is the most ancient of magic, my Alaric—from the morning of the world. Who does not know *this*, knows nothing. Small wonder you never believed in any magic but your own."

Alaric would have shrugged, had his pack not been so heavy. "I believe in the evidence of my eyes, lady. And they have seen much fakery among those who call themselves magicians and witches."

She nodded slightly. "Turning water to wine, I suppose, and plucking small animals from empty bowls. Meaningless tricks to awe the gullible into buying useless potions. Oh yes, I know something of the fools in the south.'' She turned her face to him. ''It would seem they have lost all the important knowledge of the past. The knowledge that we of the north still cherish, of the *real* power that lies all around us, like a net encompassing the world. And perhaps that is only proper, for that power issues from the north itself, and is strongest where the Pole Star's rule is strongest; and so who should be more worthy of it than the people who call that place their home?'' She looked away from him then, back to the icy way that stretched before them. ''A true witch spends a lifetime learning to use that power, and believe me, few have the ability, and fewer the patience. Yet the reward for ability and patience is great, my Alaric: the power of life and death, the power that chooses between sickness and health, between the full belly and starvation, between the storm and the calm—that is the real magic the world offers us. That is *my* magic. You had the merest taste of it, once.''

Softly, he said, ''I remember.'' And at that memory, he felt a momentary dizziness, almost as if he were back in her tent, enveloped by smoke. He blinked hard, and the feeling passed. ''I don't doubt your power, lady.''

''You don't know my power, minstrel.''

''Then I must judge it by the respect your people have for you. By which measure, it must be great indeed.''

Her mask barely tilted toward him. ''You have a flattering tongue, Alaric. It comes of depending on strangers for your meat. But leave off with me; words will not win you my favor.''

Alaric smiled a little. ''I had hopes that these many days I've ridden and walked in your service, and these many nights I've shivered, might count somewhat toward that end.''

''You have done your duty,'' she said.

He sighed. *Well,* he thought, *at least I've done the work of a good pack-deer.*

And he also thought: *I am a stranger, I must not judge what I haven't seen.* She had potent potions, that was true enough, and smoke that befuddled a man, and a presence to cow the bravest warrior. She had power, there was no denying it. But he could not help wondering if her claims might not exceed her abilities, if she might not be using her own rather potent tricks to awe the less gullible folk of the north.

He especially wondered, just now, about her ability to control the weather. For a storm was rising.

The wind came first, blowing from the north, as usual, but colder than ever, and stronger, biting deep into unprotected cheeks, penetrating furs and leather to raise gooseflesh. And with that cold wind came clouds running like sheep before the wolf: swiftly they cloaked the sky, transforming the bright and endless day to sullen twilight. The snow arrived before the travelers had finished setting up their tents—tiny flakes gusting before the wind, stinging exposed flesh like needles, and swirling and swooping as if reluctant to touch the ground. Alaric was the last man inside the larger tent, his furs thickly dusted with white motes; and as he laced the entry flaps, he saw through their narrow gap that Kata had not gone into her own shelter at all, but was still standing out in the storm, her arms raised to the sky.

In the darkness of their tent, Alaric and the other men held fast to the bottom edges of its leathern walls, to give them extra anchorage against the storm. The wind grew wilder and began to howl an eerie, high-pitched note. Intermittently, it shook the shelter as a dog might shake a rat, and more than once it found an entry, beneath a flap or at a seam, and sent a spray of snow-laden air to chill the space that had been warmed by their bodies and breath.

But for all its force, the storm was short-lived in the end, the last tatters of clouds blowing away before the sun had made an eighth part of its circuit in the sky. Though a mountain of snow seemed to have tumbled from those clouds, little of it was left behind, except for the shallow drift against the northern wall of each tent; the rest had been scoured away by the wind, scattered upon the vast flat whiteness of the ice. A summer storm, the nomad men said as they emerged from their shelter— nothing to be concerned about. Yet each of them touched one of the tent's Pole Star symbols as he spoke, and when Kata came out of her own tent, they bowed to her and

thanked her, as if she had been responsible for the storm
being so brief and mild.

Alaric thanked her, too. It seemed the proper thing to
do.

But it made her look at him long and searchingly before she ordered the march to resume.

It was the day after the storm—they had slept, at any
rate, in the interim—that one of Zavia's fears came true.

They had been walking as they often did, Kata in front,
the rest strung out at irregular intervals behind her. In
this case, Alaric was the one who trailed the group. There
was no special reason for him to lag behind—he had done
it often enough. There was no reason, either, for him to
lift his eyes above the heels of the man ahead, for he
knew there was nothing to see in any direction but the
flat white landscape. And so, when he heard a strange
creaking sound, as of a rusty hinge being forced, and
when the man he followed stopped suddenly and gave a
wild cry, he did not know what had happened.

He looked up and saw the flat white landscape. He saw
Lanri and Velet, three and four paces ahead of him. He
saw Kata, just turning back to face them.

Grem, who had walked behind her, was gone.

He took two quick steps forward, and Lanri's arm shot
out to halt him. It was then that he saw the crack in the
ice between the three of them and Kata.

From within the crack came Grem's voice, shouting for
help, echoing, as if from far away.

"Don't go near!" Kata called. Shedding her webbed
footgear, she lay down on the ice spread-eagled and
crawled to the lip of the opening. It was a man-height
wide and so long that its ends were invisible with distance. She looked down into it, then shook her head and
eased away from the edge. "We can't help him," she
said, rising to her feet and dusting a thin film of snow
from her clothing. "We'll have to look for a narrow place
where you can cross."

From within the crack came another shout, higher
pitched than before, more desperate.

Alaric pulled off his thong-meshed hoops and squirmed
to the edge of the crack, ignoring Kata's sharp "Stay

back!'' The opening was deep and heavily shadowed; he could see no bottom. But he could hear Grem clearly. And the sound of splashing water.

"Can you see me!'' he shouted, waving one arm as far over the chasm as he dared.

"Yes, yes, yes!'' called Grem.

"We must get him out!'' Alaric said.

"No!'' cried Kata. "He is lost.''

"We have the rope. Toss it down to him. There are three of us here to anchor it.'' He turned to Lanri. "You have the rope.''

Lanri glanced at Kata, then back at Alaric.

"It won't be long enough,'' said Kata. "These cracks are deep. And the freezing water brings death quickly. Get back from the edge before you fall in, too.''

"We have to try,'' said Alaric. "We can't just leave him here to die!'' He wrenched at Lanri's pack. "You won't stand by and do nothing, will you?''

"He is lost!'' shouted Kata.

Lanri hesitated just another moment, then he began to uncoil the rope. Quickly, he and Velet and Alaric each took a turn of it about their prone bodies and dropped the free end down into the crack. It was the same line that had raised their supplies to the top of the ice, and more than half of it seemed to disappear into the shadows in the crevasse.

"Grem, can you see the rope?'' called Alaric.

There was no answer.

"Grem!''

"He's lost,'' said Kata.

"Or injured, unable to catch hold of it. Grem!''

The voice was fainter than before. But the words were still clear: "Help me.''

"One of us will have to go down,'' said Alaric. He looked at Kata. "I believe I'm the lightest.''

"No!''

"You'd want me to do it if you were down there!''

She showed her teeth at that, but said nothing.

"I'll hold him fast,'' he said to Lanri and Velet. "Pull us up as quick as you can.''

Lanri nodded.

Alaric slipped out of his pack and threw off his mittens

and furs. The air was sharply cold, but he scarcely noticed it; he was sweating. He reeled the rope in, knotted
a loop in the end, and pulled it tight under his armpits.
He cast Kata one final glance. "Remember," he said,
"you made me promise. That means there's no other
way."

She said nothing.

As they lowered him into the shadowed depths of the
crack, he pulled his muslin mask down. Without it, the
shadows were not so dark as he had thought; rather, they
were blue with light filtering through the ice. To either
side, the walls were sheer, and they glittered here and
there, as if scattered with gemstones. Below, in the deepest light of all, he could just make out where ice and
water met, and the water was black as pitch. Of Grem,
he saw nothing.

When his descent finally halted, he hung in air, his
heels dangling just above the dark water. "Grem!" he
shouted, and the name echoed all around him. "Grem!"

A moment later, a splash answered him, and Grem's
head broke the surface. The man coughed and choked
and made wordless noises as he flailed weakly at the water.

"More rope!" Alaric shouted. "Just a little!"

In response, he was eased downward till his ankles
were submerged, then his knees. The water was bitterly
cold; he could feel it seeping into his boots, and it burned
his feet like fire. He grabbed for Grem, caught the man's
fur wrapping, and pulled with all his strength. Grem was
heavy, his clothing waterlogged. He clutched at Alaric,
at his arms at first, and the rope, and then, when his grip
slipped, at the minstrel's legs. Alaric tried to peel the
furs away and lighten the load, but the thongs that held
them were knotted tight with water and ice, and would
not yield. He locked his legs about Grem then, and
shouted to be lifted upward, hoping that the weight would
not be too much for the two stout men above.

Slowly, jerkily, he rose from the water. His knees were
clear. His ankles. His feet. And then, of a sudden, the
weight on his legs was too much, and the loop of rope
could not hold him—he was ripped down through it, arms
snapped upward beside his ears, and he was in the water,

deep, deep, and his mouth was full of its freezing salty taste.

The cold bit to his marrow, seemed to turn his eyes, his blood, his very heart to ice. His limbs went numb, and he knew he was sinking fast. But Grem was beneath him. He willed his arms to clutch the man, willed his senseless fingers to press into those impossibly heavy furs. They sank together, and dizziness assailed him as he felt rather than saw the yawning darkness below.

And a heartbeat later, the two of them were falling through air, falling for a long, long moment, as from the high branches of a tree, and then they struck an unyielding surface, and it knocked the breath from Alaric's lungs and the water from his throat.

Gasping hoarsely, he lay with his cheek against the ice. He was not cold; he was past that. He felt nothing but an all-encompassing languor; he knew he was too weak to move, too weak even to open his eyes. Vaguely, he heard someone speaking, but the sound was muffled, distant. Then hands were lifting him, shaking him, stripping his clothing away and chafing him all over, and wrapping him in something. He opened his eyes at last but was blinded by whiteness and closed them again. Finally, it seemed a very long time later, hands moved him again, and he saw the grayness of his eyelids darken, and he knew he was inside a tent.

Someone slapped his face. And again.

He opened his eyes. A thin line of light showed where the entry flap had been loosely laced, and it was bright enough to show the tent's interior. Velet and Lanri crouched over him, Lanri's hand raised for another blow. Alaric pulled his own hand free of its enveloping furs and caught the other's before it could strike again.

"Kata said to slap you till you woke," Lanri said in an apologetic tone.

"I'm all right," Alaric whispered, sitting up, clutching the furs about him. The languor and the numbness were passing, and now he began to shiver violently. He curled up inside the furs, knees against his chest. His teeth clacked together so hard that he could scarcely speak. With some effort, he managed to say, "How is Grem?"

"Grem is dead. Come, she said you should exercise, if you could."

"Dead? Are you sure?"

"Sure as I'm here with you." Through the furs, he gripped Alaric's arm. "Come, minstrel, we mustn't lose you, too."

With assistance from both of them, Alaric managed to don dry clothing in spite of the shivering that kept his fingers from working properly. Then Velet went out while Lanri helped him to his feet and steadied him. He could stand in the tent, if he stooped a little, and with only two of them inside, there was room for him to thrash his arms and legs till the blood seemed to thaw in his veins and the shivering subsided.

"I'm all right," he said again, firmly this time, and he gathered his furs right about him and pushed past Lanri to go outside.

The other tent was up, too, a short distance away, and Velet was pacing back and forth beside it, three steps each way. As Alaric approached, he cast him a questioning glance, and Alaric nodded, not knowing the question and not bothering to ask. At the entry to Kata's small shelter, which was laced tightly shut, he called her name.

The laces slipped from their eyelets, and the flap opened a bit to show a sliver of Kata's face. "You," she said. "Not dead, I see. And still here." She twitched the flap aside. "Come in."

Inside, illuminated by a tiny oil lamp, and enveloped by the sweet smoke that spiralled outward from that flame, lay Grem. He was covered to the neck with a fur, and above it, his face was a pale, sickly color, and his eyes were open, staring at nothing.

"You see," Kata said, "he was lost. You risked yourself for nothing. And you used your power for nothing. Even though you promised."

Alaric knelt by the man and touched his cheek; it was cold as winter-chilled leather. He licked the back of his hand and held it beneath Grem's nose and felt not the slightest breath of air. He laid his fingers against Grem's neck, where the vein of a living person would beat strong, and there was nothing.

"Oh yes, he's dead," said Kata. "And now get out and I will raise him to life again. Get out!"

Outside, he stopped the pacing Velet. "Can she really do it?" he asked.

"Sometimes," was the answer.

The sun made two complete circles of the sky while the two nomad men and Alaric waited for Kata to come out of her tent. Two complete circles while they paced the ice or huddled together in their own shelter or tried to sleep. They stayed well away from the crevasse. And they watched the ice beneath their feet quite a lot, and jumped at any sudden noise. But no new crack opened.

Finally Kata emerged, and behind her, walking shakily, came Grem.

Alaric stood very still, just staring, while the other two men brushed past him to hug Grem and babble excitedly. Grem smiled wanly; he looked like a man who had been ill for years. Slowly, he raised a trembling hand toward Alaric.

"You saved me," he said, his voice feeble and cracked.

Alaric went to him then, and gripped his hand. "Not I," he said, *"She* saved you." He turned to Kata, whose lips were curving in that tiny superior smile he had seen before. "Lady, you are a marvel. This man was dead, I swear it."

"Yes," she said. She tapped Lanri's arm with the back of her hand. "He must be exercised. But be gentle at first. Now Alaric and I must talk."

He followed her, thinking that she meant to lead him to her tent, but she walked past it before turning back to him.

"So you forgot your promise at the last, my brave Alaric," she said, her voice low and tight. "I knew if there was any excuse for it, you would."

He gave her look for look, his eyes steady. "If you knew, lady, then you should never have asked for that promise."

"I thought possibly, just possibly, you were a man of honor."

"You see no honor in saving a life?"

"You swore to obey me!"

"I don't recall it being quite like that."

"You placed yourself under my command. And then you disobeyed me!"

"There is a higher command, lady, in my heart at least."

Her mouth twisted. "Oh, brave words from the disobedient child! I know you never believed in my magic, no more than in the meaningless tricks of the south. You drank my potions and swooned, but to you it was all the same as a knock on the head. Oh, the south breeds fools! Did I not tell you your magic might ruin this journey? What is the life of one man, compared to the lives of all the people of the north? We gather the magic of survival on this journey, and you would spoil it for the little spark of one man's existence!"

Alaric crossed his arms over his chest. "I would beg your forgiveness, lady, except—what have I spoiled? You have raised the dead. Surely that proves your magic is undamaged. Working together, your magic . . . and mine . . . saved him. We are not at odds."

"You wished to prove me wrong," she said sharply. "And now you have three witnesses to swear you crossed my will and saved the man I said was lost. You think they'll forget this? You think they won't spread the tale when we return? And then what will you be but just as much a witch as before? Oh, you said you yearned to show that you were nothing compared to me, but you lied! What you really want is to sweep us all north with your power and take credit for the whole journey!"

"It would be faster, would it not? All you have to do is point the way—"

She slapped him then, so hard it rocked him back. "Who is master here?" she shouted. "Would you take my place? You ignorant lout!"

He raised a hand to his cheek. He could feel the imprint of her palm there still, and the flesh stung, and the bone and teeth beneath ached. "You are master," he said softly.

"Liar!"

"Lady—"

"You want my place! You show it in everything you do, in every step you take!"

She raised her hand to strike again, but he caught it

this time, and they stood there frozen for a moment, till Alaric opened his own hand and let hers go. Then he stepped back.

"I am not the fool," he said in a hard, cold voice. All his exasperation, and all the days and nights of the long cold journey rose in him like bitter bile. "You see me through a veil of your own devising, lady. You think I want your piddling place here in the north? Your absolute power over this insignificant flock? I could have been a prince in the south. I could have had all the wealth and power I liked, over people who mattered to the world. You saw so clearly that I could not take Simir's place, and you fear so much that I want your own. I am not the fool, lady; no. I am not the one so jealous of her own importance that she is afraid to teach wisdom to her own daughter. I gave myself to you, Kata. But if you wish, I can leave, and you'll never need to fear me again. I can find a soft life in the south, and no jealous witch to make my life miserable. Now we can call a truce, you and I, or I can go this moment. And you can say I ran away from you, if you like. But *you're* the one to choose now, not I. And you're the one to say which is stronger magic— pulling a dead body from the water, or giving it back the spark of life." He clenched his hands at his sides, and he would not allow himself to look away from her face.

She hesitated, staring at him, as if reading the soul behind his eyes. At last, more quietly, she said, "Why didn't you use your witch's power to go down into the crevasse after him?"

"I told you then: I promised. I tried to honor that promise, whatever you may think. At the end, there was no choice."

"He was no special friend of yours."

"He was a comrade on this journey. And a human being."

She was the one to drop her gaze, finally, and then to half turn away from him. "You have nowhere to go in the south," she said.

"No."

"You have stayed among us, in spite of many . . . unfortunate events."

"Yes."

"You really think this is the home you never had."

"I've thought so, sometimes. I would regret leaving it.
But I have left many places before, and I have many regrets; I have the strength to carry another. But not to
joust with you, lady. I'll have no more of that."

"You never feared me."

"I did."

"But not anymore."

"You have great wisdom, and I respect you. Respect
is better, I think, than fear. I would still serve you, lady,
if you would let me. I want to serve the good of the
people of the north, just as you do. How much better it
would be if we worked together."

She looked at him, over one shoulder. "Give me credit
for your successes."

"Lady, you raised the dead, not I. I am a child beside
you."

She smiled then, just a little. "Yes."

"You told me once that I was yours. Use me, and my
power will belong to you. And everyone will know it."

She met his eyes. "Simir would be sorry to see you
gone."

"And your daughter, I think."

"She's of no importance." She held her hand out to
him. "Shall it be a truce, then?"

"With all my heart," said Alaric, and he took her
hand. It was cold, cold as ice, but the grip was firm.

"You belong in the north," said Kata. "I've known
that for some time. I would be wrong to send you away.
You don't believe in the net of power that lies across the
world, but you are part of it just the same. Perhaps you'll
understand that by the time this journey is done." She
let his hand go at last. "I thought you were a coward,
Alaric. But now I know that you were only a child. The
north will nourish you, has nourished you, and you will
become full-grown with us."

He bowed to her.

Kata would not let them stay encamped any longer;
their goal was still too far off to let any more time pass

in idleness. Grem was still weak and unsteady on his feet, so they made him a litter of some pieces of the large tent, and each of the others took one end of a pole for carrying him. Kata and Alaric walked in front. They crossed the crack at the narrow place she had found.

She consulted her north-seeking needle often now, and when Alaric glanced at it, he noticed that the needle sometimes quivered from side to side, as if unsure of the north. Kata said that was a good sign.

A few sleeps later, Grem was walking for part of each trek, tramping beside Alaric, saying with a grin that he wanted to be near help in case anything happened to him again. Soon enough, there was no more need for the litter at all, and Grem resumed his share of their common goods.

By then, Kata's needle was quivering constantly, like a palsied finger. By then, too, Alaric was beginning to feel ill.

He said nothing to the others. He had been sick before, with coughs or mild fevers. This ailment seemed familiar enough in its symptoms, mainly a slight dizziness that came and went, that was strongest when he was tired. He thought it must be caused by the long, cold marches, or perhaps it was an aftermath of his dunking. Sometimes he felt almost queasy enough to vomit, but he fought it down. They had already suffered a delay, and he knew that Kata was anxious to keep moving.

But one day he drank too much water at one draft, and he did vomit, miserably and painfully; and once the vomiting began, he could not control it but spewed again and again; and when his stomach was empty, it continued to knot itself up, as if trying to turn his whole body inside out. Grem and Kata caught his arms and supported him while the spasms racked him, and when he was finished at last, and exhausted, they eased him to the ice, and Kata swept his mask off to look into his face.

"Pale," she said. "I should have seen it before this."

"Sorry," Alaric whispered.

She took his water bottle, sniffed its contents, tasted. All of their water was ice chipped free of the whiteness underfoot and then melted in bottles carried under their furs; she pronounced his drinkable. She tasted the dried meat in his pack and found it adequate. Then she bared her right hand, warmed it inside her clothing, and slid it into his hood to touch the back of his neck.

"No fever," she said. "How do you feel now?"

He swallowed thickly. "Thirsty."

She shook her head. "No water for now. It might bring back the vomiting. Does your belly hurt?"

"An ache here, from the vomiting." He touched his side.

"Was that there before?"

"No."

"And your head?"

"I'm . . . dizzy. Have been, a little, for a while."

"No pain?"

"No."

She stared at his eyes a moment, then prodded his middle with both hands. "Does this hurt?"

"No. I'm all right. It's nothing. Maybe the grease in the meat. It's a bit rancid. But I'm all right now. I can go on."

"You're sure?"

"Yes."

She and Grem helped him up.

"Still dizzy?" she asked.

"A little. But I can walk. We shouldn't waste time standing here."

"True enough." She gave him one last look, then said, "Grem, take his arm."

"I'm all right," said Alaric.

"Take his arm. Now let's go on."

In spite of his protests, Alaric found Grem's arm useful. He felt weak from the vomiting, and unsteady, and the hoops on his feet were suddenly much more difficult to walk with. And though he felt stronger soon and, at Kata's instructions, ate a small amount of meat and drank a few sips of water, the dizziness did not pass.

When they camped that night, Kata called him into her tent.

"It's nothing," he said. "It will pass. Probably when I wake tomorrow, I'll be fine."

She felt of his forehead and the back of his neck, of the sides of his throat and the area beneath his jaw. By the dim light of her lamp, she looked into his mouth. Again, she prodded his belly. Then she shook her head. "This is no ordinary illness." She unpinned the brooch and held the quivering needle in front of his face. "This is yourself, my Alaric. Small wonder your head is dizzy."

He frowned. "I don't know what you mean."

"Did I not say that you were part of the net of power that lies across the world? This needle traces its lines and bows to their sources. But those sources dance, my Alaric; they dance so fast that, were they visible, no human eye would see more than a blur. From far away, the dance seems small, and the needle doesn't notice it; but we are close to them, and the needle quivers because it cannot keep up. Just so are you quivering, my Alaric."

He shook his head, though that made him dizzier. "I am not a needle."

"No? Then the dizziness will pass. But I think it will not, until the dance halts. And it *will* halt, for that place and time is the goal of this journey. And that will be a good test of my surmise about you."

He smiled wanly. "Will it be soon?"

"Yes, soon. But until then, I have something that will help you." She reached into her pack and drew out a leather flask. "Give me your water bottle." When she had it open in her hands, she poured some powder from the flask into the bottle, capped it, and shook it hard. "Drink this when you're thirsty, a mouthful or two at a time. And when you refill it, I'll give you more. It will control the vomiting."

"And the dizziness?"

"Perhaps. But I think you would do well to hold fast to Grem, and not to think about your head too much. Now you'll need rest. Go to the others and tell them that it is time to use the wheel lamp."

"Wheel lamp?"

"Another bit of ancient magic. You will see."

The other men grinned when he told them, as if they were children being given a special treat. Two of them hovered at the entry of their tent while Velet went inside to fetch his pack, which was the bulkiest of them all and the only one which had never been opened in their long northward journey. When he had set it on the ice and they had all helped to untie its lashings, Alaric saw that almost the entire pack was taken up by a pyramid-shaped wooden box that measured nearly hip-high from base to apex. Two of its faces swung downward to reveal a strange device inside, held immobile by wooden chocks; with careful hands, the nomad men brought it out into the cold sunlight.

Alaric had never seen anything like it. In its middle was a six-spoked metal wheel an arm's length across, pierced by a vertical axle of the same length. Encompassing the wheel, but touching only the ends of the axle, was a seamless framework of pale green polished ceramic; a hoop encircled the wheel itself two finger spans beyond its rim, and four struts joined that hoop to each end of the axle from points spaced equally about the circumference. The whole contrivance resembled some giant, elaborate spindle, and indeed, wound about the axle on each side of the wheel were many turns of thin, tough cord.

Lanri held the thing with the axle vertical while Velet swung a brace out from beside each of the lower four struts; the braces clicked into place, making four slanted legs for the thing to sit on firmly, with the lower part of the axle as the fifth. There was a flat loop at the end of each brace, and Lanri hammered his longest tent pegs into them, making the device as stable and immovable as any structure could be on ice. Then he strapped cleats on his boots, and Velet did the same; and Grem pulled Alaric back twenty or thirty paces away from them.

"We have to give them plenty of room," said Grem.

Lanri took the free end of the cord that was wound about the axle above the wheel, and Velet took the end from the one below the wheel. They looked at each other, nodded, made a short synchronized count, and began to ease apart, the cords tight in their hands. Faster and faster they moved, their cleats biting hard into the crusty surface, till they were speeding away from each other like bounding jackrabbits; between them, the wheel of the device spun up, faster and faster, like a child's top. They were still running headlong when both cords came free of the axle, and they staggered as the cords snapped into the air like frightened snakes.

The wheel, spinning, began to glow. By the time Grem pulled Alaric back beside it, it was yellow bright and yellow hot, like the flame of a wood fire.

Swiftly, the men opened their tent up and, pulling it to the device, enclosed that glow in leather walls. Inside, the wheel lamp was like a brazier, flooding the space with light and warmth.

"I haven't been this warm since we left the band," Grem said, holding his hands out to the glowing wheel as to a flame. He had spread their ground covers between the wheel lamp's braces, to keep the ice beneath from melting too much. "This is always the best part of the journey."

Lanri and Velet nodded.

"But what is it?" asked Alaric.

"Only Kata knows," said Grem.

But all she would say was, "Ancient magic, my Alaric. And only good here in the heart of the north."

The wheel spun for a long time, longer than he would have credited; he fell asleep before it even slowed perceptibly. By the time he woke, it had halted, but even so, he could still feel faint warmth radiating from it, the last remnants of its glow. During the next march, the men showed him how, here in the heart of the north, all metal warmed, though nothing like the wheel lamp; even his knife was warm as flesh to the touch, and if his hands became numb, he could bring the feeling back by wrapping them about the blade. He did that, more than once, for the air was bitter; and he laid the blade against his cheek as well, and his forehead, for his furry hood was never quite enough to keep the cold away.

Kata's needle was quivering more violently now every time he looked at it. His own internal quivering was less, though, because of her medicine, and so was the dizziness in his head. But they weren't gone entirely. And looking at the needle always made him feel worse.

Still they moved on, heads down against the ever-strengthening wind, daggers slipped into their mittens, the wheel lamp warming their sleep. Walk, sleep, walk, sleep, and still the ice stretched onward, endless, changeless. Sometimes Alaric felt that Kata must have missed her goal long since, and they would never find it, only wander with the uncertain needle until they fell off the end of the world.

"That can't happen," Grem said when Alaric voiced his suspicions in a half-joking tone. "The world is round. It doesn't have an edge."

"I've heard that before," Alaric said, smiling with cold, cracked lips, "but it doesn't make a very good song."

And then, on a day like all the others, in a place that looked like any other place on the ice, Kata shrugged off her pack.

"We stop here," she said, and she began to pitch her tent.

The rest were happy enough to set up their shelter and thaw themselves at the wheel lamp, even though they had not walked half as far as usual. Alaric was curious to see how long the wheel took to spin down; his wakefulness had never yet outlasted it. This time, however, before he could detect any slowing, Kata called him to come to her tent.

There, she had a duplicate of the wheel lamp, though much smaller, and in a frame of polished wood where the seams and joins were easily visible. But it glowed as bright as the other, and filled her smaller space with warmth.

"Still dizzy?" she asked, gesturing for him to sit beside her.

"Yes, though your medicine helps."

"Good. You should be feeling better soon."

He smiled a little. "I hope so."

"You could always leave us, you know. I think the dizziness would vanish if you went back south."

"I can manage."

She nodded. "Then I have something to show you." From within the only cushion in her tent, she drew the wooden box he had seen once before, the box inlaid with symbols of the Pole Star. She opened it and lifted the

flask and cups out, lifted out even the mossy lining, and
showed him its bare floor. The wood was pale there, not
ebony like the rest, and burnt into it was a queer family
of symbols—first, the familiar Pole Star; next, a hexagon
with its vertices joined by internal crossing lines; and
last, a six-pointed star made from two overlapping tri-
angles:

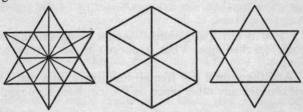

"These are the symbols of power," she said. "The
first you know—the Pole Star, ruler of the north. Ruler
of yourself, my Alaric, from the day you were born. The
second, the bound hexagon, derives from the heart of the
Pole Star and represents the powers of attraction; as iron
is drawn to the lodestone, so these powers pull upon each
other, though they never unite. The third symbol, the
triangle star, marks the Pole Star without its heart, and
represents the powers of repulsion; as one lodestone can
repel another, so these powers strive to thrust each other
away, yet they never fly apart. These are the forces around
us this very moment, my Alaric."

He smiled again. "Small wonder I'm dizzy."

"Indeed," she said. "And now I will show the deepest mystery of all." She touched something in the box,
and the pale wood that bore the three symbols fell free,
revealing another bottom beneath, and another symbol:

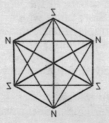

"This is a figure of my own devising, yet based on all that I learned from my own teacher, and since. It combines anew the attractive and repulsive forces of the last two figures—to show the northern heart of the net of power that overlays the world. But it is not merely a symbol, my Alaric; it is a diagram. It is a map of the land on which we sit at this moment.'' With the tip of one finger, she touched the lowermost vertex of the figure. "We are very near to this one.''

He peered at the indicated area. And not knowing what else to say, he said, "Well.''

"This is one of the net's very sources, one of the six in the north. These runes at each vertex are the ancient signs of their qualities. Look here.'' She held the false bottom of the box close to the wheel lamp and touched the empty center of the third diagram. At that angle, Alaric could make out a pair of tiny runes carved in the pale wood, that he had not noticed before:

$$\leq$$
$$N$$

"This is the sign of the lodestone,'' she said, "for it bears both qualities of power in itself, though in none but the smallest measure.''

"The two qualities . . . of attraction and repulsion?''

"Oh, nothing so simple, my Alaric. Nothing less than the powers that hold the world together.''

"Yes, I can see that would not be simple.''

"And here, in the very midst of it all, equidistant from the sources of power and held in thrall by them, is the axis upon which the sphere of the world spins. The axis, capped by the Pole Star, upon which the very sky spins. No, these are not simple things, my Alaric. I would not spend my life on simple things.''

He looked at her. "Will we be going to that axis?''

Her mouth quirked slightly. "Do you love the ice so much, minstrel?''

"Would I be dizzy there?''

She hesitated. "Perhaps not. But we won't be making

that trip. We have reached our goal, or so close that it is near the same thing. We have only to wait now until the sources of power stop dancing.''

''Will it be a long wait?''

''I think not. Midsummer Day, or thereabouts, and that is very soon.''

''And then?''

''We harvest our crop before the dance begins again, and then we go home.''

''Crop? What crop grows on barren ice?''

''A fine one, usually,'' she said. ''Of course, we can't know if this is a good year until we see it.''

He shook his head, but only for a moment, for it made the dizziness worse. ''Well, I have seen wonders with you already; why not a crop on the ice? I look forward to it.'' Then he peered once more at the several six-pointed symbols she had shown him. None seemed any more meaningful—whatever she said of them—than the Pole Star's own, and he had never thought of that as anything more than a bit of superstition. The possibility that the Pole Star, or any supposed sources of mystic power, could influence his life seemed just as unlikely as the Holy Well at Canby bringing forth jellied plums instead of brackish water. ''Tell me, lady,'' he said, ''why have you shown me these mysteries?''

''Because they are your mysteries, as much as they are mine, and you should understand them.''

''I don't understand *that.*''

She looked down at the symbols and then, slowly, she put them back as they had been, and laid the moss and flask and cups on top of them. ''I was jealous of you, I confess it. Because I have worked all my life to gain some little power from these sources and their net, while you . . . you were born with yours, you never expended a sliver of effort to gain it. Oh, yes, I was jealous. And angry, too, that you had your power but used it for such trivial things. The Pole Star does not grant many its gifts, and it expects them to be well used, and you . . .'' She shook her head. ''You were more concerned with saving your own skin than with being a witch.'' She looked at him. ''A witch has responsibilities. Or so we think in the north.'' She paused. ''They are my care, Alaric—all the bands of nomad people. That is what it really means to be a witch.''

"It is a great responsibility," he said softly.

Her eyes met his. "Once . . . I thought you were not equal to any responsibility. But now, I think perhaps you would make a proper acolyte. We have a truce, Alaric. Shall we turn it into something more?''

He felt himself recoil inside, and he looked away from her. "Lady, you honor me. But surely your daughter would be—''

"Not her. A flighty child, not worthy. The witch must choose the student carefully. I was not my teacher's daughter.''

He watched the spinning, glowing wheel as he might watch the flames of a fire. "You said you knew me, lady, but I think not, or you would not make this offer. These mysteries are not for me.''

"I thought I knew you, long ago. But you have changed.''

He shook his head again. "I thank you with all my heart, but you mistake me. Give your knowledge where it will find an eager student; I want no more than to be a minstrel.''

"But you are more already.''

"Please." He climbed to his feet, and his head brushed the roof of the tent. "I am your servant always, but my place is with the others.''

She gazed up at him, her face expressionless. "I cannot force you to learn, Alaric,'' she said, and with a gesture she granted him leave to go.

He sighed as he left her tent. He sighed and wished, not for the first time, for his lute, which was far, far away.

The nomad men had to move their tent every time they spun the wheel lamp up, but they did it cheerfully enough, for it was only a matter of paces, not of long, slogging miles. The second time, they slept afterward, and the third time, they just sat around the tent and grinned at each other. After so many days of travel, they were content to stay still. Alaric was not so content, for without walking to distract him, the dizziness bothered him; so he would walk anyway, back and forth, till his legs were too tired to support him and he could sleep soundly.

They had been two sleeps in the same spot when he woke to find the dizziness gone.

Quietly, for the other men still slept, he went outside. The wind was brisk as ever and sang against his cheeks, making his breath into puffs of smoke. He closed his eyes for a moment. Yes, the dizziness was gone, and in its place was a feeling of such well-being as he could not recall. He breathed deeply, and scarcely noticed the coldness of the air in his throat.

When he opened his eyes, Kata was standing beside him. He had not seen her since she had shown him her mysteries; her smaller lamp did not require so much effort as their larger one, and so there was no need to move her tent nor for her to come out of it. He smiled at her immediately.

"You seem well again," she said. She looked haggard herself. Her eyes were bloodshot, with dark pouches showing beneath, as if she had not had a restful sleep in days.

"I am very well.'

She nodded and held out her brooch. The needle was rock-steady. "The dance has stopped," she said. "We must move on now, and quickly."

They had never struck camp so swiftly, but still it was not swift enough for Kata, who shouldered her own pack and started off before the men were ready to follow. Running awkwardly on their webbed hoops, they were hard put to catch up with her as she strode, eyes on the brooch, ever northward. By the time they did, their goal was in sight.

"There," Kata said, pointing with one mittened hand, and never slackening her pace.

In the distance, dark against the pale snow, Alaric saw a line, like a thin smudge of charcoal. Closer, the line gained depth and broke into a scatter of dark splotches, like a small motionless herd of animals. Closer still, and the splotches resolved themselves into low, bushy plants so deeply blue green as to be almost black, growing on the bare ice.

In all his wanderings, Alaric had never seen such plants

before. They were compact, each no longer than a man could span with both arms, its tight cluster of rigid stems rising no more than knee-high, its thick, saw-toothed leaves forming a continuous cover over the top and hanging halfway down to the ice on all sides, like the jagged edge of a tunic.

Kata put her pack down in the midst of the plants and sat on it. She showed her north-seeking needle to Alaric; it swung freely now, indicating no special direction, though it dipped downward as far as its supporting post would allow. "We'll watch the plants now," she said as the other men dropped their own packs and sat down facing various quarters. "Tell me if any of them does anything."

"What are they supposed to do?" asked Alaric.

"You'll know when you see it."

Just moments later, Lanri was the first to call out.

Alaric turned in time to see that, five or six paces away, the leaves that covered one of the plants were humping up in the middle, bulging. As he watched, they parted, and a pale green globe rose slowly from among them, borne aloft by a thick stem. When it was well clear of the leaves, the globe opened suddenly into a many-petaled blue-green blossom.

It was not a beautiful blossom. It most resembled a feather duster which had fallen into a pool of dirty oil. The dark petals were thick and waxy, with tiny bristles all around their edges; they looked like they would snag a man's cloak if he brushed them. For a few moments they twitched, first one, then another, over and over again, as if adjusting their positions. And then, of a sudden, they spewed upward, as if blown by a gust from within the stem itself, flying apart as a spray of dark fragments; flying upward . . . and vanishing into thin air.

Alaric gasped. As the petals vanished, the white land about him seemed to vanish as well. In its place was the world, a sphere floating in blackness. And surrounding the world was a pulsing net of power, a net that rose from the icy north as from a clutching fist, and then spread out to envelope the globe before gathering itself back together to dive into the ice at the southern end of the world. He saw the net from afar, glowing sun-bright

against the darkness, and yet he was also a mote on the
net, sliding effortlessly from strand to strand, like a skater
on a smoothly frozen pond. The globe spun beneath him,
its surface streaming past his feet like rushing water, and
on that surface he saw all the places he had ever been—
castles and hovels, mountains and valleys, meadows and
ice—and all the places he had never been, countless
places racing by, and he knew that he could go to any of
them in an instant, this instant. For the net embraced
them all, and the net was his.

As abruptly as it had claimed him, the vision was gone,
and he blinked his eyes and looked about him. The nomad men were moving among the plants, cutting the thick
leaves free and stuffing them into bags, leaving the plants
mere clusters of naked twigs. But Kata was sitting beside
him, gripping his arm very hard.

"Can you hear me now, Alaric?" she said.

He nodded. "I had . . . a dream, I think. A waking
dream."

"Of what?"

"Of the net of power."

"Yes?"

He described the vision. If he closed his eyes, he could
recapture pieces of it, though not all. Not the movement,
nor the feeling of strength, nor the vastness of it all; no,
that had already slipped away. But the glowing net, he
knew, he would remember always.

"The sources of power have called to you," she said
when he had finished. "You should not deny them."

"But I don't know what their call means."

"Of course you do." She gripped both his arms now,
and looked steadily into his eyes. "My Alaric, we have
come here because only when the points of power cease
their dance do these plants blossom, and only when they
blossom do they produce the substance we need for the
Elixir of Life. Do they do this for our benefit? Of course
not. They do it because the blossoms need that substance
for their own journey. Do you think those petal seeds
disappeared to nowhere? No—they leaped upon the net
of power and flew instantly to the other side of the world,
to the very ice you saw in the south of your vision. The
seasons are reversed on the other side of the world. It is

winter there now, but come spring those seeds will germinate and grow and flower, and send their own seeds *here* in the very same way.

"You are like those seeds, Alaric; you leap upon the net and fly from one place to another without touching the globe in between. The net *is* yours . . . and you must learn to use the rest of its power." She was shaking him just a trifle now. "Learn from me, Alaric, and let me leave the north a great legacy in you."

He shook his head. "Lady, this is too much for me. I must think."

She dropped her hands away from him. "Yes. Think. Think hard, Alaric. This is something greater than any song."

He looked past her, to the men who were steadily gathering leaves. "Can I help you?" he asked.

She stood up. "We can do this ourselves. I think you should rest for now. We have a long journey back, and you haven't been well."

He stood, too. "I could make the journey much shorter."

She studied his face. "Yes, you could."

"I don't think it would harm your leaves. Not if they and I are so . . . intimately connected."

"No, I no longer think your power would harm them."

"Of course, the decision is yours. You would have to command me."

Her lips curved in the tiniest of smiles. "I don't look forward to all that ice, myself. But you don't know where Simir's band has gone since we left them; and there is Oltavin, and our deer. Do you propose to carry the deer in your arms?"

"I can take us to the edge of the ice. That would be a help."

She looked at him for a long time, then, and it came to him that her eyes no longer seemed cold. Wary, perhaps, but not cold. "Very well," she said at last, "I command it."

He took them one by one, with bags of leaves in their arms, and he took their packs separately afterward. They were all eager for the journey, happy to use magic to make the homeward trek shorter. Grem even asked why they hadn't used it before, to which Alaric said only that Kata had not wished it, and he was her obedient servant.

Oltavin was where they had left him, minding the deer and living in a tiny hut he had built for himself of stones and chunks of ice. He seemed less surprised to see them return by magic than to see them return so soon, but he, too, was happy to turn south at last.

True to Kata's word, they reached Simir's band before the first snow flew. Well before. And Alaric just smiled when the nomads he had carried in his arms ascribed their speed to their very own pale-eyed witch.

That, he thought, was as it should be. Holding his lute close with one arm and Zavia with the other, he felt the journey slide away from him like a shed skin. *Yes, everything is just as it should be, in the strange and magical north.*

PART SIX

THE CRUEL WINTER

The deer were restless. With autumn, and the steadily shortening days, the bucks had begun to shed the velvet of their antlers and challenge each other with tossing heads. The season of rut had arrived. For its brief duration, the nomads settled by a stream where the trees grew thick and the fish bit readily; and the deer were kept away from the camp by night as well as by day. It was a leisurely time for the band, a time when there was no need for packing and unpacking, for setting up or striking tents. A time for Alaric to laze by Simir's fire and sing and talk and laugh.

His position among the nomads had changed. Word of his quarrel with Kata had spread quickly, and the general understanding, according to Simir, was that Alaric had tried to cross her, and failed.

"Your dunking in the crevasse seems to have been a punishment," the high chief told him. "And now you are her servant completely, with your power at her disposal." He grinned. "Or so Kata says."

"I won't dispute it," said Alaric, flashing a smile. "Let them think what she likes."

Simir's only reply to that was a nod.

So he was no longer just the minstrel with a thousand songs, and no longer the new witch from the south, either. Instead, he was Kata's man. There was a new kind of respect in the nomads' eyes when they looked at him now. And the women stopped pestering him for his magic, because it was no longer his to give, but their own witch's.

But as Kata's man, he had new responsibilities, most of them requiring that he visit her tent often. He was never easy there, amid the sweetly scented smoke, but he always answered her call, carrying her messages or fetching her food. And every time he did her service, she urged him to sit for a while and learn, for his good and the nomads', and for her own future glory. He would be the greatest witch of the north, she insisted, and he and his teacher would be remembered forever.

He put her off and put her off, but nothing he said kept her from asking, from urging, from almost pleading.

Even Simir thought he should give the offer serious consideration. "We can use another witch among us," he said.

Sometimes, alone with his own thoughts, deep in the night when all the camp was sleeping, Alaric wondered himself what he should do. He could not forget the vision that had come to him on the ice, but did it mean what Kata said? Or was it simply an experience, no more significant, really, than any other of his twenty summers? He had been a minstrel so long, no other life seemed proper, and no other had ever attracted him. To change it for something else seemed a betrayal of the first person who had ever been kind to him, his long-dead mentor Dall. Yet a witch of Kata's sort was more valuable to her people, with her healing herbs and potions, than any minstrel. What was a minstrel, after all, but a meaningless diversion? Survival was the first importance. That was what Kata wanted to teach him. What did it matter if some of her knowledge seemed like superstitious gibberish? Some of it was real enough. She had chosen him, above all others, to carry that knowledge into the future, and everyone, it seemed, agreed with her choice.

Everyone but Zavia.

"Why should she choose you over me?" She hadn't needed Alaric to give her the news; she had heard it by the day after his return. She had brought it back to her tent with their breakfast, and her anger along with it.

"I told her she should choose you," Alaric said softly.

"What have I ever meant to her? Nothing! An inconvenience left over from her youth!" Her face was flushed, and tears brimmed in her eyes. "Blood of her blood, but less than nothing!"

Alaric tried to take her in his arms, but she pushed him away.

"And what are you?" she shouted. "A stranger, come to take what belongs to me!"

"I don't want it."

"You will! Don't think it won't look good to you during the winter. That's the *real* time of magic. You'll see what she does, and how they all worship her for it, and you'll want it!"

"Dear Zavia." He circled her with his arms again, and this time he held tight as she tried to thrust him away, held very tight till she stopped struggling at last and let her head droop onto his shoulder. "All I want is you," he whispered. "And as many times as she says yes, I'll say no."

"Don't lie to me," she sobbed against his neck.

He kissed her hair, her cheek, the corner of her mouth. He tasted her tears. "I'm not lying," he murmured.

Her lips opened against his, and then she pulled him down on the cushions, fiercely.

But even as their bodies clung together, Alaric found himself wondering what it was that he really wanted.

By the time the rutting season was over, the first snows had begun to fly—thin, sporadic snows, airy flakes melting when they touched the yellowing grass, but a presage of time to come. The band had been moving on for only a few days when the first of the bucks shed his antlers, and the other males soon did the same, leaving the does alone to wear their smaller racks into the winter. The shed horn provided a welcome bounty that the nomads transformed into spoons and knife hilts and needles.

Not long after, all the deer began to lose the dark tips of their coat hairs, becoming as pale as straw, as if the cold wind from the north were bleaching them out for the season of whiteness. Soon, flurries of snow became more common, and the flakes began to gather on the rolling land, untouched by a sun that, more and more often, seemed only a smear of brightness in the gray sky. The days shortened steadily, and the nights turned bitter, and seldom were the stars visible for the heavy cloud cover. Winter settled firmly over the northern plain.

Still the nomads moved on in their great circuit of the land, the circuit that would bring them, come spring, back to the ingathering and renewal of the calving grounds.

It was a stormy time. The snow, once it was well begun, blew hard for days on end and piled deep, so that soon everyone had to wear the awkward, thong-webbed hoops. But the deer could not wear this footgear, and in spite of their own broad hooves, they sank into the drifting whiteness and floundered when they walked. And walk they must, floundering or not, to find enough dead grass to nourish their bodies. When at last the snow grew so deep that they could no longer reach the frozen yellow tufts, the nomads had to take turns scooping it aside with shovels of hard-cured leather. Alaric took his own turn often enough, and he found it heavy work. But the deer had to eat, for in winter, more than any other time, they were the life and livelihood of the band.

In the warm months, hunting and fishing and gathering of edible plants had been the nomads' main sources of food. With the advent of the winter storms, the plants disappeared beneath the snow, and the hunters came home empty-handed more often than not. Tracks that would have shown well in the whiteness on calm days were quickly filled in by the wind, and the pale coats that so many creatures acquired with the season made them nearly invisible through a veil of blowing flakes. Fishing, too, offered little return, for the rivers were frozen over, and even when the ice was broken and lines could be dropped through the gaps, the fish seemed to hide from the bait. Still, without much game and fish, they ate well enough, for a large buck could feed the entire band for a day or two. The nomads expected to slaughter a goodly number of their deer over the course of the winter.

As the season wore on, though, it became clear to Alaric that they had not expected to slaughter so many so quickly. In an ordinary winter, there would have been game for the cooking pots fairly often, in spite of white coats and snow. In an ordinary winter, there would have been crisp, windless days, days when the snow left off and the land was silent and sparkling under the heatless sun. But this was no ordinary winter; it was the bad season Kata had predicted; and not merely bad, but the worst in memory.

In her tent and out of it, with sweetly scented smoke and acrid, with herbs cast upon the wind and strange words shouted into it, Kata worked her weather magic. And sometimes there would be a lull in the storm, and smiling hunters coming home with rabbits or foxes slung over their backs. But more often, she offered her witchcraft to an unheeding Pole Star, and another buck died that the nomads might live.

It seemed odd—and foolish—to Alaric that the hunters thanked Kata for the few good days but did not curse her for the bad. This was the real test of her power, he thought, this savage season, and she was failing it, even though her people did not appear to see that.

"A hard winter," the men would say, huddled about the fire in the long night, chewing their venison. "But how much worse it would be if we had no Kata."

He said nothing, not even to her, but he knew she read the doubt in his eyes, for she left off pleading with him to be her acolyte. She had no more time for teaching anyway, being busy with her charms against the storm. Sometimes, when he came away from serving her, hunters would ask if she were working her weather magic, and he always told them, with complete honesty, that she was. Sometimes, too, a hunter would go into her tent and stay some long time, in hopes of renewing his own personal hunting magic. Alaric never saw that it did much good, though, no matter how long the hunter stayed.

Quietly, he began to hunt on his own. In the south, where the snows were mild and the game plentiful, he sought the small wild deer, killing as he had always killed, by his special stealth and with his knife. Of all the band's hunters, he was the one who came home most consistently with meat. While he hunted, his venison fed Simir's own circle, and that much more of the tame meat was left for everyone else.

One night, after eating Alaric's venison and listening to his songs, the high chief went into Kata's tent. At first Alaric supposed that he was renewing his own hunting magic, but shortly he stepped out and beckoned to Alaric to join him.

Inside, Kata's own small blaze warmed the air enough that his breath did not turn to frost as it left his mouth.

She herself bent over the flames, staring into them as if
seeking the future in their flickering dance. Though Alaric knelt down beside her, she did not look at him. For
a time she did not even speak, nor did Simir, and the
tent was so silent that the crackle of the flames seemed
loud against the constant background wail of the wind.

She raised her head at last, her pale eyes red-rimmed
with lack of sleep. She had put all her energy into her
magic, and Alaric could not help feeling a pang of pity
for her at the little return she had won for so much effort.

"I warned them it would be a hard winter," she said.

"All winters are hard," said Simir, his voice low.

"They should have prepared themselves better. They
should have dried fish and game and stored roots. I
warned them."

"We had eightscore mouths to feed, Kata." There was
uneasiness in his tone. "We had no excess to put away."

"You should have found some."

Simir glanced at Alaric. "In all my time in the north,
there has never been a winter like this. Always, we've
been able to hunt in the snow. Always."

"Fool," said Kata.

Alaric looked from Simir's face to hers. "But there are
still plenty of deer in the herd. And the storms will surely
stop sometime and allow good hunting."

"Will they?" said Kata.

Simir shook his head. "We must face the possibility
that the hunting will remain poor. Perhaps for the rest of
the winter. We have deer now, but the time may come
when we must begin to slaughter the breeding stock."
He frowned into the flames. "It *is* a bad winter, but if
we eat all our deer and live through it, what will we eat
in the worst of next year? Snow?" He clenched his big
fists. "Kata is right, as always. This is my fault. I should
have pushed them harder; I should have driven them. It
meant our lives." Then he looked full at Alaric. "But if
the high chief has failed his people, their witch has not.
Her magic will save us."

Alaric tried not to let his doubts show on his face,
though he didn't think he was very successful at it.
"How?"

"It has brought you to us."

Alaric glanced sidelong at Kata and stifled the impulse to say, *Has it?*

"Long ago," said Kata, "when I knew the winter would be hard, I asked the Pole Star to help us. *He* has never failed his people. And you are his answer."

Alaric shook his head. "I'm a good hunter, in my way, but I can't feed a hundred and sixty mouths day after day. The deer of the south are small, and they hide well, even for one with my skills—"

"For *one*," said Kata, sharply. "But not for a dozen."

"A dozen?"

"You carried five people and their goods far across the ice. Why not a dozen hunters to the south, to hunt the game that lives there, and bring back meat to keep all our bellies full?"

Alaric stared at her for a moment and then, very slowly, as her notion blossomed in his imagination, he smiled. To carry hunters to the southern forest—it was a possibility that had never occurred to him. In the south, where witches were feared, he had rarely dared to use his power to transport other human beings. But in the north, where magic was welcome, he could fly them to the hunt, as giant eagles had done for the heroes of legend in half a dozen songs.

"I am a fool, lady," he said at last, "but you, as always, are wisdom itself. Command me, and we begin tomorrow."

Kata nodded. "I command you."

Wise as it was, Kata's plan contained a flaw. Though the dozen men Simir selected were eager to travel by magic to a land of plentiful game, they were accustomed to the rolling, treeless plains of the north; they found themselves confused and uneasy in the forests of the south, their hunting skills a poor match to the new landscape. Time and again, their stealthy footsteps were given away by dead twigs crackling underfoot, or their arrows were deflected in flight by low-hanging branches. Only occasionally would one rise above his deficiencies and kill a rabbit, a raccoon, or a fox.

It was Alaric who caught the real game—the whitetail deer, the wild pigs, and even a young bear, once. While his hunters crept cautiously through the southern forest, he flitted from tree to tree like a ghost, barely appearing in one place before he vanished again. In stepless silence, he visited springs and creeks, and thickets where the last berries of autumn still clung to leafless branches, and copses where the tender tips of twiglets drooped within reach of hungry deer. Yet, even with his power, the hunt was never easy. The afternoons were longer in the south, but still Alaric found himself using every scrap of daylight they offered. When he made a kill he carried it to that day's camp, then returned to meet his hunters at their rendezvous. If any of them had game, he took that north and then came back for the men. And after leaving them with their families, he often returned to the forest during the southern twilight, to stalk again in his own special way, for eightscore mouths made short shrift of rabbits, raccoons, and the small deer of the south.

He had never used his power so much—never carried so many objects or traveled so many times in so short a period. He found himself tired at the end of the day, so tired that sometimes, as darkness descended on the south, he wanted to lie down in the forest and sleep, except that he knew folk were waiting for him at the nomad camp. Often, when he returned, he was too exhausted to eat the very game he had killed. Zavia complained that he no longer had any time for her, but he just shook his head to that. He had put her aside necessarily, as he had put his lute aside. Hunting was more important now; he could see it in Simir's eyes, in Kata's, in the eyes of his hunters. With their failure, he knew it was he, the minstrel from the south, who stood between Simir's band and death.

"Perhaps it would be simpler," he said one night at the high chief's fire, when the wind roared and the snow whipped downward, making the flames sputter, "if I just took you all to better lands in the south."

The gathered nomads' only answer was a silence so profound that he did not attempt to bring the matter up again.

Truth to tell, tired as he was and hard-worked as he was, some part of him was glad that the other hunters failed so often. Some part of him was proud to be the lifeline of the band. No one had every truly depended on him before, not for more than an evening's music.

Perhaps it was his pride that made him push himself to his limits. Perhaps it was his pride that blinded him to his fatigue. No matter how weary he was, he had no trouble hunting, no trouble carrying his quarry and the hunters back to the north, and no trouble returning for another brief hunt almost every evening. But one night, as the southern sky purpled and the first stars rose opposite the sunset, when the shadows were deep and each tree seemed a many-armed sentinel standing guard over the forest, he spied what seemed to be a small bear crouching beside a boulder. He had killed a very young bear once before, and as he watched this one, all he could think was how many stomachs it would fill—juicy bear meat, still heavy with last summer's store of fat, roasting on a spit above Simir's fire. Knife in hand, he flitted to it to strike before it saw him. But when he struck, it reared up suddenly to a great height, roaring—not a young bear by any means, but a full-grown male, much taller than any man, and heavy as six or seven of the nomad hunters. Before Alaric could recover from his astonishment, before his exhausted mind could even think, the wounded beast batted him aside with the back of a huge paw.

The blow was like a log striking him square across his chest. It knocked him a dozen paces and drove the breath from his lungs. Darkness spun sickeningly about him, blotting out the twilit sky and the sentinel trees. He clutched at the ground, at the dead leaves of summer under their crisp snow cover, but could not force the wild dance of blackness to stop. He tried to breathe, but there was a terrible pain in his chest that kept the air from sliding down his throat. In the silence of unbreathing, he could hear the pounding of blood like a great mallet inside his skull. And above that, the growl of the bear as it shuffled toward him. The beast, the darkness—they seemed almost one to him, one vast living thing that was reaching out to crush and swallow him.

Where? he thought, struggling to see but failing. Failing to breathe, failing to move, as if his body no longer belonged to him. And with all his failures, another darkness began to grow inside him, as if bursting from his very heart, and greedily rushed to join the darkness outside. *Where?* he thought frantically, his mind drowning in black and icy water. *Where?*

And then the bear's claws raked him, and not knowing the answer, he leaped to escape that burning, freezing agony.

When the darkness finally loosed its grip on him, the first thing he noticed was the smell. It was sweet, pungent, smoky, familiar, though he could not think of where he might have smelled it before. Sometime later, he realized that his eyes were open, and that light flickered and danced before them—flamelight, he thought, from its softness, though he could not bring the flames into focus. Later still, a cup was placed against his lips, and an oily liquid, faintly sweet, seeped into his mouth. Like the smell, it also seemed familiar, though he could not place it. A low, soothing voice bade him swallow, and he obeyed.

He slept then. He knew he slept, because he found himself playing the lute while falling snow spangled its strings, and he knew that he must be dreaming because he would never allow such a thing to happen in waking life. And when he woke, the scent and the light and the oily liquid were with him once more.

"Drink," said the voice, and he drank.

"Sleep," said the voice, and he slept.

How much time had passed before he finally came to himself, he could not guess, not even how many times he had drunk and slept. But at last he woke and knew that he lay in Kata's tent, that the flamelight was hers, that the drink was the Elixir of Life.

"So," she said, bending over him with the cup. "You've said no to death at last."

He drank again. There was another cup for him afterward, of venison broth, rich and meaty. Its flavor drove away the pungent taste of the Elixir. "Have I been dead, then?" His own voice startled him, so weak and hoarse did it sound.

"Near enough."

He tried to shift his body under the furs that covered

him, and he caught his breath sharply at the sudden pain that lanced through his chest.

"Lie still," she said. "You've more cracked ribs than you'd want to think about, and you're half-flayed about the back. You'll carry the marks of those claws to your grave, I think."

Gingerly, he curled his hands to his middle and felt the broad leather bands that wrapped him from armpit to hip. "I came back," he whispered.

"And brought a fat bear paw with you, sliced clean off his body. He was a big one."

"Yes."

"You were foolish to try to take him."

"Yes."

She smiled just a little. "But brave."

"No," he whispered. "Just foolish." He closed his eyes again, for keeping them open seemed suddenly more effort than he could manage. "How long before I can hunt again?"

He felt her hand on his forehead, firm and cool. "Don't think of hunting now, my Alaric. You have a long rest ahead of you."

"But I must," he said, and the words were barely audible, even to his own ears.

"You must sleep. Think of nothing else. Just sleep."

When he woke again, he was being laid on a litter lashed between two deer. Above him, the sky was gray and lowering, and snowflakes danced in the air. Kata and Grem, their clothing well dusted with whiteness, were wrapping him in furs and winding thongs about him to secure him to the litter.

He tried to rise on one elbow, but the pain in his chest was too much. "Have we moved while I slept?"

Kata nodded. "And will again."

He sighed, and it was deep enough to hurt his ribs. Since childhood, he had always known exactly where he was. His mental map stretched back unbroken along his travels, with every mile, every step of the way, engraved in his deepest memory. Now there would be a blank— these miles of sleeping movement would be lost to him. But there was no help for it; this was the nomad life, and he had no right to ask that it be altered for his convenience. He sighed again, and could not keep from groaning with the pain, and then Kata gave him another draft of Elixir, and he slept.

There was a change in the nomads' routine while Alaric lay wounded. Instead of traveling every morning and camping every noon, they traveled through the whole brief day and camped for all the next, and sometimes for the one after that as well. Simir had suggested it, as a way to let the hunters roam farther across the snowy plain. It meant that his people were exhausted at the end of each long struggle against the wind and snow, so exhausted that they had no strength left to cook and were forced to eat half-frozen venison left from the previous day's meals. But it also meant that they had time to recover, time to huddle in their tents and be warm and send out the hardiest to hunt.

Simir brought Alaric the news of their hunting success.

"They say you challenged them," he said, kneeling by the pallet in Kata's tent. "But I think you shamed them into trying harder where they know the land."

"I never meant to shame them," Alaric whispered.

"Yet it was the right thing, in the end. Now they fight for their pride."

Kata nodded. "They must show they have no need of your magic."

"Perhaps there's just more game where we are now," Alaric said. "I know we've turned south."

Simir shrugged. "Whatever the reason, we're slaughtering fewer deer."

Alaric looked at Kata. "It's your magic, lady. That's the real reason."

She gave him gaze for gaze. "Of course," she said.

When Simir had gone, she brought her star-scattered box out, and at first he thought she was going to dose him with more Elixir, but no. She wanted to talk to him about the dancing points of power in the Great Waste.

He held his hand up before a dozen words had escaped her lips. "Lady, I am too weak for this. It is a deep mystery, not for the muzzy-minded."

"Yet these are good days for your schooling, my Alaric. You must stay in my tent till I call you well enough to ride, and what better time to begin your apprentice-ship?"

"Please. I am not ready."

She looked at him long then, and at last she put the box away in its sack. "I cannot force you to learn," she murmured.

He nodded, closing his eyes. "I'll know when the time comes."

"Don't be a fool, my Alaric," he heard her whisper. "Don't let my magic slip away from you."

Her magic, he thought as he drifted on the fringes of sleep. Her magic, real and delusion.

He dreamed that he passed his hand over her fire, and the flames turned every color of the rainbow. And people came to him, men he had sparred with and women whose cooking he had tasted; they came to him and crowded all around, and their faces were colored as the flames, and they told him, over and over again, that he was the great-est witch of the north. But then, jostling its way through the crowd as if it were just another human being, came his lute, calling his name in a high, singing voice, and weeping, weeping, for all his abandoned songs.

Zavia came to see him at last. He was sitting up by then, on mounded cushions, though his ribs still ached if he moved too quickly or if he tried to stand. He had not caught the slightest glimpse of her since his wounding, not even during the times that he lay swinging on his litter between the deer.

She knelt by his pallet, but scarcely half her attention was for him; she kept casting furtive glances at her mother on the other side of the fire. "How are you feeling, my Alaric?"

He smiled at her. "Better, now that I see you."

"I would have come sooner, but . . . it seemed wise to let you rest."

He reached out and took her hand. "Sometimes a be-loved face is better healing than rest."

Her lips tightened, and so did her fingers on his. "Don't you think it's time he moved back to my tent, Mother?" she said. "He claims so much of you, here. I can look after him now."

"No," said Kata. "He stays with me."

She bent her head. "As you say," she murmured.

Alaric looked past her shoulder, his eyes meeting Kata's. "May we have a little time alone together, Lady? There are things we wish to say, for no other ears than our own. Please. I know Simir would welcome your visit."

Kata frowned slightly. "She will tire you."

"I won't let her."

"Mark me, any exercise will give you pain and slow your healing. You'll regret it."

"We'll talk, no more. I promise."

Her eyes narrowed. "So you'd drive me out of my own tent, would you?"

"Lady, I would go myself, if I could."

Kata rose to her feet, drawing a fur about her shoulders. "Very well," she said. "But she *will* tire you, even with mere talk. She shall not stay long." And she swept out of the tent, leaving the flap a trifle ajar behind her, so that a thin sifting of snow blew in.

Zavia crawled to the opening and looked through it for a few heartbeats before lacing it fast. "How she hates me," she muttered. "Nothing I do pleases her. And everything *you* do does."

"Not everything," Alaric said ruefully. "She wasn't pleased that I nearly killed myself."

"You think not?" She scrambled back to his side. "Don't be a fool, Alaric. This pleases her more than anything else. Now she has you to herself, every day and every night. How much has she taught you in these days and nights of *rest?*"

"Nothing."

"Nothing?" Disbelief showed in her face. "But you are the new acolyte. You are the hope of her future." The words had a hard and bitter edge to them. "You are the one who pleases her more than the child of her body." Her fists clenched, and she looked down and away from him.

He laid a hand on her knee. "You are her rightful acolyte, my Zavia. But I can't force her to teach you."

"You could. By following Simir instead of her. Let him train you for chieftainship; he wants it as a starving man wants meat. You could be the next high chief, and I would be the next witch. We could work together for the good of the people, as Simir and Kata do now. Better!''

Alaric stroked her knee, then sighed so deep that his chest ached. ''Zavia, you think too far ahead. We have this winter to survive. Isn't it enough? No one knows what the future may bring.''

''You *want* to be her acolyte, don't you?''

''*She* wants it. I'm not sure I want anything. Except, perhaps . . . my lute. I'd play you a song if I had it, and we could stop thinking about magic and chieftainship and even winter. A song about springtime and flowers and love. That's all I want.''

She looked at him once more. ''Is it, truly?''

''And you.'' He raised his hand from her knee and beckoned her to bend closer. ''Come here, my Zavia. I've missed you.''

But instead of leaning toward him, she pushed herself to her feet. ''I mustn't tire you. I have your lute safe. I'll see you get it.'' She took one sidelong step toward the entry.

''Zavia, don't go. Stay with me till your mother comes.''

She shook her head. ''I have work to do.''

''Then give me a kiss, at least, to help me heal.''

She turned from him to reach for the entry laces and, without looking back, said, ''No. Later, when you come out of this tent. If you ever do.''

A gust of cold air marked her departure. Shortly afterward, Kata returned. She carried his lute.

For the time he remained in Kata's tent, Zavia did not visit him again. But Simir did. As Alaric grew strong enough to sit up, to feed himself, even to stand—leaning on Kata's arm—for brief periods, the high chief would stop in three and four times a day when they were camped. Sometimes he brought food from his own pot for the healer and the invalid; sometimes he merely came to make some inquiry of Kata. Sometimes he even admitted that he was there just to see Alaric, and to listen to whatever slight song the minstrel had strength for. But

Alaric fancied that when the high chief and his witch looked at each other, he could see the rivalry in their faces—the rivalry for him.

What do I want? he wondered, after one of Simir's visits. He watched Kata at her fire; the leaves of that strange northern plant had dried hard and crisp above those flames, and now she was grinding them to powder. She had tried to intrigue him with some talk about the proper treatment of the leaves—not too much heat, or they would scorch and be ruined, not too much grinding, or the precious oils would escape into the air—but he had shaken his head and plucked at the lute to discourage her.

"I am too much of a burden to you," he said. "Let one of Simir's circle look after my recovery. He'll be glad to have me in his tent."

"You are no burden," she replied. "And you wouldn't get enough rest in his tent. You would sing too much. Leave off the lute, now, Alaric; your ribs must ache."

He did leave off his plucking, but he kept the lute in his arms, a smooth but hollow comfort. *What shall I do?* he wondered. He thought of Kata's mystical stars and her shining web of power that encompassed the world. He thought of Simir, unflagging, leading his people on their great circuit of the north. He thought of Zavia, yearning, always yearning, for what her mother would not give. No matter what he chose, someone would be displeased.

What shall I do?

The winter seemed to go on forever. Day by day, the period of sunlight shining wanly through the clouds was shorter. For a time, Alaric thought that, just as there had been no night at all in the far north, there might at last be no day on the snow-swept plain. But he was wrong; the day shrank and shrank, but reached a limit, poised there a while, and then began slowly to expand. Midwinter Day had passed.

On one of those newly longer days, Alaric walked out of Kata's tent for the first time since his wounding. He did not walk far, only to Simir's fire, but he did it with just the slightest support from the high chief at one elbow and Grem at the other. Still, he was out of breath at the end of it, and his trembling legs ached almost as much as his ribs. Grem helped him to a mound of carpets near the flames and made certain he was well wrapped in his furs.

There were men gathered about the fire whom Alaric would have expected to be hunting on such a fine day. They were talking to each other with much animation, as if something unusual had just happened. Not, he thought, his own appearance, for they seemed to pay little attention to his hobbling journey.

He looked questioningly at Simir.

"A good day for you to be outside," said the high chief. "I thought perhaps you might still be too weak and would have to miss the ceremony."

"Ceremony?"

"Yes, on the first clear day after midwinter, we celebrate the sun's return. Now I must leave you here. Grem will fetch more furs and a hot drink if you get cold."

"I'm comfortable," Alaric said.

With a last nod, Simir strode back to Kata's tent and disappeared inside.

Alaric watched the bustle grow steadily all around him. It was not the bustle of packing that he had seen so often. Indeed, it seemed to accomplish nothing at all; it was simply movement and noise, a restless excitement. Even Grem, assigned to look after him, could not sit still, but bobbed up and down constantly, hurrying off to talk to people, coming back with an apologetic smile on his face, and then hurrying away once more. Alaric caught fragments of passing conversations, but all that he could make out was a sort of universal concern over who would be next to whom. As if they were all going to line up, every person in the band, and they were trying to determine precedence.

The sun stood at its low wintry noon when a hush fell upon the milling nomads, and all faces turned toward Kata's tent. Simir had emerged and was holding the entry flap aside, and every line of his body bespoke his respect for the woman who appeared there.

It was Kata, of course, but a Kata transformed. Gone were her usual skirt and jerkin of fur-trimmed leather, gone her boots and even her armlets. She was dressed, instead, in nothing but a sleeveless shift of plain white

wool. Her hair, freed of its plaits, fell loose to her waist,
her only cloak. Her feet were bare. With a firm step,
without a sign of shivering, she crossed the camp, passing Simir's fire, but sparing not a glance for Alaric sitting
there. As she walked, the nomads fell in behind her,
men, women, and children, silent and purposeful. As the
tail of the crowd surged by, Grem helped Alaric to his
feet, and they followed a few paces behind the rest.

They did not go far, only just beyond the tents, where
a wide circular space in the snow had been stamped flat.
The nomads settled all around its rim, their seats the
snow itself, no carpets here. Grem and Alaric squeezed
between a gray-haired matron and a young woman with
a baby in her arms.

Kata stood in the center of the circle. When everyone
was seated, she lifted her arms as if for silence, though
there was no need for any such signal. No human voice
had been raised, not even a child's cry; only the breeze
whispered softly about the gathered band, bringing with
it an occasional faint bawl from the distant herd. Still,
she lifted her arms and waited. Alaric saw then that her
eyes were glazed and staring, and that she did not look
at anyone, but up into the sky, to the north, where the
Pole Star would have shone, had the sky been dark.

She spoke at last, her arms still upraised, and her voice
was strong and ringing, as if she were giving commands.
But her words were the words of a tale Alaric had never
heard before:

"Long ago, in the morning of time, the people lived
in a warm and green place, where the sun had cared for
them since first they opened their eyes. And life was sweet
in that place, in the care of that good and generous sun.
But the people were wanderers in their hearts, and at last
they turned their backs on that green place, and on that
good sun, and set out into the Great Night to find another
home.

"Their journey was long, for the darkness was vast,
and homelands were as tiny and lost in it as flowers on
the grassy plain. But the Pole Star had looked upon them
in that darkness, and finding them worthy, he claimed
them for his own, and guided them safe to this sun and
this place. Yet when they came to their new home, it was

not a land such as they had known before. No, it was a land strange and beautiful, a land where magic grew in every meadow, and flowed in every river, and breathed in the very wind. And foolishly, they destroyed that magic, and made the land over in the image of their old home, which they had left so far behind in the Great Night. And they were happy in their new home, not understanding what they had done.

"But the Pole Star, who loved them in spite of their folly, preserved that magic in a few hidden places, and laid a net of his own power over land and sea, that the magic might be protected and perpetuated, forever living. And the Pole Star gave the knowledge of that magic to those who chose to dwell in his own favored domain, to hold and to use to ease their hardships. For they are wanderers, as the people were once wanderers every one, and the Pole Star has claimed them before all others. And the sign of that gift is the promise of the sun—that no matter how great the night grows, there will always be a dawn.

"Now the sun pushes back the night, redeeming the land. Now we give the Pole Star our gift in return for his."

At that, she ripped her shift top to bottom and cast it off to stand naked and pale in the center of the circle. The snow might have been grass beneath her feet, the cold wind a summer zephyr, for all the heed she paid them. Her whole attention was directed to the sky.

Simir went to her then, and placed a short-bladed knife in one of her outstretched hands. Her fingers closed upon it, and she stood statue-still while Simir waited, silent, watching her. Then with a swift, graceful motion, she bent downward and slashed at her thigh. So sharp was the knife that at first not even a line showed at the cut, but slowly the red blood began to well outward and trickle down her pale flesh; and as the first dark droplets reached the hard-packed snow, she slashed again, at the other thigh, and at her calves and her ankles, too, till the blood ran in narrow ribbons down both legs. Holding the knife high, then, she began a slow shuffling dance, and her feet smeared the redness from her veins over the pure white of winter.

After watching her for some moments, Simir tossed his own clothes aside, and with another knife, he slashed his own legs. As the blood ran down his calves, he joined Kata in her dance.

That was the signal for the rest. In twos and threes they stripped their clothes away and stepped into the circle to slash their legs and dance. Old men and young. Women with babes in their naked arms. Even children of five or six winters. There were the graybeards of Simir's circle; and there even Simir's cook. There were Lanri, and Oltavin, and Velet. There danced Zavia, straight and slim, as graceful as her mother. Only the youngest children stayed at the circle's edge, watching their elders with big, round eyes, watching them dance solemnly on the reddening snow. Only the youngest, and Alaric.

They can't expect me to join, he told himself as Grem merged with the slowly wheeling throng. *I'm not well enough to dance a dozen steps, let alone lose blood to the snow.* He shivered at the thought of the cold wind against his naked flesh, the cold snow beneath his naked feet, the cold steel. *But could I,* he wondered, his eyes on Zavia, *even if I were well?*

There was no signal to end the dance, but after a time that seemed impossibly long to Alaric, the participants began to drift outward, to find their clothing, and to become, once more, people who felt the winter wind. Soon Grem returned, smiling, as so many of the others were now smiling, as at some marvelous pleasure. He helped Alaric back to Simir's fire, where a thin stew had been left to warm over the low flames, and as they ate, Alaric could not keep his eyes from straying toward the dancing ground, where Kata still swayed and bled. She was the last remaining figure; after all the rest had put on their clothes and gone, she danced on, while Simir waited nearby, her shift hung over his arm.

She stopped finally, and let the high chief wrap her in the meager cloth and lead her by the hand to her tent. A short time later, she sent word that Alaric might come back, and when he went in, he found her fully dressed and bent near the fire with her powders and potions. She dosed him, then, as she had not for some days, with the mild form of the Elixir of Life, the form without the sleep inducer.

"You were out in the cold too long," she said.

He had to smile. *"I?"*

"You should have gone into Simir's tent."

"I was warm enough. I was wearing considerably more than you were."

She cast some powder into the fire, and sweet smoke wafted up from it. "If you can stay away from the bears, perhaps next year you will be ready to join the Star Ceremony."

He gave her a long look. "I'm not sure I'll ever be ready for it."

"You might be surprised. Simir was a stranger, and he was ready the first year he came to us."

"Simir is a much stronger man than I."

She shook her head. "It is not a matter of strength. Didn't you see the children dancing? Do you think they are stronger than you? It is an ecstasy, my Alaric. When you have given yourself completely to the north, you'll understand it."

"I *have* given myself to the north. I can't imagine how much more complete the giving can be."

She smiled just a little. "Can't you?"

He looked away from her. "Lady, my heart is here."

"Your heart is scarcely enough, my Alaric. The north asks more of you than that. It is time, and past time, to begin your instruction."

He sighed. "You have been kind to me. I am grateful, believe me. But . . . the life you offer doesn't seem to call me."

"You must listen harder, then. This is the life you were made for." She took his chin in her hand and turned his face to hers. "Don't deny your nature, Alaric. The Pole Star has made you what you are, and brought you here for this."

He saw the hunger in her eyes, as naked as her body had been during the Star Ceremony, and he understood well that she yearned for him as Zavia yearned for her magic. "Don't press me, lady, I beg you," he whispered.

She held him then, with her gaze and her strong fingers. "Do not be afraid, my Alaric. You have much to learn, but you will do well, I know it."

He tried to shake his head, but it scarcely moved, so firm was her grip. "It is not fear that holds me back; it is a dream. Surely you believe in the power of dreams."

Her pale eyes were steady. "A witch can never discount the importance of dreams." Her hand released his chin, settled lightly on his shoulder. "Tell me of it."

"It was some nights ago, but I can't seem to forget it. In the dream, my lute was a living creature, and it cried out for me; it even wept for the loss of me, because I had become something other than its master." He hesitated. "There was a large crowd around me, people who thought I belonged to them, and the lute pushed its way through them to find me."

She looked at him a long, long moment, seemed to peer into his very marrow. Then she slid her fingers along his neck, and down the line of his jaw, till they finally slipped off the point of his chin. She turned away from him, turned her back and stood very straight and stiff, her arms at her sides. She seemed to sway just a little, like a blade of grass teased by mild summer air.

"There is much wisdom to be found in dreams," she said at last, to the leather walls.

When she turned to Alaric once more, her jade eyes betrayed nothing, but one hand reached out and gently ruffled his hair. "It seems that you know your own mind." She sighed very softly, and yet the sound seemed to fill her tent, as the scent of sweet spice filled it, every corner, every crevice.

And within Alaric something answered that sigh, and a deeply buried knot loosened itself and came free.

"Perhaps it would be best if you moved to Simir's tent," Kata added, as if it were a trifle.

"As you say, lady," he murmured.

Her hand dropped away from him. "I'll call Grem to help you."

Simir's tent was a hub of activity, meeting hall by day and barracks for his closest advisers by night. Alaric did not rest so well there as in Kata's quiet shelter, but he was happy to make the move, happy to be free of the scented smoke and the colored flames, and of her pale eyes that had seemed to be watching him every waking instant. He sang a good deal more in Simir's tent, and so his ribs ached more, but he could not help thinking the trade was well worth the price.

In time, he was able to straddle a deer again, and so give up traveling on the litter. In time—though it took longer than he would have guessed—his strength returned, and he began to think of hunting. The winter storms had diminished, but game on the plains was scarcely plentiful; though the nomads tried to conserve their deer, still the herd dwindled steadily—now they began to slaughter does and yearlings, for the breeding population of bucks was getting low. When an old man died in spite of Kata's potions, there were few who mourned him long, even among his close kin, for his death meant one less belly to fill. The hunters ranged far, sometimes for days at a time, while behind their backs, a graybeard or two predicted that there would be nothing left of the herd come spring.

Simir did not want him to go. But he went at last anyway, exercising his witch's power like a cramped muscle, leaping to the horizon in a single heartbeat, and leaping as far again and again, till he found the southern mountains. A brief sweep along their lower slopes brought him to a familiar area, telling him precisely where, in the map of his life, that day's camp lay. He moved south then in one bound, to his forest hunting ground. The small buck he killed there seemed heavy to his unaccustomed muscles, but he made no complaint as he dropped it beside Simir's fire. He did promise, though, as he began to dress it out, that he would not try for bear again. Deer, he said, were quite enough.

He ranged southward almost daily after that. But as many times as he went, he never offered to carry other hunters with him, and neither Simir nor Kata ever suggested it. It was enough for them, he understood, that he was willing to go himself.

He also resumed his duties as Kata's man—helping her pack and unpack, carrying messages, and fetching her food. Now, though, she said little to him at those times; and that, he thought, was just as well, for he would not

have been able to answer her words any more than he
could answer the reproach in her eyes.

Nomad, hunter, minstrel, witch's servant—he had taken
up all his roles again. Only one thing was still missing
from his life.

Zavia.

He did not know precisely when he had lost her. Perhaps it had happened at the moment he had returned,
wounded by the bear, and Kata had claimed him. Or perhaps it had happened long before; perhaps he had been
losing her steadily since the journey to the Great Waste.
Looking back, he thought he could see a thousand signs
of her discontent. And one day, while he was seeking
deer in the south, she took another man into her tent—a
man a little older than he, a good hunter and amiable, if
a trifle dull. A man her mother would never want as acolyte.

For some time, Alaric tried to avoid Zavia, and that was
hardly difficult, for she was avoiding him—pretending not to
see him if he happened near and turning her back on his
music. Days slipped by, then more days. And when at last
Alaric tried to speak to her, she strode away, as if he were
nothing more than an insect creaking in the night.

He watched her closely after that, though he told himself he was resisting the impulse. He watched her as she
walked or rode beside her hunter in the mornings, as she
bade him farewell in the afternoons or greeted him in
the deep blue evenings. He watched with special care in
the evenings, when she linked arms with her new lover
and, smiling, led him to her tent. He looked for some
sign of performance in her manner. Every smile, every
gesture, every tilt of her head was so familiar to him, yet
strange and brittle now, seen from a distance, like a pup-
pet show grown stale from many viewings. But if a pup-
pet show, it was a deft one. Seeing her favors lavished
on someone else night after night left Alaric with a hollow feeling in his chest, a deep void like a well gone dry.
And sometimes, when he saw the tent flap closing behind
them, a painful tightness clawed in his throat.

Later, when silent darkness had settled on the camp,
he would sit alone by the embers of Simir's fire, stir them

into fitful life, and drift backward through a maze of memories . . . always returning to a more recent memory, of throaty laughter that flickered and danced like the flames themselves, and a warmth that was warmer than any blaze of gathered kindling. Someone else was hearing that laughter now, soft and breathy in his ear; someone else was feeling all the pleasures and comfort of that smooth flesh. And Alaric would put his head down on his knees and close his eyes, and sometimes fall asleep that way by the fire; and then he would dream of wandering through dead forests heaped with ash, or of crawling about in a vast, narrow prison of icicle-bound caverns far beneath the northern waste. And that dream would often end with frigid black water climbing up after him, through chamber after chamber, like some enormous hungry beast.

He caught Zavia alone at last, one afternoon when he finished his own hunting early and her new mate was still out on the snow-covered plain. He stopped her about to enter her tent, and he took her by the arm to keep her from turning away.

"Zavia," he said softly. "Let me speak with you."

She shook off his grip. "We have nothing to say to each other." She reached for the entry flap, but he moved quickly to bar her way.

"Zavia . . ."

She looked straight into his eyes then, and her lovely mouth pursed tight. "What is it?" she said, and something both desperate and angry simmered in that simple phrase.

At the sharpness in her voice, he hesitated. A confusion of half-formed thoughts surged through him. "I don't know how to say this. I don't even know what I should say."

"Say nothing, then," she advised.

He shook his head and plunged on. "I think of you so often—when I hunt, when I sing. When I'm lying in the dark."

"And when you are visiting my mother?"

He was surprised by her bluntness. "Yes, even then."

Her left hand, holding fast to the rim of the tent, flexed spasmodically. A strange light danced in her eyes, like the glint of polished metal. "Even when you lie with her?"

"Zavia," he said, "you know that doesn't happen."

"Oh? But surely that is the best way for her to pass her skills to you, especially the arts that cannot be taught by rote. And of course it's so much simpler than trying to teach her own daughter. And so much more pleasant!"

"She teaches me nothing, Zavia, and we do not lie together."

"And you never have, I suppose? She has never pressed her magic touch upon you, pretty minstrel?"

Alaric felt his innards coil like a trapped snake. This was too complex for him; there was too much at work behind her words—anger, pride, jealousy, all jumbled together. He tried to take her shoulders between his hands, but she twisted away. "Listen to me, Zavia," he said. "I am not your mother's acolyte, and I never will be. She and I are agreed on that."

"Liar. I see you go to her tent nearly every day."

"I carry food to her, and I help with her packing, but there is no instruction in magic."

"I hear no truth in your voice. Why should I believe you?"

"Zavia . . ." But he was stymied. He had no answer, and could only spread his hands, imploring her with a silent look.

"You see," she said, "you have nothing to say." She turned her face away from him. "Your lack of an answer becomes the answer; that is how the truth is finally known."

"You're wrong, Zavia," he said. He almost raised a hand to touch her cheek. But instead he said, "I love you, Zavia." Even to his own ears, the words seemed an afterthought.

"Love!" she cried, her voice strained, crackling like ice dropped into warm water. "So much is excused for love, in the name of love!" Her body swayed, and the tent frame quivered in response. She gave him a long hard look. "You claim not to be her acolyte, but those are only words. I will know it is true when she calls *me* to her tent for lessons. Now let me pass." She shoved him aside with one forearm and ducked into the tent.

He pulled open the leather flap and stood in the entrance. "You misjudge me, Zavia. Your mother's magic means nothing to me. But you mean a great deal."

She bent and scooped up her oil lamp; its tiny flame fluttered wildly in the breeze that soughed past Alaric's body. "You and I are finished, minstrel. I've found myself another keen hunter. Now go away." And she waved the lamp so close to his face that he had to step back or be singed.

"Zavia . . ."

"Go! Leave me!" She wrenched the flap from his hand, and it fell like a curtain between them.

He stood there, staring at the dark, finely creased surface of the hide. Of course, he could lift it aside again, but he understood how useless that would be. A wall more substantial than mere leather stood between them.

He thought about Kata then, who had never intended to teach her daughter anything. All of Zavia's claims on Kata's wisdom and rank were self-delusion. Even if the stranger from the south had never appeared on these rolling plains, the end would have been the same. He could explain that truth to Zavia in some detail; he could show her precisely why all her jealousies and her anger were unfounded. Perhaps he could win her back with that cold bath of reality. Perhaps.

But no, he thought. No. Her bright delusion, her hope, was the core of her being. A perfect knowledge of the truth would ravage her, would beat her to the ground as surely as a cudgel blow. And it would take a cudgel, too, to pound that truth into her skull. She wouldn't believe him; she would rant about his villainous lies. Or worse, she would half believe, and that half belief would gnaw at her like a worm in the heart.

Better by far to watch her from a distance, and never feel the radiance of her smile again, than to cause her so much pain. The leather hanging between them was not simply a wall; it was the sheer face of a cliff, which even his special power could not help him scale.

Slowly, he turned away from the tent. He would go back to Simir's fire now, and sit beside the familiar flames. And as he looked into their shimmering dance, he would recall some other time, some better time, some faraway time. He took in a deep breath of crisp winter air, and let it escape, and watched the ragged plume stream up and away and dissolve to nothing in the darkening sky.

"They choose for themselves," Simir said to him later that night when the wind whistled too loud for singing, except as flapping leather sang. "We can argue, we can beg, we can even fight each other for them, but in the end, they do the choosing."

Alaric caressed the polished wood of the lute as he might have caressed Zavia's thigh. He hadn't spoken of it, but the high chief knew of his conversation with Zavia; he supposed the whole band knew by now.

"She's a flighty one," Simir went on. "He won't be the last, not him."

Alaric shrugged.

"But there are other girls as pretty as she, and as lively. Plenty of them at the calving grounds every year."

Alaric sighed. "Let be, Simir. Men may die in songs from losing a woman's love, but I will not." He plucked a chord. "She wanted a great deal from me that I could not give. Perhaps I should only be surprised that she stayed so long."

"She's a fool for leaving you," Simir said gruffly. "An utter fool."

"No," said Alaric, and he shook his head slowly. "Probably not."

Winter on the northern plain stretched on and on, until Alaric began to think that, somehow, the mountains that marked off the nomad's land from the rest of the world were keeping spring away as well. In the south, the snow melted, and green buds showed on trees and bushes everywhere; Alaric harvested armloads of tender young shoots for the herd every time he hunted. Returning north with them was like stepping out of a dream—the contrast between soft green and bleak whiteness never failed to startle him.

But even in the north, winter eased to a close at last, with the snow becoming crusty and porous under the warming sun, and sinking away at last to reveal the dead, dry grass of the previous year. The deer feasted then, needing Alaric's southern greenery no longer. The nomads feasted as well, for game seemed suddenly to spring from nowhere—young foxes, wildcats, and countless rabbits bursting from their parents' dens to greet the mild weather and fill the hunters' bags. Not long after the last of the snow vanished, the does dropped their antlers, which made the nomads nod among themselves and talk of the calves to come. The calving grounds themselves were not far away, for during the winter the band had completed its grand circuit of the north, and now it was moving back toward the place where the herds would mingle and the fires would roar bright, and the music and dance would last half the night. With the warming of the breeze, everyone was looking forward to the calving.

This spring, though, the herd of Simir's band would be scarcely a quarter its old size. In spite of Alaric efforts, the nomads had been forced to eat seven out of eight of all the bucks and yearlings, and nearly half the pregnant does. It would be years, the graybeards said, before the herd recovered. There was talk of rebuilding its numbers by calling in debts from other bands.

At the calving grounds, though, they quickly saw that no one would be paying debts in deer.

Simir's was not the first band to arrive; half a dozen had pitched their tents already, though no one would have guessed it from the scatter of animals grazing on the new grass. Even when all the people of the north had gathered, the combined herd was pitifully small, nothing like the sea of deer that Alaric had marveled at the previous year. There would be no debt paying, no; and if the next winter were not mild as milk, there would be no deer afterward.

Simir had no need to call a meeting of the chiefs of every band. They were at his tent, every one, as soon as their people made camp. And anyone else who had no pressing work was there, too, or as close as the milling throng would permit. Alaric slipped away from the tumult early and found a fire where people who had not seen him since the previous spring were willing to share their thin venison stew in return for a song. In the end, he gave them more than that, singing deep into the night, and thinking, while he sang, how different this gathering was from last year's. It was noisy, true, but the noise was of a different kind—anxious voices, not joyous ones, and distant dance music that seemed strained and desperate rather than jubilant. And the faces that watched him were gaunt and winter-worn, and though they smiled, the smiles were forced.

Yet they were hospitable as ever, and when his hosts saw him yawn and glance toward Simir's tent, where the crowd had hardly thinned though dawn was near, they offered him a soft pallet and fur coverlets. He accepted gratefully, and only as he was drifting to sleep did he realize, faintly, that he had never asked them their names.

In the morning, there was a little cold stew for breakfast, and then Alaric sang again. He was still singing when a man with a girl-child riding his shoulders slipped in among the listeners. Alaric did not recognize the child, with her hollow cheeks and deep-set eyes, but he knew who she must be, and knew she had been plump once. When the song was done, he stood up and clasped her father's hand.

"Fowsh," he said.

"I've thought of you more than once, minstrel," Fowsh told him. "And wondered if you'd survive this hard winter with us. My mother thought not, but I see she was wrong."

Alaric smiled a little. "Tell your mother it wasn't all my own doing; I had plenty of help."

"My mother is dead," Fowsh said. "And so is my father."

"Ah, Fowsh, no."

"Just before midwinter they walked away from our camp together. They never came back." He glanced up at his daughter, then squeezed her thin leg. "They thought it would help us."

Alaric gripped his arm. "Was it so bad even in the south?"

"There was no game," said Fowsh. "Now we have no deer."

"None at all?"

"We slaughtered the last doe today. There was no point in keeping her."

"But what will you do now? Next year?"

"Join another band, perhaps. Or move into the mountains. There's always been food there."

"Raid the Red Lord's valley, you mean."

Fowsh nodded. "If Simir agrees. Nuriki's gone to ask him."

"It's dangerous."

Fowsh squeezed his daughter's leg again. "Starving on the plains is dangerous, too." He gave Alaric the shadow of a smile. "Come, minstrel, share our dinner and sing for our fire this night. We have need of your brightest songs."

"No, Fowsh, I couldn't—"

"There's fresh stew in the pot and eager ears waiting for your songs."

"But it's all you have, Fowsh. I'll sing, and gladly, but Simir can feed me."

"You cannot reject fair payment, minstrel—"

"Please. The high chief still has deer."

Fowsh pressed his lips tight together for a moment. Then he said, "Very well. Let the high chief feed you. But it will not please my wife, I promise you."

It was at Fowsh's fire, late that afternoon, that Alaric heard Simir was looking for him. He had eaten after all, pressed by Fowsh's wife, but only a small amount, and he was hungry enough that the summons was welcome. Still, he was sorry to leave, for though he had managed to bring a few smiles to the faces at that fire, they had been feeble ones.

"Tell him how it is with us," Fowsh said as he walked toward Simir's tent with Alaric. "Tell him we need his wisdom now more than ever."

"I will." They stopped within sight of the throng that still surrounded the tent. Alaric slung the lute over his shoulder and clasped Fowsh's hand. "There will be help for you. I swear it."

Fowsh nodded and let him go on alone. But he was still standing there, watching, when Alaric looked back once before plunging into the crowd.

My first friend in the north, Alaric thought, raising his hand in a last brief wave. *Would you and your family be happy where the snow is not so deep, nor the winter wind so bitter? I know a place. I know a dozen places.*

Simir's tent was even more crowded than the space around it. Twoscore men and more sat cross-legged inside, shoulder to shoulder—graybeards, band chieftains, men of experience and toughness; Alaric knew some of them from Simir's own circle, and he recognized Nuriki and several others from the previous year. They bent together, in groups of three and four, murmuring, and few of them noticed Alaric enter. Simir did, though, and gestured for him to stay at the entry. With a few words to his close neighbors, the high chief rose from his place and picked a careful path to Alaric's side.

"You and I must speak," he said. "Come walk with me among the deer."

They elbowed their way past the curious, the anxious, the questioning, and every time Simir's name was called, he shook his head and waved the caller away. When the crowd would have followed them into the fringe of the herd, he stopped it with a sharp gesture.

"They want to know what the future holds," he said at last when the deer had closed around them and replaced the babble of human voices with their own snufflings.

"Who does not?" said Alaric.

"You would know something if you had been listening to our councils."

Alaric shrugged. "I didn't think your councils needed any of my northern wisdom." He smiled a little. "As well ask one of these deer for advice. You'd probably get better, at that."

Simir looked back toward his tent. "Advice I have in plenty. Much of it would have seemed foolish, last year. Now it merely seems desperate." He shook his head. "There's not a man in that tent who didn't see his children hungry this winter, and feel his own belly gripe. Who hasn't wondered how his family—and his whole band—will survive next year." He turned to Alaric then. "We were the lucky ones. We had a larger herd and more hunters than most, even for our size. And we had you."

"I've heard," Alaric replied softly, "that some bands have lost all their deer."

Simir nodded. "Kata says next winter will be better, but it's too late for that. As a people, we've lost too much at this point, and there is no way to recover. No way as we are. So we must change. We must settle in one place and be farmers and shepherds, if we can."

Alaric stared at him. "That's a change indeed. What do the nomads of the north know of farming and sheep?"

"Most of them, nothing. But I am a farmer's son. And they can learn."

"Well, I know little enough about planting, but isn't it late in the season to begin? Even if you had grain and plows?"

"We'd be fools to plant here," said Simir. "The soil is thin and poorly watered, and the north wind blows cold too often in summer; we'd lose our harvest three years out of four. No, we must go elsewhere. And there is one place where the grain is in the ground already and the harvest is sure, where the sheep are fat, and their wool is heavy. We have all agreed on it—the Red Lord's valley."

"The Red Lord's—"

"We have five hundred warriors eager to take his castle. To make his valley ours forever."

Alaric curled a hand about the neck of his lute; its back-bent pegbox stood close beside his ear, like a friend trying to whisper good advice. He remembered the Red Lord's castle, the massive walls and pacing guards. "It's a strong fortification," he said. "With a strong complement of soldiers."

"No one knows that better than I. But we have no choice."

"No," Alaric said firmly, "there is a choice. Let me carry you south. The forest is large enough to shelter all of you, and you can clear fields and plant grain there if you want. Or you can hunt. The hunting is fine, truly, once you're accustomed to it; you'd have a new life, and no need to fight the Red Lord."

"You would carry every one of us, would you? All our hundreds, and our goods?"

"It would take time. And I could only manage the lighter deer. But it would be so much better—"

"No." Just the one word, but it cut Alaric off firmly.

The two of them stood for a moment, looking at each other. Then Simir said, ''The plan is that six of us go inside, disguised as pilgrims, and kill the Red Lord. The rest will have their best chance in the confusion that follows. Without its commander, the army will flounder.''

Alaric's fingers tightened on his lute. ''Simir, this is madness. You'll be killed.''

''What must be done, must be done.''

''Can you even be sure of killing him? The man has guards, and he's no fool to let armed men inside his walls.''

''We'll use our bare hands if necessary. But it might be easier . . . if you decided to help us.''

Alaric felt his heart shrink within him. ''Simir . . .''

''You could kill him yourself and escape without a scratch. It should be simple enough for the man who defeated Berown and bedeviled three strong young men.''

The minstrel shook his head. ''No, no, it isn't simple at all. I don't know the keep except for a few public rooms, and the tower where he tortures his victims. All guarded places; not private, like a bedroom or a bath. To kill him where guards are near would be to invite my own death. And I'm not as eager for that as you are for yours, Simir.''

''But you're quick. No one would catch you. They would be too startled.''

''Some people react with great speed when startled. They don't waste time in thinking.''

Simir caught him by the shoulders. ''You once said you *could* do it.''

Alaric looked at him steadily. ''I also said I was afraid. Neither of those has changed.''

Simir shook him a little, his big hands hard as manacles. ''*You* have changed.'' The high chief's eyes seemed to be searching his. ''Do you know yourself at all, Alaric? You've fought both a madman and a bear, you've trekked across the Great Waste, you've given all your strength to help the people of the north. You once said that your way was to run from danger. But you've stopped running! And you think you haven't changed?'' He gripped Alaric's shoulders even tighter. ''You're my son,

Alaric, no matter what you decide. But if you help us, we'll succeed, I know it."

"I'll help you and gladly, but not with this, Simir. There's a safe course open to us in the south—"

"Don't you understand, Alaric? It *must* be the valley! These are the people of the north, the Pole Star's own people. They *won't* go to your southern forest. They'd rather die here." He let the minstrel go abruptly. "If you decide not to help us, we go to the valley anyway. They have made the decision already."

"They? And what of you?"

"I abide by the will of the majority."

"But you're the high chief."

"The high chief is not the Red Lord."

Alaric clenched his fists. "You'll go, then."

"Yes. I'll be in command." He gave a small shrug. "As much as any nomad chief could be."

"And if I say no?"

"I go anyway. And I think that you and I will not meet again."

Alaric half turned away from him. "These are black choices, Simir."

"Black choices indeed, my son. Life and death."

Alaric shook his head. "Death however you look at it. One way or another, you'll water the valley grain with blood."

"I'd water it from my own veins if I thought it would save my people."

In a low voice, Alaric said, "The valley peasants were your people once."

Simir stood silent for a long moment. His mouth was firm, his eyes unwavering. "Do you pity them?" he said at last.

"I pity the ones who will die."

"They serve him. If the travelers who died in the valley could rise up and speak, they would say there is no one innocent there. Not one."

Alaric looked at him sadly. "You served him. If you die, shall I not pity you?"

He caught hold of the minstrel's shoulder once more. "If the people of the north die next winter, will you have enough pity for all of them?"

"Simir, Simir, is there no other way?"

"We can't beg them to take us in. You know that."

Alaric closed his eyes and felt the pulse pounding in his ears, felt the high chief's hand heavy on his shoulder, so much heavier than the lute. "A black, black course, Simir," he said in a whisper that was nearly a hiss.

"Our chosen course. Do you follow it with us . . . or not?" Simir's voice was not harsh, but his face looked like a carven stone.

Alaric curled his hand around Simir's thick wrist. "Father . . ."

"Are you of the north, my son, or not?"

He barely heard his own voice say, "I'll go."

Simir embraced him then, and the lute twanged as his big arm brushed its strings. Those strings were speaking, Alaric knew, giving the good advice of an old friend, but he could not hear the words. Instead, his ears were filled with Simir's voice, and a different kind of music. "You are my true son, Alaric. Now come back to the tent, for we have plans to make."

The plans, Alaric realized, had largely been made already. Most of the men in Simir's tent had been to the valley as youths, in the days when the nomads still raided, or merely in quest of the lesser Elixir plants, and they remembered all the mountain pathways and all the natural landmarks. Simir himself, with the help of those who had accompanied him the previous year, had drawn a map on deer hide to show the routes he intended, the movements, the points of assault on the castle. So certain were they all, that Alaric knew the scheme had not been hatched in a day or two, but had been germinating for years.

The young, the old, the weak, the women and children would stay behind, too far from the valley for reprisals should the nomad army fail. The rest—every man strong enough to swing a sword or bend a bow—would be part of the attack. They would creep into the valley by night, bypass all the peasant holdings that once they would have plundered, and gather about the Red Lord's fortification. Simir and his picked company would go inside, dressed as pilgrims from the south; they even had woolen cloth-

ing, laid away for years against this day, to make the ruse
plausible.

"We may be given supper and commanded to entertain
the Red Lord with tales of our wanderings," the high
chief told his party. "Or we may be thrown into prison
as soon as we arrive. It is even possible that one or two
of us may be taken to the tower for immediate torture.
But no prison, not even the tower, can hold us while
Alaric is with us."

"Can he carry even you, Simir?" someone asked.

Alaric smiled grimly. "Not easily, perhaps. But easily
enough. I'm more concerned that the Red Lord's men
will recognize me."

"That won't happen," said Simir. "Not after Kata is
finished with you."

"No one would know him now, not even a lover,"
Kata said, turning Alaric's face this way and that as she
scrutinized her handiwork. She had shaved his head, even
his eyebrows, and applied a stain that darkened his skin.
"Leave the lute behind, and they'll never guess they've
seen you before."

"I'll take the lute," Alaric replied. "We may need
music on this journey. But I won't carry it into the castle."

"You'll stain your whole body, of course, when the
time comes."

He nodded.

"And the rest of us will do the same," said Simir.
"So that we'll all seem of a kind."

"Yes," said Kata. She passed him two flasks of the
staining powder. "Remember to make the solution thin
so that the color will be even."

"I'll remember."

"I wish I could go with you, to be sure it was done
properly. And the shaving, too; it isn't easy to shave a
head."

Simir sighed.

"You'll need me, Simir. The fallen will need me."

He shook his head. "No, the decision has been made,
and we must stand by it. Who falls, falls. We must not

risk you; those who stay behind will need you all the more if we fail.''

She looked into his eyes. "I doubt that I will be enough for them, should you fail.''

"The decision has been made," he said firmly, and he turned his back on her and strode from the tent.

"He is tired," Alaric said softly.

"I know," said Kata. "We are all tired. Now listen to me, my Alaric." She curled her hand around his wrist. "You must look after him. He hates the Red Lord with a passion that you and I cannot understand.''

Alaric pursed his lips. "I think I can understand it.''

"I doubt that. For all the years he has been with us, he has never forgotten what the Red Lord did to him. First love is powerful, my Alaric. That much you *do* know.''

He nodded.

"Don't let him be foolish, my Alaric. The north needs him.''

"I'll do my best.''

"Act for him. He depends on you. You are all he has now. The boys, Marak and Terevli, were killed this winter, trying to steal deer from one of the southern bands. Now he can never call them back.''

"Kata," he whispered, catching at her other hand, holding it tight. "I can't be all he wants me to be.''

"But you must, Alaric. You must.''

The warriors chose the strongest of the deer to carry them south, and others to feed them on the journey. The rest were left with the women and children to be divided up for some semblance of the nomads' usual circuit of the plains. The farewells were quiet, Alaric thought, chillingly quiet, and as he rode with Simir at the head of the northern host, he could not help wondering how many of the women who watched their husbands leave this day did not expect ever to see them again.

Simir drove his army hard, but Alaric heard no complaints save from his own heart. For him, the days flew by too swiftly, and the nights seemed short as on the northern ice. He sang in the evenings, while fresh venison roasted over a score of campfires, and the men

crowded near to listen, but the songs seemed empty to
his own ears. He could think of nothing but the journey's
end—while he rode, as he sang, while he lay bundled in
furs watching the stars wheel toward dawn. He stared at
the blank white face of the moon one night, long after
its rising, as it floated in the darkness above him like a
silver coin. He knew a dozen legends about it; some
said it was a ball made of ice, some that it was the mirror
of a goddess and had once borne her name, Selena. But
a more ominous legend lingered with him after it passed
from his view—that the bright moon was the silver shield
of an ancient war god, set in the sky as a reminder to
men of death in combat.

He dreaded the end of the journey, and his dread sifted
like powdered snow through his veins, chilling him more
than the night air, more even than the black waters beneath the northern ice. But he said nothing, not to Simir,
not to anyone else, because he knew that no one would
listen.

The mountain passes were clear by the time the nomad
army reached them—not a trace of snow remained. The
barren rocks that Alaric remembered were everywhere
cloaked in the green of tufted grasses and hardy bushes,
and the sweet fresh scent of growing things wafted gently
on the breeze. The deer, surefooted as goats on the dry
soil, had little trouble picking their way among the
heights, and their progress was steady if slow.

Simir called a halt when they were less than half a day
from their goal, and while the nomad army rested, he
took a party of three forward to scout the valley. In case
those left behind needed to be warned quickly of some
danger, Alaric was one of the three.

At dusk, the Red Lord's domain seemed quiet enough.
High on a bushy mountainside, Simir and his companions could see the whole extent of the valley—the small
lake bordered by fields of new grain; the peasant cottages
scattered among those fields, threads of smoke drifting
from their chimneys; the slow river, gleaming in the reddish light like molten gold; and the castle, many-turreted,
its massive keep rising higher than the battlements and
darkened by strife and age. Among the cottages, they

could barely see tiny figures moving homeward with their goats and sheep.

"All peaceful," Simir murmured.

Alaric felt the dread rise within him, stronger than ever.

It was late afternoon, three days later, that all the nomad army was in place, ranged above the valley behind boulders and bushes, ready to move downward at full dark. The deer had been left behind, to keep them from giving their masters away with occasional bawling, and the men themselves were silent as the grass that cushioned their bodies. At the barest beginning of twilight, seven pilgrims, their heads all freshly shaven, their skins darkened by Kata's stain, moved down an easy slope on the southern wall of the valley. "This was the caravan route," Simir said as he fixed his woolen hood more snugly about his face. It was the route most travelers would be expected to use.

They made no attempt to avoid the nearest cottage, nor to silence its goats, penned nearby and disturbed by their presence. A cotter peered out his window and asked them who they were, strangers traveling so late in the Red Lord's valley. Simir offered their story of pilgrimage, their intention to ask for hospitality in the castle, and the man nodded and said no more. When they were well past his home, though, they saw a child running in a field not far off—running parallel to their course, but passing them quickly—and Simir murmured that it was surely the cotter's child, sent to report the strangers to the castle.

Certainly, by the time they arrived, the Red Lord's men were not surprised to see them. It was nearly full dark by then, and torches were blazing to either side of the open portcullis. In that flaring light, a dozen soldiers in chain shirts and dark leather waited, their hands resting casually on the hilts of their sheathed swords.

One of them stepped forward. "Pilgrim's bound *where?*" he said.

Alaric recognized the man from the previous year, and fought an impulse to pull his hood farther over his face. *No one would know him now,* Kata had said, and he clenched his teeth, hoping it was true.

"They say there's a shrine to the Pole Star in the

north," Simir said easily. "Where the land of ice begins."

The soldier eyed them. "That might be a very long walk."

"We are not afraid of walking."

"There are bandits along the way."

"We have nothing to steal," said Simir.

The soldier smiled just a trifle. "And you won't find any castles beyond here, to give you a night's hospitality."

Simir bowed to him. "All the more reason to seek it here."

The man nodded. "Then come inside for a meal and a decent bed. You must be weary of sleeping out in the mountains."

Simir bowed again, and all twelve guards stepped aside to let him and his companions pass through the gate. Then they formed up into an escort for the group, with the one who had spoken leading the way.

The torchlit courtyard was as Alaric remembered it—the low sprawling barracks on one side, a few sentries inside the gate and at other scattered posts, and many more unarmed idlers taking their ease everywhere. The central hall of the keep was the same as well, with its ancient faded tapestries, its fine furniture rubbed smooth by the touch of many bodies, its flagstone floor worn in a path to the Red Lord's chair by the tread of generations. Nothing had changed, nothing.

Except the Red Lord himself.

Just the year before, he had sat straight and tall in that chair, and his eyes had been gray and cold as the winter sky, his voice commanding as a drum. But no longer. Now the great Red Lord slumped in his seat, as if the weight of his crimson clothing, or of his own gaunt body, were too much for him to bear. Now his eyes were rheumy, and his voice issued from a throat grown corded and thin, a voice that quavered with every word.

"Pilgrims," he muttered, as if unsure of the meaning of the word. "Is there truly a shrine in the north? I do not recall it."

They had knelt with their escort some half-dozen paces from the chair, and he had not given them leave to rise.

On his knees, Simir said, "My lord, we have been told it is a very holy place."

"I've heard of holy places in the south. But the north . . . the north, you say?"

"Not far beyond the mountains, my lord, so we were told."

"Beyond the mountains?" In a peevish tone, he added, "Where is he? He knows the north. Has no one called him? You laggards, call him now! We know how to punish laziness! Where *is* he?"

"Here, Lord," a voice called from behind the nomads.

Alaric felt his whole body stiffen. He knew that voice. He reached for Simir's arm and felt the tension of the muscles: he saw his own alarm mirrored in the high chief's face as it turned. He heard steps coming near, heard boots on the flagstone, and saw the quivering, torch-spawned shadow fall across Simir's body. And at last he, too, twisted round toward the unexpected presence.

"Hello, Father," said Gilo.

He was gaunter now, strong new hollows showing in his cheeks, but the old familiar arrogance lingered in his eyes. He wore a tunic of the Red Lord's own crimson above his dark leather trews; he was the only other man in the room who wore that color, and he carried himself as if it meant a great deal.

"Pilgrims," he said, and he smiled a hard, cold smile. "My lord, you know well what that betokens." His eyes flicked to the leader of the soldiers. "Seize them."

At once the soldiers sprang to their feet, swords gliding from their scabbards. Seven of them took a nomad each by one elbow and dragged him upright. From the stone stairway at the far end of the room, half a dozen more men stepped forward, pikes at the ready, to form another circle about the prisoners.

Gilo crossed him arms over his broad chest. "You shouldn't have waited, Father. You weren't going to get any closer to him than you are now. You see, he doesn't let travelers kiss his ring anymore, not since I told him about your plan."

"These are the proper pilgrims, then?" the Red Lord said in his quavering, cracking voice.

"Oh, very proper, my lord," said Gilo. He scanned the dark-stained faces. At Alaric's he paused, his eyes narrowing, and then his mouth twisted into a sneer. "I see you brought the best help you could find." He stepped closer and took hold of the minstrel's tunic at the throat. "I have a debt to pay to you, my brother."

Alaric looked into his eyes and saw the hate there, dancing like reflected torchlight. "Have you?" he whispered. "It seems to me you've come out of it all well enough."

With a jerk of his powerful arm, Gilo threw him to the floor. "Yes," he said, and his teeth showed for a moment, like a snarling animal's. "And you will be the first to see just how well." He looked up to the Red Lord. "This one to the tower," he said.

Of course, thought Alaric; *he doesn't know about me.*

The old man rose from his chair, his legs unsteady beneath him. With one hand, he gripped an armrest, and with the other, which shook like a storm-blown leaf, he touched his neck where the pale scar showed above his collar. The scar that Simir's knife had given him. "No," he said, his voice suddenly strong, as if all the force of his body were being focused in it. "Your father and I have an older debt between us."

Gilo's mouth tightened for an instant, and then he stepped back, away from the prisoners. "As you will, my lord." He gestured sharply to the soldiers. "Take the big one to the tower. Carefully; he's as strong as three men."

Three guards prodded Simir toward the stairway.

The Red Lord eased back into his seat, his breathing heavy. "I'll go to the tower as well," he said weakly.

"My lord . . ." Gilo began.

"It will give me strength." He made a small, beckoning sign with one hand, and the two largest pikemen went to him and slid their pikes through slots beneath the seat of his chair; standing one before and one behind him, they gripped the pikes and gently hoisted the sedan thus created. As they started toward the stairway, he made another small gesture and said, in a voice barely audible,

"Take the rest to the cells for now." He did not look back to see that the remaining soldiers glanced at Gilo for a confirming nod before they moved to obey.

When the iron-banded door had shut behind them, the prisoners huddled together in the farthest corner of their cell. Their only light came through a small, barred window to the corridor outside, scarcely enough to show the dimensions of the chamber. Shoulder to shoulder, with their cloaks drawn about them, their hoods up, the nomads resembled nothing so much as a huge pile of dirty laundry. No one glancing through that window could have guessed that where there had been six men huddled, now there were only five.

The weapons they had left behind lay wrapped in leather on a night-dark mountainside. Alaric scooped the waiting bundle into his arms and, a moment later, spread it before his companions, exposing lightweight swords, unstrung bows, and quivers packed tight with arrows. When the others were all armed, he strapped his own blade to his waist, and Simir's beside it, and then he vanished once more.

He had guessed that enough time had passed for even the Red Lord's sedan chair to reach the tower. At its summit, he recalled, was a ring of four small wedge-shaped rooms, each accessible only from its immediate neighbors—individual storerooms, for silver, gold, jewels, and ravaged human flesh. He appeared in the first, the silver chamber, ready to leave instantly if anyone were there. It was empty, save for its many chests of silver, but the sound of human voices, of shuffling things and the rustle of metal against metal, told him that people were near. And one was in shackles.

He pressed himself to the nearest wall and edged quietly to the open door of the gold storeroom. Peering in, he saw no one there and flitted inside. The next door, which also stood open, led to the jewel room; it, too, was unoccupied; but standing in its farther doorway, the one that led to the final bloody chamber, was a man-at-arms. He was a pikeman, his weapon tipped back against his shoulder, its point barely clearing the lintel. His back was to Alaric. From beyond him came Simir's voice, proud and challenging. Alaric could not make out the words, and did not stay to try.

In the cell, the men were ready. One after the other, they threw off their cloaks, and then Alaric carried each of them to the gold room, scarcely pausing for breath between trips. When all were in place, ranged on either side of the farther door, they looked to him; five pairs of eyes, five swords, awaiting his signal.

He set his teeth together and gave a nod.

They burst through the doorway, the last man heaving the door shut and throwing the heavy inside bolt; by then the first of them had stabbed the pikeman through the back and charged ahead. Alaric took in the scene forming beyond the last doorway—the falling man, and past him the startled guards, just turning toward their attackers; the Red Lord, his whole attention still focused on his captive; and Simir chained to the far wall, every line of his body shouting defiance. In the next instant Alaric was beside Simir, grasping the high chief about the thighs, lifting with all the strength he could muster, moving them both out, away.

They appeared just beyond the locked door, in the gold room, and Alaric staggered as he let his burden drop. One glance told him that, in spite of his haste, Simir was whole; even the shackles had come with him, as well as a large chunk of the stone to which they were bolted. Alaric grasped a wrist cuff in each hand, moved a pace away in his own fashion, and the high chief's arms were finally free.

As Simir slid his sword from Alaric's belt, the door made a soft noise, and the high chief leaped to one side, motioning sharply for Alaric to do the same. The heavy panel opened just wide enough for a pike head to slip through, like some strange iron viper giving challenge. Simir's hand shot out and grabbed the shank as he lunged against the door, forcing it inward.

Alaric had raised his blade like an ax, both hands on the hilt. His palms were clammy, and the sweat poured down his face and neck and spine like a freezing rain. As Simir pushed into the jewel room, Alaric braced himself to meet anyone who might rush past the high chief's bulky frame.

But the men beyond the door embraced Simir. They were his own.

Only the Red Lord was alive in the final chamber—alive and still seated in his chair, with a dazed look on his face and a gag torn from his own red tunic sealing his mouth. Four of his men lay crumpled at his feet, their blood smeared darkly across the stone floor. The other—the first pikeman—was sprawled like a shadow at the threshold; one of the nomads kicked his feet aside as they all stepped back into the torture room.

Simir stood before the master of his youth, and as he looked down into that gaunt, pale face, there was contempt in the set of the nomad chief's mouth. "It's good that you know me," he said, and with a single thrust of his blade, he pierced the Red Lord to the heart. "I wish there had been time to give you a taste of what you gave so many others," he added, wrenching the blade free and wiping the blood on his trews, "but we must not be fools." He signed to the others to follow as he started toward the door.

They were just entering the gold room, Alaric only a step behind Simir, when they saw Gilo through the opposite doorway. And he saw them.

He was alone, and he came to a halt as if striking some invisible barrier, his face betraying his astonishment. Then he turned abruptly and ran, shouting an alarm. Simir started after him, the others at his heels, but Gilo reached the door to the silver room, pulled the massive panel closed behind him, and turned the key before they could get there.

"Alaric!" said Simir. "Stop him!"

Alaric took a deep breath and leaped to the other side of the door. Gilo was already bounding down the stairs, still crying for help, and from far below there came the sound of soldiers running to meet him. *Stop him,* Alaric thought, and abruptly he was on the stairway, and Gilo was crashing into him. The impact bowled them over, and they fell a dozen steps, clutching each other.

They came to rest on a narrow landing, Gilo on the bottom, his back to the cold stone. He caught Alaric's wrists, one in each hand, his grip tighter than any rawhide. His face and lips were bloodless, and all the arrogance was gone from his eyes, replaced by terror. "What *are* you?" he whispered hoarsely.

"Don't you know, Gilo?" Alaric said softly. He glanced down the stairway; he could hear the soldiers climbing fast, their chain shirts jingling. He hooked a leg behind one of Gilo's knees.

"Wait," Gilo said, his voice breaking. "Let me go. I'll leave now. You'll have the castle, the treasure. I'll never bother you again. I swear it!"

Alaric looked hard into those wide eyes, once so full of malice. "Too late, my brother. Much too late." And with these words, he saw the old Gilo slide back into those eyes.

Suddenly Gilo twisted, releasing his grip on Alaric's left wrist, and scrabbled for the knife sheathed at his waist. Alaric knocked his hand away from the blade and, before he could try again, swept the two of them up to the silver room. They dropped a hand-height, landing with a thump on the stone floor. Gilo froze, and Alaric used that instant of astonishment to ram a knee into his groin and roll free.

A moment later, the nomads were crowding close, their swords making a palisade about the high chief's eldest son as he lay curled on the floor, gasping. Simir himself stood by Gilo's head. He glanced at Alaric, just a flick of the eyes. "Never hesitate," he said, and he thrust his blade through Gilo's throat.

Gilo made a gurgling sound, as blood frothed and spewed from the wound. It might have been any word at all, or none. Then he lay still.

"Where's your sword?" Simir said to Alaric.

The minstrel tore his eyes from Gilo's body. "I must have lost it on the stairs."

They could hear the thumping of dozens of boots on the steps now, a thumping muffled by the heavy door. Simir strode to the door and threw the bolt. "They'll waste plenty of time trying to open that." He pointed toward the torture chamber with his blade. "Get yourself a weapon, and let's go elsewhere while these rooms attract so much interest."

Alaric took a sword from one of the bodies. Its hilt was bloody, but he wiped it on his tunic. Then he wiped his own hands as well, though they seemed just as slick afterward.

"The courtyard," Simir said to him. "Find us a shadowed place."

Alaric nodded and was gone.

He appeared beside the soldiers' barracks, its stone wall to his back, its overhanging wooden eaves making a pool of darkness in the torchlit yard. Immediately, he stepped deeper into that shadow. Before him, in the open space between keep and castle wall, the men who had been idling not long ago were beginning to cluster and to murmur inquiringly among themselves. Word of some disturbance in the keep had reached them, but no one seemed to know what it was. A few of them drifted toward the keep's main entrance, while others were moving uncertainly toward the barracks, where their weapons were stored.

Alaric returned to the tower. "Thirty or forty men in the yard, but most still unarmed. I've found a good spot, though I doubt it will stay so for long."

Simir nodded. "Take me first."

When all of them were there, shadows among shadows, Simir pointed to the sentries at the winches for portcullis and drawbridge; they were no more than two dozen paces away. Then he gave the signal.

Six nomad arrows took down the winch guards, while a seventh, Alaric's, its oil-soaked, cloth-bound tip lighted at the nearest torch, was shot straight into the sky. As the flaming arrow reached its zenith, a wild howling commenced in the darkness beyond the castle walls—nomad warriors rushing to the fray. Simir's party slipped from the shadows to encircle the winches, and though there were shouts from the ramparts concerning the bridge and the portcullis, no one seemed to notice that the men who might have done something about them were lying in the dust. Only when the first company of northerners sprinted across the bridge, rough wooden shields held above their heads against a rain of arrows, did the defenders' attention truly turn to the courtyard. As those first invaders fought their way through the guard at the gate and rushed to the winches to reinforce their comrades, the Red Lord's men ran to engage them from their posts at the base of the wall and the doorway of the keep, and those newly armed flooded from the barracks.

Alaric moved through the chaos like a ghost, now here, now there, dodging and feinting in his own special way. He never paused to strike a mortal blow, but still he was worth a dozen men to the nomad side, in startlement, confusion, and distraction. Twice he slammed the barracks door in the faces of men about to dash out with drawn blades. Then he caught up a fallen pike and swung it wide at ankle height as he flitted from place to place across the yard, tripping soldier after soldier. By the time he lost the pike in the melee of scrambling feet and falling bodies, he had lost his new sword as well. He pulled another from a mail-shirted corpse, but his hands were now too slippery with sweat to hold it fast; a soldier, turning suddenly, struck it a powerful blow near the hilt and knocked it spinning. Alaric leaped away, his whole arm burning from the impact.

He flattened himself against the shadowed barracks wall, his breath coming hard and fast, the pain pulsing from wrist to elbow. The confusion of the courtyard seemed to waver and blur before his eyes. Bitter bile rose in his throat, and he fought it down. He knew he mustn't stay long in one place, and with an effort, he focused his eyes on a shadow on the opposite side of the yard and moved to it. He was farther from the fighting there, and he leaned against the cold stone of the castle wall, shaking his head to clear it. He rubbed sweat from his forehead with the back of his left arm and squinted toward the winches. He could just make out Simir, taller than most of his opponents, his sword rising high for every stroke.

Then he heard an odd sound, as of a heavy weight falling from a great height.

The portcullis had slammed down.

But we have the winches, Alaric thought, and then he saw that at the top of the wall, where the thick cable should have passed over a last wheel before attaching to the portcullis, there was no cable. It lay instead on the flagstones, where men surged back and forth across it in their struggles. Someone had cloven it in two.

Perhaps a hundred nomads were trapped inside the castle, and though four hundred others still howled beyond the walls, there was little they could do to help.

Alaric glanced at Simir again and felt the heart shrink inside his breast. He felt sick and dizzy, and every instinct screamed at him to get away. Then he scanned the courtyard one last time and willed himself . . .

. . . to the portcullis.

Four men had been crushed by its fall; he appeared standing on their bodies, and he caught at the massive iron grate with his good hand to keep from slipping. Men were fighting on the other side—the Red Lord's soldiers with their backs to him, hard-pressed by the nomads. As he stood there, one man was hacked through, and the blade glanced off one of the iron crossbars after cleaving his body.

Alaric embraced the portcullis with his whole body, pressing himself to it, feeling its cold strength, its immobility, through his clothing and against his naked cheek. He embraced it and called up all his own strength, and he willed himself to move.

He felt himself falling in darkness—no, not falling, but being *pulled,* and he thrust the weight of metal away from him, or thrust himself from it, he was not sure which. He fell anyway, and slammed his injured arm on something hard, and cried out with the sudden rush of pain. Then he lay still and began to sob, the helpless tears flooding from him, half physical hurt, half the anguish of his heart. The portcullis was beneath him, a hard bed on the grassy mountainside. The night was dark, and the shouts from the Red Lord's castle were the merest breath on the summer wind.

Alaric lay limp on the cold metal, weeping and alone.

It was morning when he limped across the drawbridge. The portcullis was still down, what was left of it—broken bars on either side, leaving room for five men abreast to pass through. A dozen nomads were guarding the opening with the Red Lord's pikes. They greeted him wearily, but he said nothing to them, only walked on.

The courtyard was a charnel house, corpses everywhere, blood everywhere. The flies had begun to gather already: they buzzed round Alaric's face, but he didn't bother to brush them away. Two men came out of the keep as he entered; they carried another corpse between them. He didn't look to see if it was Gilo, or perhaps the Red Lord, or even someone who had ridden beside him across the snowy plain. He walked on.

Simir and some others—band chiefs and influential men—stood talking where the Red Lord's chair had been. They saw the minstrel when he was ten paces into the room.

"Alaric!" Simir cried, striding toward him. "We've been looking for you half the night! You're hurt!"

Alaric cradled his right arm with his left, as if it were a baby. Swathed in cloth—in his own cloak, retrieved from the dungeon—it made a large bundle. "My arm is wrenched. The rest are just bruises."

Simir circled the minstrel's shoulder with his own big arm. "Come into the kitchen. Have something to eat, and we can look at it."

In the kitchen, tables and stools had been pushed aside to make room for the nomad wounded. These lay on straw pallets on the floor, covered with blankets or cloaks, or with tapestries ripped down from the walls, and they were tended by nearly as many of their uninjured fellows. At the great hearth, the Red Lord's cooks bent over half a dozen simmering caldrons and ladled the Red Lord's food onto trenchers for his conquerors. The old woman who served Alaric was dull-eyed, her movement slow and stiff. He wondered if she had seen the carnage in the yard. He wondered if perhaps her own son was there, or her grandson.

Simir unwrapped Alaric's arm, and several chunks of ice fell free of the swaddling cloth.

"Where did you get ice at this time of year . . . ?" he began, and then he nodded. "Of course."

The arm was swollen from knuckles to elbow, and the hand and wrist were beginning to discolor. Simir probed the joint gently, then moved the fingers and the wrist itself, as Alaric grimaced. "A bad sprain," he said at last, wrapping it up with the ice again and fashioning a sling from a fragment of drapery. "You won't be playing the lute for a time. But perhaps we can make it a short one—we've found the Red Lord's private store of wine,

and steeping in the bottom of each barrel, a bag of dried
leaves which smell of the valley's Elixir plants. It won't
be one of Kata's potions, but it's better than none at all.
A better remedy for this, I venture, than it ever was for
an aching heart.''

"I don't want the Red Lord's wine."

"I think Kata would want you to drink it."

Alaric looked away from him and shook his head.
"What Kata would want no longer matters. I won't be
seeing her again."

Simir gripped his good shoulder suddenly. "Why do
you say that? Has something happened to her while we've
been gone?"

"No. Not to her; to me."

"To you . . . ?"

Alaric turned his face to Simir's. The high chief was
exhausted, that he could see. And there was a cut on his
cheek, a line of beaded clots and a faint smear of red.
But it wasn't a bad cut. "I'm not staying, Simir," said
the minstrel. "I'm going back to the south."

Simir's grip loosened; then, stiffly, he rubbed Alaric's
shoulder. "You're tired, my son. You need rest. We all
do."

Alaric looked into the high chief's weary eyes and saw
everything that the north had been to him. He saw Zavia
and Kata, and Grem and Fowsh. He saw Gilo and Berown. And above all, he saw Simir himself, and those
nights of song and laughter at his fire. "You've been very
kind to me. I won't forget you."

"Alaric, don't be foolish. This is the beginning of our
new life. You can't leave now. Why, Kata wants to teach
you all her lore, and Zavia—I wager she'll take you back.
She's already tired of that other one, and you will be her
hero, as you will be to all our people."

"Will I?" *As if that matters.*

"We took this castle because of you, you know that."

He closed his eyes. "I didn't kill anyone last night.
Not a single man. And yet all their deaths are on my
head. Every one."

"And through their deaths, we live." Simir's voice
softened. "It's a hard world, my son. Only the strong
and the clever survive. Surely you've learned that in your

wanderings.'' He hesitated. "It is something a high chief must never forget, for his people's sake.''

Alaric looked into his face again, then. "That's what you would have me be, isn't it? The high chief after you.''

Simir smiled a little. "You'd make a fine one.''

"Simir, you don't know me.''

"Oh, I think I do, my son.''

"No. You know what you wish me to be. But what I am inside''—he tapped his chest with his good hand—"you don't know that. If you did, you'd understand why I must go.'' He gripped Simir's arm. "I have loved you all, Simir, never doubt that. Especially you.''

Simir's smile faded slowly as his red-rimmed eyes searched Alaric's. "You're all that I have left, Alaric,'' he said softly. He caught Alaric's good wrist in his big hand.

The minstrel gave him look for look. "I'm sorry,'' he answered, as gently as he could.

"Stay at least till your arm heals.''

Alaric shook his head.

Simir's mouth tightened for a moment, then worked once, twice, as if he were about to say something but stopped himself. At last he did say, "What shall I tell the others?''

"That the minstrel has traveled on, as minstrels do.''

"And Kata? She had such high hopes for you.''

"I think . . . Kata knows already.''

Simir looked at his swaddled arm. "Where will you go, Alaric? How will you earn your meat? You can't play. . . .''

"There are people who will remember my songs and give their hospitality for that memory's sake. I'll manage.'' He took a step back from the high chief, slowly shedding his touch. "Farewell, Simir.''

"What, now, this very moment? But you're far too tired to travel, surely.''

"Not in my way.''

Simir's mouth curved, but the expression was joyless, nothing like a smile this time. "You're very stubborn, minstrel,'' he whispered. "It's a northern trait, gift of the Pole Star. Perhaps it means the Pole Star will look after you, even in the south. You are one of us, after all. You always will be.''

Alaric felt the sadness deepen inside him. ''No,'' he said softly. ''I never was. But thank you for thinking it. Father.''

A heartbeat later, he was on the mountainside where he had left his lute, and then he was in the southern forest, in a bower he had used in former times. Feeling drained of life, he lay down upon the thick cushion of last year's leaves, the lute held fast in the crook of his good arm. But sleep was slow in coming, because his injured arm throbbed, and because the future seemed so bleak. The southern sun was warm, and it helped him to rest; but in his heart, Alaric felt the winter of exile closing about him again.

ABOUT THE AUTHOR

PHYLLIS EISENSTEIN is the author of six novels including SORCERER'S SON and the Balrog Award-winning BORN TO EXILE. Her work has been nominated for both the Hugo and Nebula Awards several times. A graduate of University of Illinois at Chicago, she currently works as a freelance writer.